THE SOUTHERN BELLE BREAKFAST CLUB

Phyllis f. McManus

McManus Hill Productions 2017

First Original Edition

singncountrygirl@aol.com
Facebook – Author Phyllis f. McManus

McManus Hill Publications 2020

Dedicated to my friends in our
Southern Belle Breakfast Club
Gail Bourgeois
Becky F. Carter
Sue Griffin
Dot Jackson
Barbara Summers
They brighten my day with not only a cup of coffee,
but words of inspiration and encouragement.

In memory of Becky Couick
You are truly missed,
but we know Heaven rejoices with your presence.

In honor of
Lynn Austin Petty
Evelyn Hobbs
Sadie Westcott
"Lifelong friends are truly a gift from God."

Thank you, Don.
You believe in what I attempt to achieve
and you encourage me to push forward
when I am lost for words.
God creates friends in many different forms,
including a husband.

Chapter 1

Southern women have a style of their own.
They proudly speak their mind and stand by what they believe.
This is a story of a group of women determined to stand by one another,
no matter what the consequence might be.
Welcome to the lives of the women in "The Southern Belle Breakfast Club."

Sadie sat patiently, waiting for her friends to arrive at the restaurant. Over the years, it had never changed. She had always been the first to arrive. This did not anger her. It gave her time to reflect on the things she needed to do after the group went their separate ways for the day. Sadie was known for her virtue of patience. She had never quite made up her mind if this was a blessing or a curse.

She knew that Stella and Tilly would soon make their entrance, with JoBeth and Hannah following close behind. Gracie would be the last to arrive. She would always apologize before anyone had time to ask her why she was once again tardy.

It was strange how the lives of these different women had intertwined over the years.

Sadie smiled as she sat quietly, thinking back of just how each of them met and entered the group enlarging it to six members.

Sadie and Tilly had started the group. They had met at a Parent-Teacher Association meeting at their children's school. They were voted to host a teacher luncheon together. They did so well with the project that they were voted to serve on many more, thus throwing them into a friendship that would appear to last.

The phrase that opposites attract definitely applied to them. Sadie was a strong leader and always was polite to everyone, whether he or she deserved it or not.

Tilly was a woman that seemed to find fault in everyone, especially if that person did not humor or agree with her. She seemed to find happiness in being a drama queen.

Tilly met Stella at a charity benefit and quickly recruited her into the club.

Stella was the wife of a high-profile lawyer. She never wanted for anything or though she made it appear that way.

JoBeth and Hannah were the next in line to join. They both belonged to the local exercise gym, where Stella was a faithful member. Stella questioned the already established group if they could join, and everyone quickly agreed. Thus, this enlarged the group to five.

It was apparent that the gym was an everyday must for JoBeth, but Hannah only went for the socialization. She considered herself a fluffy woman, not caring how many extra pounds she had put on over the years.

Gracie was the last member of the group to join. It had been a very strange encounter. It was a very cold, rainy morning when the group met at their usual time and restaurant for breakfast. This mysterious woman, Gracie, had walked in soaking wet from the rain and sat down at a table beside them. She was alone and appeared very sad. Sadie was the first to notice and quickly asked the group if she could invite her to join them for breakfast. They nodded, and so Sadie invited her to have coffee with them.

She remembered how Gracie had seemed surprised but gathered her wet raincoat, her freshly poured cup of coffee and walked slowly to their table. She introduced herself and made small talk about the weather. When they invited her to join them each week, she slowly nodded in agreement. Several months later, she told the group how by chance, she came into the restaurant on that rainy day. Her husband, Reece, had died of cancer in the early hours of the morning. She had left the hospital in a daze, not knowing how she was going to live without him.

They had sensed an air of mystery about Gracie that day, which had remained over the years.

Sadie's daydreaming finally ended when she saw Stella and Tilly enter the restaurant.

Tilly made a waving motion with her hand to Sadie and then gave Stella a gentle push toward the table.

"Sorry, we're running late. Stella decided she needed to change into another outfit at the last minute," stated Tilly, with a smirk.

Stella boldly came to her own defense, "Tilly, you know it didn't happen like that." She turned to Sadie and continued, "I spilled my liquid makeup on the front of my blouse and didn't realize it until Tilly brought it to my attention. I could have put a scarf around my neck, and no one would have known the difference, but Tilly disapproved. So, it's her fault we are late."

Sadie chuckled to herself. She could not understand why Stella always agreed to carpool with Tilly to the restaurant. Stella could save many arguments by jumping in her new BMW and driving herself. Deep down, Sadie felt Stella liked to be controlled, but she would never share this thought with the group.

"Where in the world are the others? They know what time we are supposed to meet. It's not as if we haven't been meeting at the same time and the same place for years. It seems they are getting later and later," complained Tilly.

"It doesn't matter, Tilly. It will not hurt any of us to miss a meal, except for maybe JoBeth. I am worried about her. She seems to be losing a lot of weight lately," Sadie said, with concern in her voice.

"I brought that to her attention the other day when we were shopping," Stella said. "She almost bit my head off. So I'm not bringing that subject up to her again."

"Finally, here they come. Let's order breakfast," Tilly impatiently said.

"Gracie isn't here yet. Let's wait a while longer," suggested Sadie.

"Good grief," Tilly muttered under her breath.

JoBeth and Hannah hurriedly took their seats.

Hannah was the first to speak, "I saw Gracie pulling into the parking lot as we were walking in the door. She's right behind us."

"About time," Tilly mumbled, but no one acknowledged her remark.

Gracie quickly walked in the door, gave a hello wave to the server, and walked toward the group.

"Sorry, I'm late. Now wouldn't you all like to have a dollar for every time I've told you that?" She said calmly.

"It's all right, Gracie," Sadie said as she motioned for the server.

The server quickly came to the table. "Good morning, ladies," she said. "Will it be the usual for everyone this morning?"

Everyone nodded except for Gracie. She politely said, "Yes, thank you, Ida, that would be great."

During the past thirty years, the group had known only three servers. Ida had been working at this restaurant for the past twenty years.

Ida swiftly came back, pouring coffee for everyone at the table except for JoBeth, who had ordered hot green tea for months. Then she left to finish placing the order for the group.

"Well, now since everyone is here, I've just got to tell you all the news," Hannah said, beaming. "I'm an empty nester. I don't know how I'm going to fill up my days now."

"My gosh, Hannah. Your son is thirty-one years old, and this will make the third time he has left home. You need to wake up and smell the coffee. He'll be back in less than a year," Tilly stated as if enjoying her remark.

Sadie reached under the table and pinched Tilly on the leg. Tilly didn't flinch but quickly quit talking.

"That's great, Hannah. I'm sure that this time he will be able to make it on his own. After all, it is hard these days to make a living," Sadie said, trying to reassure her.

The others agreed, except for Tilly. She was still rubbing her leg from the pinch Sadie had given her.

It hadn't bothered Hannah that her son kept coming back home to live. Her husband, Gordon, had left her years earlier for a younger woman, so having her son home was security for her. She did not like admitting this to anyone, not even herself. Her son moving out was another void in her life, and also though she tried to sound happy, it had made her extremely sad. This feeling was something she did not want to share with the group.

Sadie looked around the table and realized that each one had more time on their hands at this point in all their lives than they should have.

"Ladies, I have an idea. I would really enjoy seeing you all more than one or two times a week. Do you think that we could continue to eat breakfast here on Wednesday, and everyone comes over to my house for breakfast on Monday?"

They all quickly agreed, except for Gracie. She sat quietly but finally answered with a tone of sadness, "I'll do my best to be there."

This surprised Sadie. She wanted to question Gracie but not in front of the group. She would wait for another time.

"Finally, here comes our food," Tilly stated angrily.

Sadie leaned over and whispered, "Tilly, don't make me have to pinch you again."

Tilly swiftly moved away from Sadie and gave her a slight smile. Tilly knew she was quick to say whatever she was thinking. She had made a mental note on several occasions to try to change this habit. It was not working.

Ida placed the plates of food in front of them, poured more coffee, and then left.

Everyone seemed to be enjoying her meal, except for Gracie. She took a few bites and then moved her food over her plate, making it look like she was eating.

Sadie watched as she did this but did not question her.

JoBeth was the first to finish. "Excuse me, ladies, but I must go to the powder room," she said, excusing herself from the table.

Sadie watched JoBeth walk into the bathroom and close the door behind her. She excused herself as well and followed JoBeth. Sadie reached for the bathroom door and quietly entered. She stood at the sink for several minutes, not saying a word. She could clearly hear JoBeth making herself throw up and then flushing the toilet several times.

Finally, JoBeth opened the door wiping her mouth with a wet paper towel.

She looked at Sadie with shock in her eyes. "How long have you been in here?" JoBeth asked, with her voice trembling.

"Long enough, JoBeth, long enough."

"I got sick on my stomach. I think the eggs must have been bad," JoBeth said, stuttering.

"JoBeth, you forget I'm a retired nurse. You can't fool an old fool," Sadie said sternly.

She continued, "Do you know what you're doing to yourself?"

"I can stop any time I want, but I'm so fat. I have got to lose at least two dress sizes. Don't tell the others," she pleaded.

Sadie took her by the shoulders, turned her around to face her, and said, "They are already noticing things. You cannot hide a thing like this. You should realize we notice when you wear oversized sweatshirts over a blouse when it is hot enough to fry eggs on the pavement. Don't fool yourself, JoBeth. You need help."

JoBeth lowered her head and then quickly pulled away from Sadie. She looked in the mirror to make sure she had wiped her mouth.

"All right, Dr. Sadie, I admit it. I have a problem. Now are you satisfied, and what do I do about it?"

"I'm giving you a time limit. If you have not put on at least a pound by Monday, you are checking into a hospital to help you fight this.

Do not think I will not weigh you on my scales before the girls come for breakfast. You make sure you get there early if you don't want them to know."

"I don't want them to know right now. I will tell them, but just not right now. I don't want them to think I am weak," JoBeth confessed.

"Weak, JoBeth, after all these years, we know each other like an open book, except for Gracie. Sherlock Holmes could not figure out the secrets she is carrying around, but that is all right. When she gets ready for us to know her business, she will tell us. You should have come to us when you got it through that thick skull of yours that you had a problem."

Sadie turned JoBeth toward the mirror and said, "Look long and hard at yourself, JoBeth. Those beautiful green eyes of yours are not looking as bright as they once did. Your hair seems thinner. Just how long has this been going on?"

"Not long, Sadie. I will stop. I promise," JoBeth said as if trying to convince herself as well as Sadie.

"Let's get out of here before they come looking for us, but remember I'm on to you, and you are going to stop this crazy act one way or the other."

Sadie hugged JoBeth and could feel the bones in her back. She felt sick to her stomach. Why had she not questioned her before now?

She was going to help her fight this disease, whether she wanted help or not.

Together they walked from the bathroom. Immediately, all eyes from the Southern Belle Breakfast Club women were focused on JoBeth and Sadie. The look that came across the face of Sadie let them know that they were not to ask questions at this time.

Chapter 2

Life is complicated with choices that we each have to decide on.

You choose wrong, and life can be a battle.

You choose wisely, and life can be manageable.

Early Monday morning, JoBeth was standing at Sadie's front door knocking, furiously.

Sadie, with an encouraging smile, opened the door wide.

"Since when did we start knocking on one another's door before we entered?" Sadie quickly asked. "I can tell that you are mad, so get over it."

JoBeth hurriedly walked right by Sadie and commanded, "Let's get this weigh-in finished before they get here. I'm not ready to get a scolding from the group and especially the negative comments I would get from Tilly."

Sadie nodded. She knew Tilly would be the first to tell JoBeth exactly how she felt. Still, at this point, JoBeth needed a professional to discuss the problem with her.

JoBeth went straight to the bathroom, quickly undressing down to her undergarments.

Sadie could not get over how skinny JoBeth was. She could count every rib in her body. It was much worse than she had thought.

JoBeth slowly placed one foot on the scales and looked down.

"Both feet, JoBeth, it doesn't work unless you have your entire body weight on the scale."

She gave Sadie a sharp look and continued to get on the scale. She looked down to see her weight, but Sadie quickly grabbed a towel and threw it on top of the scale.

"I don't want you to know how much you weigh this morning," Sadie said. "When was the last time you weighed?"

"I weighed last week, and it was awful. I weighed 135 pounds."

She looked at Sadie to see if she believed her. Sadie frowned and then tossed JoBeth her clothes.

"Put them on quickly. We have some talking to do before the group gets here."

Having said this, Sadie walked from the bathroom and headed toward the kitchen.

JoBeth swiftly got dressed, looked at herself in the mirror, and headed toward the noises she heard coming from the kitchen.

She quietly slid into the chair and waited for Sadie to begin her speech, but Sadie continued to work and did not say a word.

JoBeth finally spoke, "Okay, Sadie, I lied again about my weight. I guess I'm asking for help."

Finally, Sadie stopped what she was doing and walked over to JoBeth. She hugged her with all the strength she had.

"That is exactly what the nurse in me needed to hear. Until you realize you need help, no one can help you. Until you truly make that decision to get help, nothing will change."

Sadie pulled a card from the Carolina Treatment Center from her apron pocket and handed it to her. JoBeth looked it over and then placed the card inside her pocket.

"You're going to be the last one to leave here today. I don't care how long it takes. We are making that call together, and you are going to make an appointment. These are professionals, JoBeth. They can give you the help that you desperately need right now. You are skin and bones, and I could kick myself for not saying something to you about it before last week."

"Have you said anything to the others?" JoBeth asked sternly.

"They aren't stupid. We have noticed your weight loss, but it didn't go any further than that. Looking back over the months, I am surprised someone didn't question you about it."

Sadie reached for the coffee pot, poured JoBeth a cup, and handed her the cream and sugar bowls.

JoBeth started to push the cup away, but Sadie quickly put her hand toward the cup and said, "No green tea in this house, JoBeth."

If looks could kill, Sadie would surely be sprawled on the floor, waiting for the medical examiner to pronounce her dead. JoBeth did not like this idea of being told what to do. She wanted to be in control of her body, even if it meant wasting away.

Sadie sternly said, "You can look at me with those killer eyes if you want, but I'm still going to stick to my guns. You're going to get past this whether you want to or not."

JoBeth reached for the sugar bowl, took the spoon, and proceeded to add sugar to her coffee.

Sadie smiled to reassure her that she was not mad. She knew that the days ahead for JoBeth were going to be hard ones.

JoBeth sipped on her coffee while staring at all the food Sadie had prepared for the breakfast club.

Sadie slowly stirred the butter she had just placed in the big pot of grits she was cooking. Large slices of ham sizzled in the frypan, just waiting for her to make red-eye gravy to go along with it. There would be no toast on Sadie's table this morning. She had already made a pan of biscuits that would be served with honey and butter. She pulled a jar of her homemade blackberry jam from her pantry and placed it beside the biscuits.

JoBeth asked sarcastically, "What's wrong, Sadie? Did you not have time to cook eggs this morning?"

Without saying a word, Sadie pointed to a large covered bowl.

"I should have known," JoBeth said, sounding a bit less sarcastic.

Sadie did not reply. She would let JoBeth have her pity party for now. She knew exactly what she was trying to do, and it was not going to work. No matter how rude JoBeth would get, it would not change Sadie from helping her get the help she needed.

"Hello, my friends, what a great smell coming from this kitchen," Tilly said as she walked in with Stella by her side.

"The kitchen smells and looks as if Paula Dean has paid you a visit. My goodness, Sadie, by the looks of things, it appears you have been cooking all night," Stella said as she lifted the lid from the pot of grits.

Sadie knew that having the group over for breakfast was another excuse for enjoying her passion for cooking. She had always enjoyed cooking large meals for her family in the past. When her husband, Mitchell, died and her two children already moved out on their own, she had found it hard to cook just for herself. Therefore, she continued to cook large meals and share with her neighbors. Old habits never seem to die, and this was certainly one of them.

As Sadie scooped the ham from the pan, she tried to shake the feeling of depression that was trying to work itself into the corner of her mind. It had been nearly five years since she had lost her husband due to a heart attack. Every day, she felt the emptiness of not having him by her side. She knew she would never get over the feeling of missing him.

"I'll be right back, ladies," Sadie said while walking toward the living room. She felt she needed to leave the room and be alone for a few minutes. She had never wanted people, not even her closest friends, to see her when she stepped into this side of gloom.

She slowly walked toward the fireplace mantel and looked at the picture of her and Mitchell. It had been taken on their thirty-sixth wedding anniversary.

She reached for it, placed it to her chest, and whispered, "Oh, honey, we thought we had the world in the palm of our hands."

Memories of the love they shared engulfed her. She wiped the tears from her eyes but quickly smiled as she thought of the life they had shared. They had two children that had made them proud as they had grown into adults.

Sadie carefully placed the picture back on the mantle and then reached for another picture frame. It also was from the same day as their anniversary party. It was a picture of their daughter, Savannah, and their son, Travis.

She beamed with pride as she thought about the life they had made for themselves.

Savannah had worked many years to become a defense lawyer and now worked with a large firm in New York. Travis was a freelance photographer who successfully had his photographs cover the front of many magazines.

She had too many happy memories of Mitchell and their life to let sadness overtake her. She would shake it off for now as she had done many times in the past.

"A penny for your thoughts, sweetie," Hannah said as she reached for Sadie and hugged her.

"I'm sorry. I didn't hear you come in," Sadie admitted.

"As many times as I have walked into your house over the years, I surely know my way around. I have been standing in the doorway for a while. Are you all right?"

"I'm fine, Hannah," Sadie said, faking a smile.

"You do know, Sadie, that you don't always have to be the strong one of the bunch of us. It wouldn't hurt every once in a while to let us take care of you."

"I'll remember that," Sadie said as she locked her arm in Hannah's and led her from the room.

Tilly was busy placing dishes on the table. As Sadie and Hannah entered the kitchen, Tilly said, "I know we aren't going to start until Gracie arrives, but I thought it might speed things up to have the table ready."

"No need to wait then," Gracie said as she entered the kitchen. "Hand me a plate, and we can get started. It appears I'm only a few minutes late this morning, so maybe my record is improving."

"Now, how does that old saying go, better late than never?" Tilly asked.

"My goodness, are you not fussing at me for being late this morning?" Gracie asked, with a puzzled look on her face.

Tilly continued to place cups and saucers on the table and did not say a word. After all, she didn't want to change her reputation of being an outspoken person in just one day.

Everyone took her place around the large table.

Stella was the first to speak, "Sadie, you have outdone yourself today. There is more food here than you can shake a stick at."

Sadie smiled, "Dig in before it gets cold."

Hannah quickly said, "Join hands, ladies. I want to say the blessing this morning."

Everyone grabbed for the hand that was beside her as they had done for years and held tightly.

Hannah began, "Bless this food, dear Lord, for the nourishment of our bodies and bless the one who prepared it. Help us, dear Lord, as we attempt to do Your will in our daily lives. Amen."

Sadie continued to hold JoBeth's hand. She gave it a slight squeeze and then turned and smiled at her. JoBeth returned the smile.

Sadie realized she had forgotten the grits. She quickly slides her chair from the table, excuses herself, and hurries to the stove. As she picked the bowl up, she realized someone had walked up behind her.

She slowly turned to see Gracie staring right through her.

Gracie whispered in a sad voice, "Sadie Sue, do you think God hears all prayers?"

Sadie took a deep breath. Gracie was the only one out of the group that had ever called her that. She was not sure why Gracie called her this only at certain times. She felt that at some point in time, Gracie would let her know why.

"Yes, I do, Gracie. I truly do." Sadie expressed slowly.

Gracie paused and asked, "Do you think he answers all prayers?"

"In His own way and time, I do, Gracie."

Sadie placed the bowl once again on the stove and reached for Gracie's face. She cuffed it softly in her hands and looked right into her eyes.

"Is there something you would like to talk about, Gracie?"

Without hesitation, Gracie whispered, "Yes, in my own way and time."

She pulled away from Sadie, carefully reached for the bowl of grits, and took them back to the table.

Sadie knew without a doubt that her concerns were valid. Something was bothering Gracie. There was something incredibly wrong. Gracie had finally made the first step with this question, but Sadie knew it would have to be Gracie to make the next step. She would wait for Gracie to approach her again, but she would not wait long.

Sadie returned to the table and watched her friends enjoy the meal she had prepared. JoBeth was trying to put on a good show of pretending to eat. Sadie had noticed several times that Tilly had completely stopped eating to look at JoBeth.

Sadie felt a nervous feeling start to form in the pit of her stomach. She knew Tilly was a ticking time bomb with a question she wanted to be answered. You cannot be friends as long as this group had been and not be able to know what the other was thinking. She knew Tilly was going to make a comment, but she didn't know when or what it would be.

Several more minutes passed with laughter filling the room, and then it happens. Tilly placed her coffee cup slowly down on the table and turned to JoBeth.

Tilly went right to the point. "JoBeth, I love you to death, but you look sick."

This time Sadie did not even want to pinch Tilly for saying what popped out of her mouth.

JoBeth looked straight at Sadie and accused, "You told me that you weren't going to tell them."

"Tell us what?" Stella questioned.

"Sadie hasn't told us anything, JoBeth, but I think we all know what you are talking about. You've been trying to hide your drop in weight from us for weeks." Hannah said in a stern voice.

Gracie reached for JoBeth's hand and begged, "We all need help sometimes in our life. Now, let us help you."

"Sadie, tell them. It appears this is your doing," JoBeth insisted calmly.

"JoBeth, I didn't betray you. I told you I wouldn't say a word, but if you can remember, I did say they had noticed changes in you." Sadie paused and waited to see what JoBeth was going to say.

"Ladies," she announced. "Sadie feels I have an eating disorder. I'm still not convinced I do, but it appears she wants me to go to a treatment center."

JoBeth reached in her pants pocket, pulled out the card that Sadie had given her, and started to crumble it up.

Hannah quickly grabbed the card and blurted, "You do have a problem, JoBeth. I have noticed changes in you when we go to the gym together. I have wondered how in the world you were able to work out on those machines with those heavy sweats. I should have known you were trying to cover up your body."

Stella looked around the table and ordered, "Let's get the table cleared and the food put away. Then we are going to listen while JoBeth makes a phone call."

Everyone followed Stella's lead except for JoBeth.

She stood up, and as she headed to the bathroom, she stated, "I am calling them tomorrow."

She opened the bathroom door and was surprised to find Sadie standing at the sink. She was slowly taking her finger and pretending to stick it down her throat.

Calmly, she questioned, "JoBeth, I guess I am doing something wrong. Is this the way you do it?"

"Stop it, Sadie!" JoBeth cried out.

Sadie reached for JoBeth and pulled her into her arms. JoBeth cried harder than Sadie had ever heard her cry before.

When there seem to be no more tears, they walked out of the bathroom together.

Outside the bathroom door stood the rest of the Southern Belle Breakfast Club women waiting to help.

Gracie took JoBeth by the hand, and together they walked back to the kitchen. She pulled a chair close to the phone and directed JoBeth to sit down. Hannah placed the card in JoBeth's hand while Tilly handed her the phone.

Stella softly urged, "It would be best if you make the call yourself. We will do it for you if you can't, but if you truly feel you need help, you will make the call."

JoBeth was shaking so intensely that she could barely hold the phone.

"Hold the card for me, Hannah, while I dial the number," JoBeth stated in a scared voice.

Hannah smiled with encouragement and held the card as JoBeth punched in the numbers. She sat patiently while waiting for someone to answer.

Finally, JoBeth said softly, "Yes, I need to speak to someone that can help me. I think I have an eating disorder."

She raised her head and looked at all her friends that were already giving her their support.

She quickly changed her statement and continued talking on the phone, "I have an eating disorder, and I want help."

Sadie stood in the corner of the room, smiling. JoBeth had finally completely admitted she needed help. This was a beginning step in her recovery.

JoBeth continued to answer questions. Several times she would repeat, "I understand" and "Yes, I will."

Everyone continued to stand around her with a questionable look on their face.

She finally handed the phone to Hannah and said, "They want me to come this afternoon."

"I think that would be a wise decision," praised Sadie.

"I'll go home and pack me a bag. They said I might be there for several weeks. They will discuss the type of treatment when I get there."

She suddenly became very quiet, and a look of fear once again spread across her face.

"I am driving you to your house and help you pack. Then we will drive to the center," Hannah stated.

"There is no need for that. I can pack and drive myself."

"Trust me. You're not strong enough yet to walk in the doors willingly." Sadie continued, "Maybe, it is still the nurse in me talking, but I feel you need our help."

"That's right, so let's get going," Hannah commanded in a tone that the women were not accustomed to hearing from her.

"Your car will be safe here. I will put it in the garage. It will be waiting right here until you get back," Sadie said before JoBeth had time to use this as an excuse for driving herself.

JoBeth nodded. She knew there was no way she could change their minds. It had to be today. There was no turning back.

"All right, Hannah, get me home," JoBeth blurted.

Sadie pulled Hannah into the corner of the kitchen and whispered, "Don't let her out of your sight. She still has the food in her that she ate for breakfast. I don't fully trust her at this point, and I know she cannot trust herself. She will try to get rid of it by making herself throw up. Also, let her pack whatever she wants because they will check her suitcase when she gets there. I am positive she has been eating laxatives like we eat candy, but they will search her carefully."

"I'll watch her. I promise, Sadie," Hannah stated proudly.

Sadie smiled at the way Hannah was taking control of the situation. She could not get over the change that had been coming over Hannah in the last few weeks. Hannah had not shown this much confidence and control since before her husband had left her. He had called from his office and told her that he was leaving and he would not be back. His words were that he had found someone that had made him complete. He had definitely used the coward's way out by not returning home to get his clothes or any of his belongings. It was as if he was walking away from everything, wanting to make a completely new life and leaving the old one behind.

Sadie suddenly had a flashback of the things Hannah had to face when her husband left. She had been so heartbroken she had taken to her bed for several weeks. It made every one of the women go to her house and drag her from the bed. She had even talked of suicide. Therefore, they took turns staying with her making sure she was not going to hurt herself.

They had watched her improve over the years, but at times, it was evident that she blamed herself for his leaving. He had made her believe he left due to her not taking care of herself. His actual words were that she let herself go, and he did not want to be around someone that always looked like a slob. He told her that if she had been more of a woman to him, he would have never walked away from their marriage. This was his way of controlling her right to the end. She believed him, so she blamed herself for the divorce.

Sadie was thankful for the change she had seen in Hannah today. She was determined to find the underlying cause once they had gotten JoBeth settled in the treatment center.

Hannah took JoBeth by the arm and walked out the door.

She turned to the group and said, "It won't take me long to help get her packed. We will meet you in the parking lot at the treatment center."

They hurriedly got in the car and drove off with the group still standing on Sadie's front porch, watching as they sped away.

Tilly was the first to speak, "What in the world has made Hannah become the commander and chief?"

"So you noticed, also?" Stella giggled.

"I have to admit the new attitude looks good on her. Bless her heart. It's about time." Gracie said, smiling.

Sadie took a deep breath as she thought about the situation at hand. JoBeth was going into a treatment center, Gracie was still a mystery, and Hannah was finally becoming her own woman. She could not decide at this point, which needed her attention, the most. That funny feeling in the pit of her stomach worried her. For some reason, she felt Gracie's need was the worse.

Chapter 3

*Life has proven that true love between a
man and a woman*
needs to be shared equally.
*When one strays, it destroys all memories
of the happy past*
that once was
*and destroys all hope for what could be in
the future.*
*When the love and hope turns into hate, it
can leave ugly scars,*
especially when the hate is for yourself.

"I don't think we are ever going to get
through this traffic, Stella. You are driving like
an old woman heading to a bingo game,"
complained Tilly.

"I promised Trace I would be careful and
not have another accident," Stella expressed
sharply.

Tilly leaned toward Sadie and whispered,
"He would just buy a new car instead of having

the dent fixed. Now, you see why I usually do all the driving. No, she just had to drive this morning. She almost had a hissy fit when I told her I would drive to your house."

"Tilly, I'm hearing everything you are trying to whisper to Sadie," Stella said while looking at them in her rearview mirror.

"Please, Stella, keep your eyes on the road." Gracie begged and then, with a sigh of relief, continued, "I see the treatment center on the left over there."

"Remind me to kiss the ground when we get out of this car," Tilly whispered, making sure Stella did not hear her last remark.

Stella drove toward the large building and found a parking place. It resembled the looks of a hospital. Sadie could not help but think this was going to intimidate JoBeth. She had disliked hospitals since her husband, Cody, had died. He had gotten too sick for her to care for him at home, so he was moved to a Hospice House. She would faithfully stay by his bedside days at the time. She continued this for five months until one morning, he didn't wake up. He had died in his sleep. Every night for months, she had pulled her chair as close to his bed as she could and hold his hand the entire night. That night had been no different. The next morning she awoke to the touch of his cold hand. This was a feeling that did not leave her heart for years.

Stella pointed toward the front of the building and stated, "There is Hannah, but where is JoBeth?"

Sadie frowned, "I was scared of this. I bet she is in the car and won't get out."

They swiftly got out of the car and walked toward Hannah.

"I have done everything I can think of except threaten to drag her out of the car by her hair. She will not move," Hannah said, almost breathless.

"Well, maybe that is what we will have to do, but she is going into that building," Sadie said in a stern voice.

They walked toward the car. JoBeth looked at them and bravely locked the car door.

"That's not going to work, JoBeth," Hannah stated as she held the keys and dangled them back and forth in the air.

JoBeth quickly unlocked the door, put her head down, and her lips out in a pouting motion.

Sadie opened the door and then kneeled down toward JoBeth. "I know you are scared, but we are behind you on this. We promise we will stand by you. Have we ever let one another down all these years?"

Gracie took JoBeth by the hand, gently pulled her from the car, and said, "You're killing yourself, and we won't allow it. We have too many years together to sit back and watch you slowly die due to an eating disorder."

"That's right, Gracie, get right to the point," remarked Tilly.

Sadie smiled as she watched each one take part in walking JoBeth toward the door. She reached into the car, got JoBeth's suitcase, and hurried to catch up with the group. She wondered if JoBeth had tried to sneak laxatives in with her, but she knew the staff would soon find out.

Stella held the door open as Gracie, arm in arm with JoBeth, walked inside first.

Sadie faked a smile as she walked toward the nurse behind the front desk.

"Hello, we called earlier in the day." She looked toward JoBeth and continued, "This is JoBeth Walker."

The nurse came around from the desk and greeted her, "Yes, JoBeth, we were expecting you. If you follow me, I will take you to Dr. Roberts's office. He is anxious to talk with you."

"Come on, girls, we will go as far as we can with her," Sadie said.

Immediately, the nurse remarked, "I'm sorry, but you will have to stay here."

"Don't be sorry, honey, we are going to go with her to talk to the doctor. Then if he tells us to leave, we will leave," Tilly stated in a voice that made the nurse know there was no way these women were going to change their minds.

A frown quickly appeared on the nurse's face, but she did not try to stop them. She kept walking with the little army of women behind her. Everyone stayed silent as they walked down the hall.

Finally, they came to the doctor's office. The nurse opened the door wide and announced sarcastically, "Dr. Roberts, here is Mrs. Walker and her friends."

He smiled and said, "Good afternoon, ladies, come on inside. I'm afraid I don't have enough chairs for everyone to sit, but I can have some brought in."

"That's all right. We can stand," Sadie said, smiling back.

He sat back in his chair and began, "All right then, which of you nice ladies is Mrs. Walker?"

JoBeth, without saying a word, slowly raised her hand as if she were in a schoolroom.

Dr. Roberts stood up, reached for her hand, and slowly shook it.

"I am delighted to meet you, but more importantly, I am glad you have decided to get help. The nurse you talked to on the phone filled me in slightly, but I am very eager to talk to you myself. I can tell you right now that you are a fortunate lady to have all these friends standing by your side."

JoBeth nodded but continued to stay silent.

Dr. Roberts slowly questioned, "Do you feel comfortable enough for them to wait for you outside while we talk alone?"

JoBeth continued to keep her head down but finally, in a whisper, said, "Yes."

"Ladies, I can show you where to wait, and I will call you back as soon as Mrs. Walker and I have a little talk."

"I think she would rather you call her JoBeth," Tilly snapped sharply.

Sadie looked at Tilly and drew a deep breath.

JoBeth slightly laughed and confessed, "Yes, I do prefer being called JoBeth. I feel so old when I am called Mrs. Walker."

The doctor laughed with her and said, "Good, JoBeth, it will be."

Sadie drew a sigh of relief. This time Tilly had not put her foot in her mouth.

Dr. Roberts walked them from his office and said, "Ladies, go right down this hall and turn to the left. The first door on the left is a little café that has great coffee. I'll send someone after you when JoBeth and I have talked. Please, trust me, she will be all right."

"We trust you, Dr. Roberts, but we have to admit we are scared for her. She will not eat," Hannah said, sounding worried.

Dr. Roberts smiled and then whispered softly, "I can fix that."

"Thank you so much, Doctor Roberts, that is so sweet of you," Stella said in a flirting manner and then started walking down the hall with a twist of her hips that would make even a sailor blush.

They followed behind her in disbelief while shaking their heads.

Tilly was the first to speak, "Stella, do you think you need some fries with that shake? And another thing, you were flirting with the doctor."

"I was not. I was just friendly," she said, trying to defend herself. "Tell her, Sadie."

"I'm sorry, Stella, can't help you on this one. I got the same feeling as Tilly did." Sadie admitted, frowning.

Sadie's statement did not seem to affect Stella in one way or the other. She raced ahead and then motioned for them to come, "Here it is, and I can smell the coffee from outside the door. Oh, could I ever use a cup!"

It was clear the subject was changed and wouldn't be discussed again today. This was a side of Stella, the ladies had not witnessed before. It was a side that Sadie disapproved of.

Stella opened the glass doors of the café wide, and the girls walked inside. It did smell good, with the aroma of different kinds of coffee filling the air.

Gracie questioned, "Can we order and then sit outside on the patio? It is such a nice day, and maybe that will put us all in a better mood."

"I agree, Gracie. Lead on, and we are right behind you." Sadie said.

Within minutes, they were all sitting around a wooden table with a large umbrella shading them from the afternoon sun.

Sadie breathed a sigh of relief and eased back in the comfortable chair. She slowly brought the tall glass filled with sweet ice tea with a lemon wedge sitting alongside the rim toward her lips. It felt good going down her throat.

"That looks good, Sadie. After this cup of coffee, I might just have to have a glass of sweet iced tea myself," Gracie said, smiling.

"Something tells me we are going to be here for a while. I am going to go back to the café and see if they have some cookies we can munch on," Tilly said.

"I'll go with you. I love to window shop, especially when it is for food," Hannah admitted, giggling.

Tilly and Hannah quickly went back into the café.

Gracie immediately spoke, "Hannah has gradually been changing the last few weeks. It is a good change. She seems happier than I have seen her in years."

"You would think she is in love," Stella remarked while watching the door for their return.

"There is only one way to find out, and we have all afternoon to see if she will talk about it," Sadie stated.

"Well, here they come with a tray of what I suppose is sinfully good sweets," Stella said, smiling.

Tilly walked toward them with the tray and placed it in the center of the table.

Hannah took her seat and stated, "We can at least tempt our sweet tooth with all these sweets while we sit and talk about what to do next for JoBeth."

"Actually, Hannah, there is not a thing more we can do for her at this time except give her our moral support. We were hoping that you would fill us in on what is going on in your life right now." Sadie said without hesitation.

"What do you mean?" Hannah asked, trying to act surprised.

"Your whole attitude has been changing over the last few weeks. It is a change for the better, Hannah. We are proud of the way you took control of the situation with JoBeth. It is also other things. You have had a sparkle in your eyes lately," beamed Stella.

"You're in love, Hannah! You cannot hide a thing like that. We should have known. Who is he?" Tilly kept pressuring. "Who is he, Hannah?"

"I'm not in love, but I have been talking to a man for several weeks."

"Wait a minute. Have you been talking to a man? That sounds like an internet talk. Is that what you mean? Don't even go there, Hannah. That is dangerous. You may think you are talking to a man, and it could turn out to be a woman or worse," fussed Tilly.

"Wait, everybody, give Hannah a chance," Sadie stated, trying to calm the situation down.

"Thank you, Sadie. Yes, I met him through a dating service on the internet. We have been communicating back and forth only on the computer except for a few times when he has called me on the phone."

"You gave him your phone number?" Tilly lashed out.

"Hush, Tilly, let her continue," Sadie once again said.

"He seems to be a very nice man. He wants me to meet his mother."

"Yep, I just bet he does, and she probably lives with him!" Tilly blurted.

"As a matter of fact, she does," Hannah said as if she was losing her newfound confidence.

Sadie looked sharply at Tilly, letting her know to ease up.

"It hasn't been easy for me all these years. All of you, except for Stella, have lost your husbands due to death. They did not choose to leave you behind. Gordon had a choice, and he decided to walk out of my life. Do you know how that made me feel? I went through a period of grieving, just as you all did but in a different way. Your husbands went to their grave, still loving you, and mine is still alive, walking around, making me feel like a failure."

Gracie reached for Hannah's hand and squeezed it.

Hannah continued, "Yes, it's been several years, and each one of you helped me live again, but deep down inside, I continued to hate myself. He belittled me all the years we lived together. I would walk past a mirror and hate every inch of my body. Do you know how it feels to hate yourself when you should hate the one that has wronged you?"

"You don't have to explain to us, Hannah," Sadie urged, trying to make her know they understood how she felt.

"I'm honestly not trying to be mean, but why did you live with him all the years you did?" Tilly asked, with sympathy in her voice.

Hannah reached for her coffee cup, took a small sip, and then continued, "It was very simple for me to continue to live with him. I had a son to raise, and I did not want him coming up the way I did. This is something I have never told anyone because I was ashamed, but I never knew who my father or his family was."

Tilly sharply said, "Hannah, I remember when your mother was very sick, and I went over there with you. There were pictures all over the house. I remember seeing a picture of your dad in an army uniform, a picture of your grandmother, and maybe even some cousins. Your mother had a picture of your dad right on her bedside table right up to the day she died. I remember those pictures. Why would you say you never knew your dad?"

"I knew a father that my mother wanted me to know. She had a fairy tale life and brought me right into it. She told me that she had met my dad at a church gathering that her church was giving for the men in the military. She saw him from across the room and knew they would be together for life. They spent every minute together that he had left on his leave. Then right before he had to go back, the justice of the peace married them. She told me they had two wonderful years together."

"Did you ever question her about the years you never had with him?" Gracie asked.

"Of course, I did. I asked all the questions a child would ask about the daddy she never knew. Mother always had an answer. When I asked her about a grandmother or grandfather that I never met, a picture would appear on the mantel within days. She would tell me that she had received a letter from my grandmother with pictures."

She paused, took a deep breath, and then continued, "On birthdays and Christmas, I would always have a small gift from the grandparents I had never seen. Mother said they lived far away, but we would save money someday to go and visit them. That someday never came."

Sadie calmly asked, "How did your mother explain the reason that you never got to meet your father?"

"At a very early age, I remember her telling me that he was on his way home from the army base, and he had a car wreck. She told me that seven months later, I was born. Therefore, he never got to hold me in his arms, and I could never call him daddy. That satisfied me. I simply believed everything she said. After all, she was my mother, and mothers never lie to their children."

"Did your mother finally admit to lying to you?" Tilly questioned.

"Of course not. I had to find out myself."

"Well, don't stop now! Tell us how you found out." Tilly commanded.

"I was about thirteen years old. A classmate and I were voted to go and buy our schoolteacher a Christmas gift. Everyone in the class voted to buy her a picture frame, and then we would put our class picture in it as a gift.

We took the money that was collected, and her mother drove us to the local mall. We went into a novelty store with dozens of picture frames, and up on a shelf sat a picture of my grandmother. I was in shock. I went and looked on another shelf, and there was a picture of my make-believe grandfather. I could not believe what I was seeing. I looked through all the picture frames looking for a picture that was supposed to be my father, but I guess it was so outdated that the picture wasn't used anymore."

She took another sip of coffee and then continued once again, "Well, it didn't take me long to realize what was going on. My life, as I knew it was a total lie. I had been looking at pictures all those years that were duplicated in thousands of picture frames. I guess my mother would go into a store, pick out the picture of a family member that she thought we needed, and buy it."

"Did you confront your mother on this?" Sadie asked.

"No, I never did. I guess I was a mature little girl or just stupid. After I got over the shock, either I realized that Mother didn't know exactly who my father was or something terribly wrong because she didn't tell me the truth. Maybe I didn't want to know the truth at that time. I was happy living in her fairy tale, so I fantasized that my father was very famous. One day Father would be Elvis, and then on other days, I would let him be the president of the United States. It made life easier for me."

"You're a better woman than me," Tilly admitted. "I would have done something."

"Well, I can't admit I was a perfect little angel. I got so upset about her lies that one day I asked did I have any cousins. Within two days, there were pictures on the mantel that magically became my cousins. She even gave them names that I could call them. The strange thing is that as I got older, Mother would go out and buy pictures that seem to age, also. My cousins grew older, as I did. I finally quit asking about my father's family."

Hannah sighed and then questioned, "Now, Tilly, does that answer your question?"

"Yes, honey bun, you have answered my question and much more. I also realize now that I should have never made a comment about your son coming back home to live with you. I apologize. I will never tease you about it again. I think he realizes how his dad made you feel all the years he was growing up, and he worries about you even at this age."

"If you didn't speak your mind about things, you would not be Tilly," Hannah said, laughing. "You are probably right, and I need to do something about that to let him realize it is time for him to live his own life and quit worrying about mine."

"We are still worried about this internet guy. Don't jump into something to prove to your son that you have a life of your own," Gracie urged.

"Gracie is right, Hannah. You need to take it slow, and if it is meant to be, you will find happiness. A dating service from the internet is not a safe place to find your perfect mate. So, you can see why we are worried about you," Sadie said, honestly

"I promise I will take it slow, and I won't do anything without first running it by all of you. Now, can we change the subject?" Hannah asked.

" I am not ready to change the subject right yet. I would like to know if you have forgiven Gordon for leaving you for another woman," Stella asked.

Hannah lowered her head and slowly answered, "Yes, I suppose I have. Forgiving just keeps life moving in the right direction. Forgiving doesn't change what he did to me, it doesn't change the past, but it does help."

"One more question, and we will leave you alone," Gracie said quickly.

Hannah looked at Gracie with a smile. She was not one to ask many questions, so Hannah felt it was all right.

"Have you ever tried to find your father?"

"No, but there have been times I did give it a lot of thought. I didn't want to try to find him before Mother's death. I admit growing up and wondering just what happened played with my heart and mind. I would wonder about the possibility of Mother being raped, or maybe the man was married when they met. I would have all kinds of thoughts of why a father wasn't in my life, but it doesn't matter now. At this point, he would probably be in his middle eighties, and more than likely, he is dead."

"Well, we know for sure that Elvis was not your father," Tilly said. "It is obvious after the display that Stella gave us with the shaking of the hips in front of the doctor that Elvis is her father. Shake, rattle, and roll are the things Miss Stella had on her mind today."

"You are as mean as a rattlesnake, Tilly. All right, I admit I was flirting," Stella admitted, in a huff.

They all grew silent, looked at one another, and then busted out laughing.

Sadie was the first to speak, "I do declare girls, after all these years, we can fuss at one another one minute and then be laughing together the next."

"That's what best girlfriends do. You can laugh together but also cry on one another's shoulder. You can also trust them with a secret that you would prefer to take to your grave," Gracie softly said.

Again, the girls grew quiet in hopes that Gracie would continue, but the mystery woman once again went silent. She picked up her coffee cup, brought it toward her mouth, and said, "Looks like I need a refill."

Suddenly, a nurse opened the door to the patio and announced, "Excuse me, ladies, but the doctor is ready to talk with you now. Please follow me."

They jumped from their seats and filed in behind the nurse.

Tilly caught up with Sadie and whispered, "What is going on with Gracie?"

Sadie shook her head and placed her finger on her closed lips. This let Tilly know not to ask any more questions.

The doctor was waiting at the door of his office. JoBeth was nowhere in sight.

"Come on in, ladies. I have found each of you a chair to sit in," he said as he motioned them toward the empty chairs.

"I know you are wondering where JoBeth is right now. She has checked herself in and has already been signed a room."

He sat back down in his chair and turned to the group once again, "I know you are not going to want to hear what I am going to say, but here goes. She cannot have any contact outside of this center for at least three weeks, and then we will talk about a visit."

Sadie spoke up, "I think we all knew that was coming."

"She has told me that I can speak freely about her condition with all of you. You ladies must all have an exceptional bond with one another."

He continued with his voice sounding serious, "Sadie, I understand you are the nurse in the group. So, you know just how bad her condition is, don't you?"

Sadie nodded her head, yes.

"Her condition is known as Anorexia Nervosa. It can cause heart and kidney problems and even death. Her treatment will involve monitoring, mental health therapy, nutritional counseling, and maybe medicine and ....."

Suddenly, Tilly stopped him in mid-sentence, "Could you get down from your stethoscope for just a minute? I don't understand some of the words you are using."

"I bet you're Tilly," he said with a low chuckle.

"Yes, but how did you know?"

"Let's just say your name came up while JoBeth and I were talking."

"What caused this to happen to JoBeth?" Stella asked before Tilly could think of something to make her stumble over outspoken words again.

"In some people, we find that having a negative self-image and a high level of negative feelings, in general, will create this. Undergoing a stressful life change, such as a new job or move, events such as rape or abuse, and sometimes a sudden death in the family can trigger this to happen. That is what we are going to have to figure out. The short time JoBeth and I have talked has given me absolutely no clue. She is definitely in denial and is unreliable in terms of providing accurate information. I was hoping the five of you might be able to shed some light on this."

"Her husband, Cody, died a few years back. They were extremely close. When you saw one, the other was close by. They had a very special relationship. Maybe that is a part of the problem," Sadie suggested.

"That gives me a place to start. You ladies have done the most important step, and that was getting her to come here. Later, I am sure she will feel very blessed that her friends helped her search for help early. Now, let me begin my work on getting her well. Sadie, I will call you and let you know her progress, and I'm sure you will pass it on to the others." He rose from his chair and said, "It was nice meeting each of you, but now I need to go make sure JoBeth is settled in."

He shook each of their hands, and out the door, he went.

They remained silently seated, staring at one another.

Hannah was the first to speak, "Are we not going to be able to hug her and tell her, bye?"

She wiped away the tears that had started running down her cheek.

"I can almost bet you that she doesn't want to see us right now. We are the ones that forced her to come, and by tonight, she will be extremely angry with each of us. They will immediately be encouraging her to eat and actually watch her eat. Then they will make sure she does not force it back up later." Sadie explained.

"The only thing we can do now is go on home and hope she will want the help being offered her," said Stella.

"We need to be sending up a lot of prayers for her. She is going to need every one of them," Sadie pointed out in a scared voice. "She has a rough road ahead of her, and we can't be here to help her."

Chapter 4

Secrets are like fireflies that have been caught and put in an
old mason jar.
As long as the lid is tightly secure, they will fly around
anxiously, but not hurting anyone.
Once the lid is removed, they quickly flutter out in
all directions.
Sometimes secrets would be best kept as fireflies
in a mason jar.
Once the secrets are released, they too,
as fireflies, flutter around
from one place to the other.
Unlike the fireflies, secrets can change the lives of many,
even destroying what once was a happy memory.

Once again, the ladies were seated at their usual table at Midway Restaurant, eating breakfast. The only difference was that JoBeth was not in attendance.

"It feels funny not having JoBeth among us," Stella admitted.

"I had an update from Dr. Roberts this morning." Sadie happily stated.

"Fill us in on the report. I sure hope it is good news," Tilly said.

Sadie smiled, "The doctor said that she was making progress. If she continues in this way, we will be able to see her in a couple of weeks."

"Our prayers are being answered," Hannah stated. "We should feel blessed."

Gracie touched Hannah on her shoulder and softly said, "I hope you still feel like that when I tell you what I have been doing the last two weeks."

Looking puzzled, Hannah asked, "What do you mean, Gracie?"

Gracie slowly picked up her coffee cup and brought it to her lips. She took a long sip as if trying to gather enough courage to continue. She finally placed the cup back on the saucer.

She kept her head lowered, and without giving Hannah eye contact, she said, "I know who your father is."

"You what?" Hannah shouted.

The customers that were sitting around them became silent.

Ida quickly came to their table and said, "Hannah is everything all right?"

Hannah politely apologized, "Ida, I'm sorry. I didn't mean to startle anyone. I was just told something that shocked me. I'm going to be fine."

Ida chuckled and then said in a whisper, "I love the mornings you ladies are here. You all make this place come alive with your laughing and talking."

Filling their cups with fresh coffee, she continued, "By the way, let JoBeth know I miss her."

"Thank you, Ida, that is sweet of you," Sadie said.

Ida smiled and walked away to continue to pour coffee for her other customers.

Gracie once again put her attention to Hannah, "We can forget that I ever made that statement, and I will never bring it up again."

All eyes were on Hannah. No one at the table was saying a word.

Finally, Tilly broke the silence, "Hannah, you may not want to know, but I surely do. Can Gracie tell me?"

Hannah sternly stated, "I didn't say I didn't want to know. I am just scared that it might change the lives of a lot of people, with me being one of them."

"Of course, it's going to change your life. You will finally be able to put a real picture of your father in one of those picture frames." Tilly said.

"What do you think I should do, Sadie?" Hannah asked in a pleading voice.

"If I were in your situation, I would want to know everything that I could find out about the man that helped bring me into this world. You can always keep the information you find out to yourself. It doesn't have to be shared."

Hannah turned to Gracie and stated, "Start at the beginning. I'm ready to hear everything."

"It was effortless. I paid a little visit to the courthouse. I had all the information I needed to find your birth certificate, so that is what I did. Right there in black and white was the name of your mother and your father. I was concerned that your mother might have put down a false name for your dad, but she didn't."

"How do you know it was a real name?" Tilly asked.

"I went straight from the courthouse to the library and used the computer. You just put the name of the person you are looking for in search and click. His name came up very quickly in several places. He was a history teacher for many years and later became a principal of a school right here in the county."

"You mean he has been living right under my nose all this time?" Hannah asked, almost in tears.

"That's exactly what I mean," Gracie said.

"What is his name?" Tilly asked excitedly.

"Hannah, it's your call. Do you want to know who he is?" Gracie questioned.

Without hesitation, Hannah questioned, "Yes, Gracie, what is the name of my father?"

"His name is Kenneth Reed and Hannah, and he is still alive."

"I can't believe this. Kenneth Reed was my son's history teacher. I can remember him as plain as day. Travis was having a lot of trouble with his grades, and Mr. Reed made learning fun for him. He turned my son around when it came to enjoying school. He was a favorite teacher of all the kids," Sadie said in amazement.

"Seemed like everyone knew and loved Kenneth Reed except for his daughter," Hannah said softly.

"Is this where we stop and put the secret back in the past?" Gracie questioned.

"It sounds like you got all this planned out, Gracie. What do we do next?"

"Well, Hannah, I guess you can say I have already taken care of that."

"Sounds like you have been a busy little beaver, Gracie. I like your style, girl," laughed Tilly.

"What did you do?" Stella questioned.

"Well, I then printed out every bit of the information that the website had to offer. It told the school's name he had taught at and the school where he had become a principal. It covered a lot of information about his life."

"What did you do then?" Tilly asked impatiently.

"I called the school where he had been a principal many years ago. I told the secretary that he had been my history teacher, and I wanted to put together a class reunion. I wanted my favorite teacher to attend. This was a way of finding out if he was still living or not. She was happy to tell me everything that she knew about him. Hannah, the way she talked, he was a very kind and gentle man."

"Well, again, that is something I wouldn't know. He certainly didn't want me in his life," Hannah stated angrily.

"Stop that, Hannah. You don't know if he even knew about you. Give him the benefit of the doubt." Sadie ordered sternly.

"Well, let's go meet Father. We have a lot of catching up to do."

"It's not going to be that easy, Hannah. He is at Meadowview Nursing Home. He has been there for many years. He is in the Alzheimer's Care Unit." Gracie informed.

Hannah started to weep, "So, I come this far and may not learn why he abandoned Mother and me?"

"Things aren't always the way they seem," Sadie said.

"You are certainly correct about that," Gracie stated, looking at Sadie with that mysterious look that always appears out of nowhere.

"Let's go see him, Hannah. Please say you will. Meadowview Nursing Home is only about twenty minutes from here." Stella said, almost pleading.

"Hannah, there is something else I was able to find out," Gracie informed her.

"You are just a wealth of information, Gracie," Tilly teased.

"Tell me, Gracie, don't leave anything out at this point," Hannah said sadly.

Gracie reached for Hannah's hand, placed it in hers, and softly said, "He had two sons and a daughter. His daughter died when she was six years old. His wife died of cancer over ten years ago. As I said before, the secretary at the school had only kind words to say about him."

"Well, we will see," Hannah said while reaching for her pocketbook. She reached inside, found tip money for Ida, placed it on the table, and said, "Well, ladies, what are you waiting for? Let's go find my father and see what he has to say about me."

Soon, they were walking through the wide doors of Meadowview Nursing Home. It was a beautiful place with bright shiny floors and large comfortable looking furniture placed carefully around the room.

In the corner was a large fireplace with a wooden mantel. Hannah could not help but notice all the pictures in bright shiny frames that were placed on top. It brought back memories of her childhood home with the make-believe pictures of her make-believe family that lined their mantel. She was sure these were real people with real lives.

Suddenly, Hannah felt a wave of sadness that engulfed her entire body. She turned and started walking toward the exit door.

She felt someone touch her lightly on the shoulder.

"If you leave now, you will never forgive yourself," Sadie said. "You will always hold on to the questions that you've held in your heart all your life. It will eat away at you like cancer. Don't walk away from something that might change your life for the better."

"Sadie," Hannah whispered. "I know you are right, but I'm scared. I am almost fifty-eight years old, and I am getting ready to meet my father for the first time in my life. This is tearing me apart inside."

Gracie walked toward Hannah and stated, "We can stop anytime. Remember, you are the one controlling this."

She smiled and continued, "Sometimes life is full of surprises as well as secrets. Our lives are not always what they appear to be to other people. Give this moment a chance and see what might be in your future beyond these doors."

Sadie stood silently, trying to figure out the statement that Gracie had just made. It somehow appeared to her that she was talking about her own life.

Hannah did not question Gracie. She grabbed for her arm and whispered, "Walk me to the front desk. I am as weak as a kitten."

Gracie wrapped Hannah's arm carefully in hers and walked toward the desk. The others followed close behind.

As they got closer, Tilly whispered to Sadie, "What are we going to tell the nurse the reason for wanting to visit this man?"

Sadie whispered back, "Something tells me that Gracie has everything under control."

"Hello," Gracie said, with a broad smile plastered across her face. "We would like to see Kenneth Reed if it is possible."

Tilly joined in, talking rapidly, "He was my favorite teacher in school, and we are doing a section in the local newspaper about him."

The nurse looked puzzled at the statement Tilly had just made.

Sadie walked toward Tilly, put her arm around her waist, and said, "She means Mr. Reed was her son's favorite teacher."

"Oh, yes, that's what I meant. I guess I am having one of those senior moments again," Tilly said with a slight laugh.

The nurse smiled, "We definitely understand senior moments around here. I am glad you picked today to visit him. He is having a good day. He may even remember the name of your son. On his good days, he is a wealth of information and a joy to talk with. He is a very nice man."

Hannah whispered to Gracie, "I'll be the judge of that."

The nurse pointed, "Continue walking down this hall, and you will be at the lounge. He will be in his wheelchair sitting close to the large window. He tells us that the sun beaming through the window makes his tired old bones feel better, bless his heart."

"Thank you," Sadie said as they started walking slowly down the hall.

Hannah continued to hold tightly to Gracie's arm.

As they opened the lounge door, it seemed that the warm morning sun filled every corner of the room.

They stood and looked around.

"There must be a dozen old men in wheelchairs in here. Which one is he?" Tilly asked while taking a few steps away from Sadie. "I didn't mean anything by that, so don't pinch me, Sadie."

Sadie could not help but smile.

Gracie seemed to know exactly where to go. She continued to hold on to Hannah, walking her straight toward a man that had his back turned from them. He was staring out the window as if he were in another place and time.

"Excuse me, Mr. Reed, how are you today?" Gracie asked softly.

He slowly placed his hands on the wheelchair, making it turn to face them.

"I am doing fine. Thank you, young lady." He paused for a few seconds looking at each of them and then continued."Do I know you, nice ladies?"

Hannah's heart melted. She was not ready for the reaction she was having. It was as if she were looking in a mirror. She knew now where the color of her eyes and the shape of her nose had come from. This man was definitely her father.

"You don't know us, but we sure know you. You taught some of our children when you were a teacher at Parkwood High School," Gracie said as if she had been practicing for this question.

"Oh, that seems like a lifetime ago. Please pardon me if I don't remember their names, but I will try." He said as if trying to bring back those years from his memory bank.

"It isn't important that you remember their names. We are interested in you. We would like to do an article on your life as a teacher during the years that teachers were allowed to teach the important things." Gracie said as she continued to play the game.

Suddenly, a strange look came across Mr. Reed's face as he put all his attention on Hannah.

He finally spoke with tears running down his cheeks as he rolled his wheelchair toward her.

He looked up at her and said, "Young lady, could you humor an old man for a moment?"

He reached for her hand, and Hannah quickly grabbed for his. She kneeled on one knee beside his wheelchair.

He reached toward her face and softly cuffed it in his hands.

"You remind me of someone very important in my life," he said.

"I do?" Hannah asked, fighting back the tears that were building up inside her.

"You remind me of someone I knew many years ago. She meant everything to me. I didn't fight hard enough for her. When you love someone, and they are suddenly taken out of your life....." He stopped in mid-sentence. A blank look appeared across his face, and he said, "Do I know you, nice ladies?"

Without acknowledging their presence in the room, he slowly pulled his hand from Hannah's face and rolled his wheelchair back toward the window. It was evident that the Kenneth Reed they had just met was no longer with them.

They could hear him softly saying, "The warm sun coming in the window makes my old bones feel good."

"What just happened, Gracie?" Hannah asked.

Gracie placed her finger across her lips in a motion for Hannah to stop talking. Hannah knew immediately that someone was standing behind her. She turned around to face a man that appeared to be in his middle forties. He was a striking man with salt and pepper hair that resembled her newfound father.

"I can see that Father has once again gone into that silent shell of Alzheimer's. The nurse at the front desk told me that you were hoping to talk to him about his early teaching years. I'm sorry if you didn't get enough information."

He smiled and extended his hand to Hannah, "I'm Derrick Reed. Kenneth Reed is my father."

Hannah reached for his hand and softly held it as she talked, "You have a charming and interesting father. I know you are very proud of him."

He nodded and then turned and walked toward his father. They watched as he hugged his father.

He turned back once again to them and slowly walked toward Hannah.

"I hope he didn't upset you with his talk of a lost love. He does that quite often now. We don't know if it is a part of the Alzheimer's or a real person who was once in his life. We just know that it seems to calm him down when he talks about her, and so we sit and listen."

"He was such a great teacher, and I am sure he is a great father as well," Hannah said, trying to get as much information as she could from her half-brother.

"Yes, he is. I miss the way he was before, but I just try harder to hold on to the memories of when I was a young boy. Did he tell you I have a brother, and I also had a sister?" Derrick asked.

Hannah suddenly became silent. Gracie realized that she had to do the talking for her.

Gracie quickly said, "He didn't mention them, but I am sure he would have if we had longer with him."

"Yes, when he is having a good day, he tells everyone about his family. My brother's name is William. We had a sister, but she died when she was only six years old. I didn't get to know her because I came along much later after her death. I can remember Mother telling me that she was the bright light of Father's life. In his eyes, Mary Jo could do no wrong."

He continued, "It would have been nice to grow up with an older sister in my life. Sometimes life plays you a bad hand of cards, and I guess that is what happened. She had a rare form of cancer that took her quickly. Mother told us later that Father almost lost his mind when he lost his little angel. Even to this day, when he starts rambling, he will talk about his angel, Mary Jo."

Suddenly, Hannah found new strength to talk once again, "Derrick, do you mind if we come back to revisit your father?"

"No, I hope you do. He doesn't get many visitors anymore. Mother has been dead for many years, and he has very few friends left that are his age. So please, feel free to visit anytime."

He smiled and once again continued, "It was nice meeting each of you, but I need to get back to Father. I don't have long to visit today. I need to get back to the office. I just felt the need to come today if not, but just for a few minutes."

He turned, reached for a chair, and pulled it close to his father.

Hannah stood watching as he reached for her father's hand and placed it softly in his. Derrick talked to him as if he could acknowledge everything he was saying.

She quickly turned and walked out of the room with the others right behind her. She didn't stop at the front desk.

When she was safely outside, she turned to them and cried, "Mary Jo was my mother's name. He named his daughter after my mother. That proves he loved Mother, and I know if he had known me, he would have loved me, also. I have got to know the truth."

Gracie said firmly, "Then it is time to get the rest of the story from your aunt."

"How do you know that I still have an aunt living?" Hannah questioned.

"Let's just say that I have my ways," Gracie said and started walking toward the car.

"Here we go again trying to figure out what the mystery woman means," said Tilly.

"After all these years, I don't think we will ever figure out Gracie," said Stella.

Sadie smiled and whispered to herself, "Yes, someday we will."

Chapter 5

When you live your life with secrets,
there is always emptiness you feel in your
heart and mind.
The thoughts of 'could have been, should
have been,'
continue to haunt you into the winter of
your years,
and you are never, ever the same.

Within twenty minutes, they were pulling into the driveway of Hannah's aunt. The car ride had been a silent one, with Hannah trying to let everything she had just found out sink in. There were still many unanswered questions, but she was determined to find them out one way or another.

"Hannah, before we get out, I just have to know why you never questioned your aunt about this all these years," Tilly said, bluntly.

"I guess I thought I would be disrespecting Mother," Hannah admitted. "I have had very little contact with my aunt. I guess my life went in different directions. Then, after I got married, I put everything I had into making my marriage work."

"Well, we see where that got you," Tilly blurted out.

"I don't need a remark like that at this point, Tilly. You are much too opinionated."

"Well, that's your opinion," Tilly said, smiling.

"I give up on you, Tilly," Hannah said.

"No, you don't, and actually, I was trying to pay you a compliment. It just didn't come out right. What I meant to say was that husband of yours wasn't worth trying to save. You are better off without him."

"I agree with Tilly on that one," Stella chimed in.

"Are we going to sit in the car all afternoon and talk about Hannah's ex-husband or help her find out the truth about her father?" Sadie questioned.

"Hush, ladies, and get out of the car. Hannah, your aunt, is sitting on her front porch, probably hearing everything we are saying," Gracie said calmly.

They quickly got out of the car and headed toward the white-haired woman rocking back and forth in an old wooden rocker.

Sadie rushed to Tilly's side and whispered, "Do you know you can be a nuisance at times?

Hannah has been through a lot today, and we still don't know what is facing her once she questions her aunt. Now, you are trying to start something about her failed marriage. You beat all I have ever seen."

"Yes, I know I can be a nuisance, but you still love me," Tilly whispered

"Yes, but you sure are making it hard," Sadie admitted.

Tilly gave her a sneaky look and then ran to catch up with Hannah. She put her arm around her shoulder and said, "Once again, I apologize for my big mouth. I want you to know I've been very proud of you today. I don't think I could handle things the way you did at the nursing home."

Hannah smiled and said, "I hope you continue to feel that way after I've finished talking to my aunt. I am determined to get the truth out of her, even if I have to become a Tilly."

Tilly smiled, but the smile quickly changed to a puzzled look. She turned to Sadie and asked, "What did she mean by that?"

Sadie laughed and said, "Now, Tilly, what do you think she meant?"

Hannah swiftly walked up the steps and greeted her aunt with a hug, "Hello, Aunt Bella, how are you doing this nice sunny afternoon?"

"I'm doing just fine, Hannah. What a nice surprise to see you, and you have brought friends. This is certainly a pleasure for an old woman."

Hannah introduced each of them, leaving Tilly for last. Tilly sensed this but did not say a word.

"Please find a rocker and join me," she said, pointing to all the extra rockers that lined her front porch. It was obvious that in the past, she had done a lot of entertaining.

She continued, "There won't be very many sunny days left to take advantage of before it starts to turn cold. These bones of mine don't like the cold."

Hannah's thoughts immediately went back to her father's comment about the sun making his bones feel better. She knew that for the rest of her life, feeling the warm sun against her skin would bring her father's words back to her.

She put these thoughts from her mind, pulled her rocker close to her aunt, and said, "Aunt Bella, this isn't just an ordinary visit I have come for."

"I didn't think it was. I've wondered all these years when this day was going to come," she said, continuing to rock slowly back and forth.

"There are many questions I need to be answered, and I think you are the only one that can answer them. They are unanswered questions I have lived with all my life."

"Ask away, child, and they will be answered the best way I know how."

"Today, I met a man named Kenneth Reed. It turns out he is my father."

"That he is, my child," she said calmly.

"Why was this kept from me all these years? I had the right to know," Hannah said with a stern tone in her voice.

Aunt Bella looked straight into Hannah's eyes and said, "Yes, you did, but it's not that simple. I don't want you to blame your mother for not being honest with you. Mary Jo did what she thought was best for everyone concerned at the time."

She continued, "Would you like to talk to me alone, or are your friends here to learn about family secrets as well?"

"I have nothing to hide from them," Hannah said.

Aunt Bella took a deep breath and then slowly began to help Hannah fill the void she had in her life.

"My sister met Kenneth Reed at school. I honestly feel it was love at first sight for both of them. Father disapproved of him. Grant you, Father could be a good man, but it was a side he hardly ever showed. I guess you could consider him a bit of a snob. Are you familiar with the old saying, the other side of the tracks?" Aunt Bella asked.

Hannah nodded.

"Well, Father, let it be known that he felt Kenneth was from the other side of the tracks and wasn't good enough for his daughter. He forbid Mary Jo to see Kenneth. This almost broke her heart. The only time she was able to see him was at school. This was enough for both of them, but soon school was out for the summer. They had absolutely no contact at all then."

She paused, took a deep breath, and then continued, "I'll never forget the day Kenneth came to our house, walked right up the steps, and knocked on the door. Father must have seen him walking up the sidewalk because he just sat in his big leather chair and gave us strict orders not to go to the door. I swear, I think Kenneth knocked for five minutes. Then he started calling out Mary Jo's name. That made Father's blood boil. He jumped up, grabbed for the door, and flung it open."

Hannah asked quickly, "What did my father do then?"

"He stood there looking like a block of stone, and then he slowly asked to speak to Mary Jo. That angered Father evermore. He screamed at the top of his lungs at Kenneth. He told him that if he ever stepped foot on his property again, he would have him arrested. He told him he was never to try to see Mary Jo again. Then he slammed the door right in his face."

"What did Mother do then?"

"She ran for the door, but Father grabbed her arm and pushed her up against the wall. She screamed out that she hated Father and ran to our room with me right behind her.

Father screamed right back, telling her not to come out of the room until she was ready to apologize for her outburst."

She drew another deep breath and continued as if she needed to tell Hannah everything without stopping.

"We both ran to our bedroom window and watched as Kenneth slowly walked down the street with his head bowed low."

"So, Mother, let him walk away?" Hannah questioned.

"My goodness, no. The next thing I knew, she was opening the window, jumped out, and ran right into his arms."

Aunt Bella closed her eyes tightly as if she was trying to see the past played out once again, "I can still see them now embraced in one another's arms. Then they took off running as fast as they could down the street."

"Where did they go?" Tilly asked quickly.

Aunt Bella looked at Tilly and smiled.

Then she turned her attention back to Hannah and said, "I never asked your mother where they went, but I sat at that window all night long waiting for her to return. Father never came to our room that entire night. After all, he told her not to come out until she was willing to apologize." She laughed and then said, "Well, it didn't appear she was ready to apologize."

Everyone sat silently, waiting for Aunt Bella to continue her story. Tilly wanted to ask more questions but knew now wasn't the time.

Finally, Hannah broke the silence with another question. "When did Mother come back?"

"The next morning, around nine o'clock, she came crawling back through the window. She made me promise not to tell. It wasn't a hard secret to keep. We were very close, and I would never betray her trust."

"But, I don't understand...."

Aunt Bella stopped Hannah in mid-sentence.

"Humor me, child. I will help you to understand. Just be patient. Your mother continued for several weeks, sliding out that window to meet her love. Father never knew until one hot August morning. We were gathered around the breakfast table when suddenly, Mary Jo got very sick on her stomach. She took off, running to the bathroom with Mother hot on her heels. Within five minutes, Mother came out screaming that she knew Mary Jo had to be with child."

"That child was me," Hannah announced, smiling.

"You're so right," Aunt Bella said, smiling. "Well, Mary Jo was rushed off to a doctor in two states away to get her pregnancy confirmed. Father didn't want anyone in our town to know that his daughter had disgraced him."

Tilly said under her breath, "He was a real royal snob."

"I'm old, Tilly, but I'm not deaf. You are right, though. My father was what he called the pillow of the community, and he wasn't about to have his daughter pregnant and not married."

"Then why didn't he let them get married?" Hannah asked.

"Are you kidding? That would be giving in and allowing his daughter to be married to someone that was beneath her. Father was determined that would never happen."

Sadie felt like it was her time to ask a question. She couldn't hold it back any longer.

She asked, "What did he do when they got back from the doctor's office?"

"Well, Mother came in with Mary Jo, slowly walking about five steps behind her. She announced that Mary Jo was definitely pregnant, and her life as a teenager was over. Father went straight to our room, packed a suitcase, grabbed Mary Jo by the arm, and walked her straight to the car. He drove down our street as if he was going for an afternoon drive. I didn't see Mary Jo for several years after that day."

Once again, Aunt Bella became silent. She reached in her apron pocket, pulled out a handkerchief, and wiped the tears from her eyes. After all these years, this reflection of the past still upset her.

Stella couldn't hold her silence anymore, "Can you tell us where he took her?"

She nodded and said, "She was taken to a home for unwed mothers. Of course, Father called it home for sinful girls that disgraced their families. He told our neighbors and his friends that Mary Jo was finishing her education in a private school in England."

Sadie questioned," Did they believe his story?"

"If they didn't, they would never question him. Father was the type of man that no one would question any of his actions. He planned that Mary Jo would have the baby, give it up for adoption, and return home after a few months. Then he would tell his friends that Mary Jo was too homesick to study in England and decided to come home. Oh, he was a smooth talker, that father of mine."

"Well, it is obvious she didn't give me up for adoption."

Aunt Bella smiled and said, "Your mother was a brave and determined woman. She gave birth to you, and in less than four hours, she walked right out of that place, holding you tightly in her arms. She went straight to a battered women's shelter."

"I've got to know the truth, Aunt Bella, no matter how much it will hurt. Did my father ever know about me?" Hannah asked softly.

"No, child. Father saw to that. For weeks, after Mary Jo was sent away, Kenneth would come to the house pounding on the door. Father continued to tell his lies. He convinced Kenneth that Mary Jo decided to go away. She didn't want to have anything else to do with him. After several months, I suppose Kenneth finally believed him. You have to remember he was only sixteen. What could he do? He believed that Mary Jo was in England. There was no way he could jump on a plane to England and beg her to love him again. He didn't have enough money for a bus ticket, let alone a plane ticket. I remember the last time he came begging for information about Mary Jo. Father kept repeating the same lies with a very calm voice. Kenneth's hopes were crushed, and it showed all over his face. He left, and Father had finally won."

Hannah stood up and walked to the edge of the porch. She took a deep breath and then suddenly started to cry softly. Sadie went to her side and hugged her.

"It's a happy cry, Sadie. I finally know that I had a father that would have loved me if only he had just known I existed."

Aunt Bella spoke up, "Mary Jo had all intentions in letting Kenneth know about you, but Father refused to let her come back home after you were born. She continued to stay at the shelter until you were about eighteen months old. I honestly don't see how she did it. She managed to find a cheap apartment, got a job, and raised you on her own."

"Did she ever try to contact Kenneth after Hannah was born?" Tilly asked.

"Yes, she tried before and after Hannah was born. She wrote letter after letter, but Kenneth never got them."

"How do you know that?" Tilly questioned once again.

"Because I went and talked with Kenneth's mother. After all, Mary Jo was my sister, and I knew she and Kenneth loved one another very much."

"Could his mother not help them be together?" Stella asked.

"Father was a very important man in this town, and he threatened them. He could make a single phone call and have Kenneth's father fired from his job. You have to remember they were very poor, and he couldn't afford to lose his job. Kenneth's mother told me that Mary Jo would write letter after letter. Still, as the letters arrived, she would immediately burn them. It was easy to keep the secret from Kenneth. After the last talk Father had with him, he lied about his age and joined the army."

"Did your father ever find out that you went to Kenneth's mother for help?" Sadie asked.

"No, but finally, she asked me not to come back. She was that scared of Father. I honored her wish and never went back, but I did call her several times. I had to find out about Kenneth and the life he was living without my sister. I promised her I would never let anyone know we communicated."

Hannah looked puzzled, "I still can't understand why Mother didn't eventually tell him the truth."

"Your mother was a proud woman, and that's why she kept the secret. She continued to live away from our parents for two more years. She had a plan to save money, come back, find Kenneth, and make a life with him. Then I found out he had gotten married while he was stationed at Fort Sill, Oklahoma. I wrote to Mary Jo, letting her know. I didn't receive a letter from her for several weeks. I didn't know what to think. I finally received a letter telling me she would never try to contact him. She wasn't going to break up a marriage. She knew how it felt to lose someone you love, and she didn't want this woman to feel the heartbreak she had known for the past few years."

Hannah was full of questions, and she was not about to quit asking them now, "How did Mother end up moving back to Monroe?"

"Well, when you were a little over two years old, Father died. Mother decided the house was too large for just the two of us. She found a house that suited her needs about forty miles away. So we packed everything and moved. Mother wanted her granddaughter in her life. She had felt this way the entire time, but she was ruled by Father and his wants. So she kept her feelings to herself until after his death. I called Mary Jo and convinced her to come back home. She agreed completely with me. The two of you lived with us for about six months, and then she rented a house that was just a five-minute drive from us. Mother was on cloud nine. She kept you while Mary Jo worked. She loved you, Hannah, and I truly believe she tried to make up for the grandparents you didn't know and have."

"She loved me. I never doubted that while growing up." Hannah admitted.

"Mary Jo gave Mother and me strict orders never to speak of Kenneth Reed in front of you. She told us what we were allowed to say about her life. We were just so happy to have you and her in our lives that we agreed. She would go to the department stores, buy picture frames, keep the pictures already in them, and insist we should acknowledge them as your father's family. Therefore, we did. She felt since we didn't live in the same house or community that Kenneth would think we had moved to another state."

Hannah decided not to let her Aunt Bella know she knew about the make-believe family in the picture frames. It wouldn't make any difference at this point. She quickly made eye contact with each girl, giving them a look that let them know not to bring it up. She mostly gave Tilly the "hush' look before she could remark. Tilly acknowledged this by giving Hannah a quick thumbs-up motion.

Aunt Bella softly said, "Hannah, I'm feeling a little tuckered out. Why don't you gather up your friends and let's go inside."

Hannah looked at her watch. They had been talking for almost two hours.

"Aunt Bella, forgive me. I didn't realize how long we had visited."

Hannah reached for her aunt's arm and helped her from the rocking chair. For the first time since she had arrived, she realized just how frail her Aunt Bella appeared.

Sadie opened the screen door wide as they all walked in.

Immediately, memories engulfed Hannah's mind. The house was filled with the aroma of sweet potato pie. She could remember visiting her grandmother's house, and it was always smelling of fresh-baked bread or gingerbread cookies. She felt a feeling that she hadn't experienced in many years. She smiled. She wanted to hold this memory in her thoughts as long as she could.

Aunt Bella smiled and said, "Tilly, my new friend, why don't you help Hannah get us all a glass of sweet ice tea. There is a sliced turkey in the refrigerator. Sadie, something tells me you can throw together a salad in a flash. Stella, look on the counter and get that fresh sweet tator pie I cooked this morning."

She paused, laughed aloud, and then continued, "We will have us a little party. I don't get many visitors, and for some reason, I don't get invites to parties anymore. I still do a lot of cooking. I guess when you grow up in the time I did, it just comes naturally. Women in my time grew up learning to cook before they were tall enough to reach the wood stove."

She continued to laugh as she turned and went to her bedroom.

Tilly announced in a harsh voice, "She's just plain bossy."

Gracie quickly came to Aunt Bella's defense. "No, Tilly, she is old, lonely, and actually opening her house to us. She is a true Southern woman. I like her style."

Tilly changed her opinion, "I didn't say I didn't like her. Hannah, you have a lovely aunt."

Hannah nodded, turned, and gave Sadie a quick wink. Once again, Tilly had been corrected for her sharp tongue.

Everyone got busy doing the task Aunt Bella had wanted each one to do. In less than ten minutes, a feast of sandwiches, fresh salad, and sweet potato pie was placed on the dining room table.

Hannah could not help to notice several pictures that were placed on the buffet. She smiled as she picked the one up that held a photo of her and her grandmother sitting in a porch swing.

Sadie walked toward Hannah and softly said, "Nice looking family."

Hannah nodded and then replied, "Yes, now I can honestly say they were."

Aunt Bella walked slowly toward the dining room, carrying what appeared to be a massive photo album.

"You all did a good job. You've brightened up an old woman's day."

She sat down, reached for her tea glass, took a sip, and said, "Hannah, this is for you. Mary Jo wanted me to keep it in a safe place many years ago. She told me not to give it to you unless you had questions about your father. This may unlock many questions you had about him and what he did with his life."

Hannah carefully reached for the photo album. She placed it on the table and opened it to the first page. Her eyes began to fill with tears.

"Child, should you wait?" Aunt Bella asked.

"I can't, Aunt Bella. I've been waiting all my life for this day," she said while trying to wipe away the tears.

The others started to eat while keeping a close eye on Hannah. Tilly wanted to join her in looking at the photographs, but Sadie kept giving her *the look*. This lets her know that right now, it was for Hannah's eyes only.

Suddenly, Hannah said excitedly, "Aunt Bella, this is the picture of a man in uniform that Mother kept by her bedside. She told me it was my father, but I didn't believe her. I don't understand. You told me they never saw one another after the day Mother was sent away."

"That's right. I was able to get the pictures, or I guess I should finally admit I stole them."

"You what?" Tilly asked loudly.

"Several months after Kenneth joined the army, I went to see his mother. She was showing me several pictures that he had sent her. I sort of put two of them in my pocket when she went into the other room to answer the phone." She admitted with a grin across her face.

"I'm so glad you did," Hannah softly said.

"I have always regretted grabbing them up and not looking on the back of them," admitted Aunt Bella.

"Why is that?" Stella questioned.

She once again gave a slight chuckle and said, "Well, he had signed one on the back for his mother. He had carefully written, *To Mother, with love, Kenneth.* Mary Jo wanted that one to put in her frame at home and this one to put in the photo album. She felt by doing this, she had his handwriting to cherish as well as the picture."

"Hannah, that was smart thinking on the part of your mother," Tilly said while reaching for another turkey sandwich.

Hannah began to take a few bites of the food while turning to another page. Her mother had kept clippings from every newspaper she could find about the life of Kenneth Reed. He had been selected teacher of the year several times. He had served as chairperson on many projects that helped the community. He had been the principal of a high school that received many honors. There was page after page of his achievements.

Mary Jo had even saved the obituary of Kenneth's young daughter. Hannah's thoughts went immediately to her mother and how she must have felt knowing that he had named his daughter after her.

The last page in the album was an article the newspaper had done about his life and accomplishments. It had stated that he was living now at Meadowview Nursing Home and welcomed friends and colleagues to visit. Underneath on a small piece of paper, Mary Jo had written, *I will go to my grave – loving you.*

Hannah could not hold back the tears any longer.

"Aunt Bella, Mother spent her entire life loving a man she could never have."

"That's right, Hannah. Your mother was a good woman that was certainly not going to destroy another family to get what she wanted. She would never be as evil as Father was. She took all the secrets she could to her grave. If she hurt you in the process, it was not her intention. You were the only part of Kenneth she had, and she cherished you. That is why she walked out of that home just hours after giving birth to you. They were going to take you away. Father had already signed papers."

Aunt Bella reached for Hannah's hand, held it softly, and said, "You will never know the pain and heartache your mother went through all her life. It is hard living a lie, Hannah, but sometimes you do in life what you think is best. That is exactly what Mary Jo did."

Hannah closed the photo album, wiped the tears that were still running down her cheek, and said, "I think I'm ready for a slice of your famous sweet tator pie."

Everyone at the table laughed except Gracie. She sat quietly, looking at the food that remained on her plate.

Aunt Bella was the first to notice. "Child, you look a little pale. Has all this sad talk been too much for you today?"

"Goodness no, Miss Bella. I just feel a little nauseous on my stomach. The doctor said I have an ulcer, and I guess it is trying to show itself today."

Sadie said with concern, "When did you find this out?"

"I went to the doctor a while back. I didn't want everyone to be concerned, and that is why I didn't say anything. If you could just wet me a paper towel so I can blot my face, I will feel better."

Sadie started to get up, but Aunt Bella placed her hand on her shoulder and said, "I'll get it for her, Sadie."

She left the room, but within seconds was back with a white lace handkerchief that she had wet with water. She walked to Gracie and placed it on her forehead.

"Thank you, Aunt Bella, but this is much too pretty to use. All I needed was...."

Aunt Bella stopped her and said, "My new friend can't be walking around, dabbing her face with an old paper towel. It is yours, Gracie. I want you to have it."

"Thank you," Gracie said as she touched the sides of her face with the wet handkerchief. "I feel much better already."

Sadie knew by looking at Gracie that she was not honest with everyone. It was her way of not wanting to spoil the party that Aunt Bella thought she was having.

They all soon noticed Gracie's condition and, without saying a word, began to clear the table.

Hannah reached for her photo album and then walked toward her aunt.

"Aunt Bella, all the words in the world could not begin to let you know how much I love you. Thank you for helping Mother keep her secret, but also, thank you for sharing it with me today."

She reached for Hannah's hand, held it softly, and whispered, "I wanted to tell you just one more thing. I did see Kenneth one more time."

Hannah looked puzzled, but Aunt Bella continued, "A strange thing happened about a year after Kenneth joined the army. I was at my bedroom window, enjoying looking at the leaves beginning to turn their color. I saw Kenneth walk up the street and turn onto our sidewalk. He stopped and just stood there. I swear I think he didn't move for ten minutes. Oh, he looked so grand in that uniform. It was as if he was debating what to do. I stood behind the curtains looking out, making sure he didn't see me. At that point, I had made so many promises with Mary Jo and Kenneth's mother that I didn't know what to do. Therefore, I did nothing. He finally turned and walked back down the street."

Hannah sighed, "I wonder how lives would have been changed if he had just walked to the door and once again tried to talk to someone?"

"Don't question life anymore, Hannah. You're still young and can turn whatever heartache you have had into happiness. Just always remember your mother was not about to change the life of Kenneth's new wife. It takes a special woman to look beyond her wants and desires for someone else's happiness."

"I've never thought of it that way. Mother was an exceptional woman, wasn't she, Aunt Bella?"

She nodded and then smiled.

"I'll be back for another visit, Aunt Bella. I promise I will, but right now, I think we need to get Gracie home. I think she is feeling worse than she is letting on."

Aunt Bella turned to them and said, "This old woman needs some rest, so you spring chickens get on home before it gets any darker. I've enjoyed getting to know each of you, and I expect to see you walk up on my front porch again real soon."

They all promised and then walked out the door, except for Gracie.

She reached for Aunt Bella, hugged her, and said, "Thank you for this day and my handkerchief."

Aunt Bella continued to embrace Gracie. She softly whispered in her ear, "You need to see another doctor to make sure of what is ailing you. I know you don't want to worry your friends, but sometimes it is best to talk about things. After today, I think you as well will realize that. Now, get on out of here and catch up with those wacky friends of yours before you make this old woman cry."

Gracie smiled and did as she had asked.

They quickly got in the car and gave one final wave to Aunt Bella.

Aunt Bella continued to wave until the car was completely out of sight. Then she looked up toward the evening sky and said, "Mary Jo, now I can rest. I kept your secret in my heart for you all these years. Yes, now I can rest."

Suddenly, from the silent car, Hannah said, "Girls, I have a father, and he is a wonderful man. Thank you, Gracie, but how did you find out all this information? You never asked my aunt a single question. It was as if you already knew the answers."

Gracie turned her head toward the window and stared out into the darkness. She didn't say a word.

Complete silence engulfed the car. There would be no more questions asked today.

Chapter 6

One seeks happiness in many forms,
a baby's laugh,
the morning dew on fresh-cut grass,
a mother's hug,
even
the smile from a stranger.
You will never be happy if you look past
every day
happenings.

The weeks seemed to have dragged slowly by, but the girls were finally on their way to get JoBeth. The doctor had called Sadie, letting her know he felt secure enough to let her go home.

Sadie sat quietly in the back seat of the car listening to Stella complain about Tilly's driving.

Hannah was busy attempting to text her new male friend that she had met on the internet. This relationship seemed to be going much too fast for Sadie to feel comfortable.

Sadie tried to think positive about this. Hannah had been happier than she had been in many years. Sadie knew that most of her newfound happiness had been due to finally knowing who her father was, even if she could not acknowledge it to the world. Her new friend from the computer was just icing on the cake.

As usual, Gracie sat very quietly as if she were in deep thought.

"A penny for your thoughts, Gracie," Sadie said as she touched her softly on the arm.

"Oh, just hoping that we will get there safely. Tilly is not the safest driver we could have put at the steering wheel."

Sadie knew that Gracie was not completely honest, but she did not question her. She knew, once again, there would be no use in doing that.

Finally, they were there. Tilly pulled into a parking place. They got out and ran up the steps of the building as if trying to see who would be first to see JoBeth.

As they entered the building, they saw her standing at the desk with a suitcase in hand.

She let it fall to the floor and ran to meet them, "It seems like years since I have seen you all," she said with tear-filled eyes.

"I have great news to fill you in about!" Hannah said excitedly.

"I can't wait to hear about it, and I've got a lot to tell you all as well."

"Hello, ladies," Dr. Roberts said as he walked toward the group. "I see you have all come out to take your friend back home. JoBeth, you are a fortunate woman to have friends like these. Now, if I could take a few more minutes of your time JoBeth, I would like to talk to you and your friends."

He turned and walked toward his office with the Southern Belle Breakfast Club following close behind. Stella looked at the others and sped toward Dr. Roberts so she could be the one right behind him. She turned and gave them a slight smirk.

"There she goes again," said Tilly.

Sadie chuckled and then whispered to Tilly, "Well, at least Dr. Roberts can't see the fool she's making out of herself."

Finally, they reached his office. He had brought in enough chairs that each had a seat.

"I knew you would all come, so I had chairs brought in for you. First, JoBeth, I want to let your friends know that I am very proud of you. You made unbelievable progress in the weeks you were admitted. I questioned your desire to get better the first few days you were here. I will let you decide how much you want to tell your friends about the treatment. You will need to come in once a week to continue your counseling. I know you would have done this on your own, but I didn't feel like you would mind your friends knowing about this."

He looked toward Sadie and then continued, "It might be hard the first few days by herself, but I know I can depend on each of you to be there for her."

They nodded.

After saying this, he stood, walked to JoBeth, and gave her a slight hug.

"Now, JoBeth, live life, love life, and enjoy life, and I will see you next week," he said.

Each of them shook his hand, and out his office door, they went.

Hannah rushed down the hall to get JoBeth's suitcase.

She smiled at JoBeth and said, "I helped you pack this suitcase, bring it in that first day, and I am going to carry it out for you. JoBeth, I don't want you or this suitcase ever coming back here in the shape you were in several weeks ago."

JoBeth stopped, turned to face her friends, and said, "I promise I will never be like that again. Now, let's go eat breakfast."

It felt good for them to be together again. As they walked into Midway Restaurant, they waved at Ida. She quickly came toward them and hugged JoBeth.

"So glad you are back. I've missed you," she said.

JoBeth smiled, "Thank you, Ida. I've missed you, too."

"Your table is not taken, so you go on over, and I will bring you your usual beverage."

JoBeth looked at the others and smiled. "Ida, can you please bring me a cup of coffee instead of my usual green tea?"

"I sure can. So that will be six coffees coming right up."

As they sat down, Sadie was the first to speak, "JoBeth, we didn't tell anyone where you have been."

"Thank you for that. It would have been all right for Ida to know, but I want to be the one to tell her. I just don't want to tell her right now. Enough about me, Hannah, you said you had to tell me something. I am sitting on pins and needles. What is going on?"

Suddenly, Ida appeared with an oversized tray with all their orders on it. She placed their plates on the table.

"After all these years, I know exactly who orders what. Now, eat up, ladies, and I'll be back shortly with refills on your coffee."

"Thank you, Ida," Gracie said as Ida was walking away.

"I would love to be the one that blesses this food today. It has been a long time since I have wanted to bless food, let alone eat," JoBeth said with a slight laugh.

They each grabbed for the others' hands as JoBeth said, "Thank you, Lord, for this food and a very special thanks for my friends that sit around this table today. You have blessed me beyond what I deserve, but I thank You for your blessings. Amen."

Tilly said quickly, "Well, could someone pass me a Kleenex? I think I have something in my eye."

"They call them tears, Tilly," Stella said, teasing. "I think we could all use a Kleenex right about now."

"No, tears, please. I am just so happy to be back with you. I have to tell you that eating is still a battle for me, but I take it day by day. So, if you see me not eating as much as you think I should, don't worry. I'm getting there slowly but surely."

Sadie agreed, "We know you will, JoBeth. We will try not to be mother hens and give you your space to take your own baby steps."

"Hannah, now, please tell me your news," JoBeth said excitedly.

For the next forty-five minutes, Hannah told her everything that had happened over the past few weeks with her father. She had visited him several more times at the nursing home. She told them that he had some good days, but for the majority of them, he was an empty shell of the man he once was. She would still sit patiently in the warm sun at his favorite window, hoping his mind would once again come back to the day and time. She enjoyed his company, pretending he was a beloved teacher of her son. Neither he nor anyone else outside of her circle of friends would ever know the truth behind the visits. She was content with this arrangement.

JoBeth listened carefully, and then she said, "Hannah, this is like a fairy tale that has a happy ending. I know you would never let your father know the truth, but this is as close to a happy ending as life gets."

"You're so right," said Hannah. Then she paused, smiled great big, and said, "I can't hold this back any longer. I also have something else to tell you and the others."

Tilly said, "Hannah, you are becoming a drama queen. Tell us what is going on before you burst."

"I have a date tonight with Bruce."

"You what?" Tilly questioned loudly.

"Hush, talking so loud, Tilly, and calm down," Sadie said. "Hannah, are you sure about this?"

"Do you even know his last name?" Tilly once again questioned but in a lower voice this time.

"Of course I do. It is Smith. His name is Bruce Smith, and he has the nicest smile."

Hannah said while reaching for her pocketbook to find his picture.

Laughing, Tilly said, "Smith, do you know how silly that sounds? He could have come up with something better than Smith. At least, he didn't tell you his name was Bruce Jones."

"What do you mean by that, Tilly?" Hannah asked.

"Honey, she means that there are many people that make up their last names, and they use Smith or Jones," Gracie said, trying to inform Hannah.

"Well, it isn't a made-up name. Thank you, Tilly, and here is a picture of him that he sent me on the computer," Hannah said as she passed the picture around the table.

Tilly grabbed for it quickly and said, "He's not particularly handsome."

"You're getting on my last nerve, Tilly," Hannah said sharply.

Sadie reached for the picture and said, "He has a nice smile, Hannah."

"Yes, he does, doesn't he? I bet in person it will be even nicer." Hannah said, beaming.

JoBeth quickly joined in, "Hannah, where are you and he going tonight?"

"We are meeting at the Branding Iron Steak House in Monroe at six o'clock."

"That's a good idea to meet him the first time in a public place," Stella said, adding her feelings about the conversation.

Suddenly, Hannah's cell phone rang.

She quickly reached for the phone and said, "I am sorry, girls. I know we have always agreed no cell phones switched on while we are eating, but Bruce said he would call to confirm our date. His mother hasn't been feeling well, and he might have to cancel. I'll just step in the bathroom and talk to him."

She left the table with a broad smile plastered across her face.

"She is acting like a young school girl on her first date. We can't let her go and meet someone by herself like that. He's telling her he has a sick mother as well. She must be over a hundred years old. Hannah has fallen for his story, hook, line, and sinker. She is just too naive," Tilly said.

Sadie looked sternly at Tilly, "Don't hold anything back, Tilly, just tell us exactly how you feel about this."

The others couldn't help but laugh at Sadie's comment.

Gracie was the first to speak, "Yes, she sees the good in everybody, and if it is naïve, so be it. We can't let her go by herself, though. So, what do we do, Sadie?"

"We keep an eye on her and make sure she is all right. You all meet JoBeth and me at my house at five o'clock, and we will drive on over to that steak house before she gets there. We will keep an eye on them. She will never know."

"Sadie, does that mean I am going to spend a few nights with you?" JoBeth questioned, smiling.

"Yes, please, JoBeth. Again, I am not a mother hen, but we all would feel better if you can just let us take care of you for a while."

"We all need to be taken care of sometime in our life. It's your time now, JoBeth. Later, you might have to take care of one of us," Gracie said softly.

"By the way, Gracie, what is the doctor saying about those ulcers of yours?" Sadie asked.

"Hush, girls, she's coming back," Stella said quickly.

Rushing back to the table, Hannah cheerfully said, "Well, our date is certainly on. Bruce said his mother was doing much better. Now, I don't want any of you to worry about me. I will tell you all about our date tomorrow."

"Well, I can see there is no changing your mind about this. So, I'm not going to waste my breath anymore trying," Tilly said in a huffy tone.

"That's right, and so change the subject." Hannah smiled in a conquering way and then continued, "JoBeth, Dr. Roberts said something that has had me puzzled and concerned."

"What was it?" JoBeth asked.

"He said that he would let you decide how much you wanted to tell us about your treatment. I didn't know what he meant. Is it something we could help you with?"

JoBeth took a slow sip from her coffee cup and then said, "I can surely talk to all of you about it. I had to sit in a circle with a group of strangers for all those weeks and admit my past to them."

Stella, with compassion, said, "You don't have to talk about it today."

Hannah added, "No, JoBeth, I didn't mean to hurt you or sound nosey."

"Honey, you could never hurt me. I am ready and willing to tell you all everything. It helps me. I guess I need to start at the beginning. The counseling that I had finally helped me realize where my eating disorder began. I realize now. It started when I was a little girl. I had a loving daddy, but he was a perfectionist. He wanted to be perfect and everyone in his life as well. He wanted a model wife and his kids to be a perfect Ken and Barbie doll example. He was constantly telling me what to eat and how much. I was chubby at one point, and I wanted to be Daddy's little girl. Therefore, I would watch what I ate. Sometimes, I wouldn't eat solid food for days at a time. I had a menu, and I wouldn't stray from that menu no matter what."

"What do you mean, you had a menu?" Stella asked.

"It certainly wasn't what a normal menu should be. I realize that now. It was a cracker for breakfast, a small amount of rice for lunch, and maybe some lettuce for supper. I would allow myself a stick of gum only if I got very weak."

"My goodness, how long did you continue that?" Tilly questioned.

"I would do that until Daddy would comment on me being his perfect little girl. Then I would know I had pleased him, and I would start back eating smaller amounts of food. I would always make sure not to eat enough to make me fat again."

Gracie placed her hand on JoBeth's and said, "When did you decide to stop?"

JoBeth looked each of them straight in the eyes and said, "I continued this eating pattern until Daddy died. I finally realized I was slowly killing myself as well, and I quit. I didn't look back and moved on with my life. I met Cody, and I grew even stronger. He loved me for me. He would look in my eyes and see me as JoBeth, not a chubby woman or a skinny woman, but me. He loved me for whatever I was and for however I looked. He made me feel proud to be me. Does that make sense?"

Sadie smiled and said, "It makes complete sense, honey. You had a very special husband."

JoBeth continued, "I have realized in therapy that I hid the emotions I had as a young girl. They stayed in the back of my mind for all these years but didn't surface. After Cody died, they came back. I grieved over him, and that grief brought all the other emotions that I had tried to hide all those years back to the surface. I let the eating pattern take over my life again. In a way, I could not control the grief that I was feeling in my mind, but I could be in control of my body by the food I wasn't eating. I thought I was in control, but in reality, I wasn't. Hannah, my dear friend, now you know what he meant. He wasn't sure if I had enough courage to tell you all how I really felt. He wasn't sure if I would admit that Daddy helped me get this way. See, sometimes you can love someone so much that you put them on a pedestal, and nothing they do or say makes you think they are wrong. In therapy, I am learning Daddy was wrong. I also realize now that what I was doing was a senseless act of destroying myself. That is why I will be meeting with the group once a week for as long as it takes. I want to get completely well, and it is going to take therapy to do just that."

"JoBeth, I hope you realize that we are very proud of you and the way you are overcoming this problem," Sadie said while dabbing the tears from her eyes.

JoBeth smiled, "Thank you, my dear friends. Now, I think it might be time we get out of here. We have used up this table for over two hours this morning. Poor Ida has missed out on a lot of tip money by us sitting here for so long. Hannah has got to get home and start getting ready for her date. I need to get settled in at Sadie's, and I am sure that the rest of you have got something you have to do."

"JoBeth is right. Let's get going," Sadie said quickly.

Each one reached into their pocketbooks, bringing out the money for Ida to have a huge tip.

They walked out the door when suddenly JoBeth turned to them and said, "I know I said we needed to go, but there is one other thing I need to do. Can you just give me a couple of minutes?"

They nodded, walked toward the car, and got in. They nervously watched as JoBeth entered the restaurant once again. They looked at one another with the same thought in their mind.

"I can't stand it any longer. I have got to make sure she is not repeating her little act in the bathroom, making herself throw up," Sadie said, quickly getting out of the car.

"Do you need us?" Gracie asked.

"If I'm not back in five minutes, come after me."

Sadie rushed to the door, opened it, and stood in shock. JoBeth was having a conversation with Ida. Then she watched as

JoBeth gave Ida a huge hug. Sadie knew that she had told Ida where she had been the last several weeks.

Sadie raced back for the car, jumped in, and said, "There is no need to question her about what she was doing. It's all right. Remember when she said she wanted to tell Ida where she had been herself? Well, that was what she was doing. Here she comes, so everybody act normal."

Stella looked at Tilly and said, "Try to act as normal as you can, Tilly, even if it hurts."

Everyone chuckled except for Tilly. She pretended to pout, but after all these years, they knew that was just another one of her acts. Tilly could dish out teasing and jokes but couldn't seem to take it in return. This was a part of Tilly they accepted and loved.

Chapter 7

The search for happiness can lead you down a road to disaster
or a life filled with bright new beginnings.
Happiness can sneak into your heart without noticing it.
Open a door – there it is!
Walk around a corner – there it is!
Pick up a ringing phone
and you might find it on the other end just waiting to say "hello."

Tilly was trying to be extra careful as she drove away from the restaurant. She was still pouting from the remark Stella had made, but she was not about to pout for long. It was not getting her any sympathy from the others.

Everyone stayed silent, deep in their thoughts, when suddenly, Tilly announced, "Hannah, I'm taking you home first. You seem anxious about getting ready for that blind date of yours."

"It's not a blind date," Hannah insisted.

"Have you met him in person before?" Tilly questioned.

"No," Hannah answered.

"I rest my case. It's a blind date."

"All right, have it your way, but I'm going on that date and enjoy myself. Do you know how long it has been since I sat across the table with the opposite sex, had a meal, and a nice conversation?"

Sadie urged, "Tilly, please pay more attention to your driving and less to Hannah's social life."

"Yes, Miss Sadie, I'll do just that," Tilly said sarcastically.

Sadie looked over at Gracie and giggled softly.

Tilly had finally reached Hannah's house. She pulled into the driveway and said, "Hannah, if he turns out to be an ax murder kind of person and he kidnaps you, we will be watching for your picture on the back of a milk carton."

Hannah got out, stuck her head back in the car, and spoke loudly, "Tilly, the laugh is on you. They don't put missing people on the back of milk cartons anymore."

After saying this, she slammed the door, walked directly in front of the car, and waved bye with a smile on her face. Then she turns around, bends over, and shakes her bottom back and forth. This made everyone in the car laugh, except for Tilly.

Tilly rolled her window down and shouted, "Love you too, Hannah."

Then she backed the car out of the driveway and continued the drive.

"Tilly, why did you fuss with Hannah about her date? We are going to be watching over her. She's just not going to know," said Stella.

"That's right, so everyone remember to be back at my house at five o'clock. Please, don't be late." Sadie pleaded while looking directly at Gracie.

Gracie stood in Sadie's hallway and announced, "Well, guess I got here before anyone else."

JoBeth came from the kitchen with a cup of coffee in her hand and handed it to her.

"Good for you, Gracie. Sadie is in the kitchen, making us all a thermos of coffee. I sure am glad that I can be in on this adventure."

"Me too, JoBeth," Gracie said, smiling and checking her coffee to make sure it was not too hot.

JoBeth walked toward the window and looked out.

She called to Sadie, "Tilly and Stella just pulled into your driveway. I guess it's time to get this show on the road."

Sadie walked into the room with a large thermos and a small picnic basket. She smiled at Gracie, letting her know, without saying a word, that she was glad she was on time.

"Let's go out and meet them. We better get started now in case we get into some heavy traffic," Sadie said while walking toward the door.

Gracie and JoBeth smiled at one another. Sadie always seemed to be in control, but she did it with class and that Southern charm of hers.

"Hello, everyone. Are we ready to go and take care of this internet man once and for all?" Tilly said, with her fists in the air making a boxing motion.

"That is all she has been talking about the entire drive over here," Stella said. "She has herself all worked up, and I can't calm her down."

"That is exactly why I am doing the driving tonight. So everyone, get in my car," Gracie said while dangling her keys in the air.

Gracie seldom voiced a command, so everyone did as she said.

Tilly quickly got in beside Sadie and announced, "I'm sitting beside Sadie. She has the basket of food, and I am about to starve."

Gracie slowly pulled onto the highway, and away they went. The traffic was heavy, but she seemed to be making good time.

"All right, ladies, we will be there in less than ten minutes, and we need to get a plan here. What are we going to do if she sees us? What will we say?" Stella questioned.

"I think we will come up with something between all of us. The best thing for us to do is get there and make sure we have a parking place that is close to the shrubbery and as far away from the front entrance as we can get. That way, maybe we can stay hidden." Sadie suggested.

"That place usually stays crowded. Maybe we can get there before it gets too busy." Gracie said while stopping for another stoplight.

"Oh my goodness, look at the clouds. They are turning gray. I sure hope it isn't going to storm," Stella said in a nervous voice.

"Well, Sadie is always prepared. She might have umbrellas in that basket," teased Tilly.

"We're not getting out of this car, so why would we need umbrellas?" Sadie was quick to comment.

Gracie put her turn signals on and made a slow turn toward the right. "We're here, ladies. Start looking for a place to park."

She continued, "I was scared of this. Look, the lot is full except for a few parking places right there at the front door. What are we going to do now?"

"What time is it?" Sadie asked.

Looking at her watch, Gracie said, "It's about ten minutes till six. I knew that last traffic light was going to make us late."

"Quick, pull over in the Lowe's parking lot. We will get as close to the restaurant as we can. When we see them go in, we will attempt to find a parking place in the restaurant lot again." Sadie said nervously and then continued. "We will look for Hannah as you pull around."

"Oh my goodness, Hannah is pulling in now. Do you think she sees us?" Tilly asked as she lowered her entire body in the car seat.

"There is no use in trying to get down in the seat, Tilly. If she saw the car, she would know it is us," Gracie said, shaking her head as if she could not believe what Tilly had just done.

Stella laughed aloud and said, "Hide Tilly, I think she saw you."

"Okay, Okay. I think I get the point. It's just that this is making me nervous." Tilly said as she sat back upright in the seat.

Everyone in the car started to giggle.

"If she saw us, then we will be completely honest and tell her that we were concerned for her safety," Sadie said, trying to reassure herself with the plan.

Tilly confessed, "Well, I don't think she would be very happy if she sees us."

"Why do you say that?" JoBeth asked.

"All this with Hannah was depressing me. So, I called her after I got home this afternoon. I was attempting to convince her one more time that this meeting tonight was a bad idea. It was apparent she wasn't going to cooperate or come to her senses. She even told me to mind my own business for a change. Can you imagine that?"

Stella nodded her head and said, "Yes, I can see where she would have come up with that suggestion."

Tilly gave Stella a long look but didn't say a word.

"This is as close as I can get," Gracie said as she parked the car and switched the motor off.

Sadie grabbed for the picnic basket, opened it, and brought out a pair of binoculars.

"Here, Stella, you have the best eyes of all of us. See if you can see her from here and tell us what is going on."

Stella placed the binoculars to her eyes and started the search.

She suddenly screamed, "There she is. I can see her. A man is walking toward her. Oh my gosh, they are hugging one another."

Tilly grabbed for the binoculars, yanking them from Stella's hands.

"Why did you do that, Tilly? You just about put my eyes out." Stella lashed out.

"Quickly, find them, Tilly!" Sadie yelled.

"I don't see them," Tilly admitted.

"It's probably because while you were yanking the binoculars from Stella, they went on in," Gracie said in a stern voice.

"Tilly, now we don't know if they went inside or got in his car," Sadie said in a nervous voice.

"Did you see the car that he got out of, Stella?" Tilly asked quickly.

"No," Stella said.

Tilly immediately jumped out of the car and ran toward the restaurant.

"What in the world is she doing?" JoBeth questioned.

Sadie said, "Use the binoculars and watch her, Stella. I sure hope she doesn't blow our cover. After Tilly calling her today, I'm sure Hannah would not appreciate us doing this."

Suddenly, it was as if the gray clouds that had been hanging low opened up. It started raining with a vengeance.

"I can't see a thing now. It's raining too hard." Stella said while removing the binoculars from her eyes.

Gracie turned the windshield wipers on in hopes they would be able to see Tilly.

"Here she comes, and she is wet from head to toe," JoBeth said.

Quickly, Tilly opened the car door, allowing rain to spray all over Sadie.

"What in the world were you thinking, Tilly?" Sadie asked while wiping the rain from her face.

"I wanted to make sure she didn't get in the car with him and ride off. Hannah is very gullible right now, and if we don't watch after her, who is?

"Tilly, you are becoming almost human." Stella teased.

"Did you see them without them seeing you?" Sadie asked.

"Oh yes, they were still in line waiting to be seated. They wouldn't have seen me if I walked right by them. They were too busy talking to one another. I opened the door, peeked in, and then turned and got myself back here. By the way, Sadie, I'm not trying to change the subject, but I wished you *had* brought an umbrella."

Sadie just shook her head. She could not get over how fast Tilly could go from one subject to another and not think a thing about it.

Gracie looked as hard as she could through the pouring rain toward the parking lot of the restaurant.

"I think I can get us a parking place in the lot now where Hannah won't see us. I guess the rain is a blessing in disguise, after all, tonight," Gracie said as she drove the car slowly toward the restaurant.

JoBeth pointed toward an empty parking place and said, "Gracie, there is one that is far enough away from her car that she shouldn't be able to see us. That large clump of shrubbery will be good coverage for us. We will just hope we aren't parking beside his car."

"Something tells me we are going to be here for quite a while." Stella smiled and continued, "I sure am glad you brought a thermos of coffee, Sadie."

Sadie passed around cups, and each poured themselves a cup of coffee. Then she brought out peanut butter cookies she had made earlier in the day.

Tilly said, "Hannah doesn't know what she is missing."

Suddenly, the car filled with the girls giggling.

Sadie continuing to laugh, said, "Now, Tilly, think about it. I think that right now, Hannah would much rather be with him than all of us sitting in a packed car drinking coffee with the rain beating against the windows."

Tilly decided she would remain quiet for a while. She reached for the thermos for another cup of coffee.

"Honestly, Tilly, we all are worried about Hannah, but I think you are truly worried the most. Showing emotion looks good on you. Maybe you should try it more often." Stella said calmly.

Tilly continued to remain silent. She was concerned. Some of the decisions Hannah had made in the past were not smart ones.

It had turned pitch dark, and the rain was still coming down hard.

Gracie tried to look at her watch to see what time it was. She didn't want to turn on the light inside the car. They could be coming out at any time, and she didn't want to take the chance of being seen. She remembered that she had a flashlight in the dash of her car.

"JoBeth, can you reach inside the dash and get the flashlight?

She did as Gracie had asked.

She turned the beam of the flashlight toward her watch and announced, "They have been in there for over two hours."

"My bladder feels like they have been in there for over four hours. I knew I should not have had that last cup of coffee. Sadie, I feel like I am floating. I have got to go to the bathroom," Tilly said in a pleading voice.

"Tilly, I can't help you there. Just stop thinking about it," Sadie suggested.

"With all this rain beating against the windows and the coffee that I have drunk, well, I can't stop thinking about it," Tilly said, moving around in her seat.

"Look, everybody! They are standing at the entrance of the restaurant. All eyes stay on them this time. We have got to make sure she gets in her car," Gracie said, once again in a take control voice.

"What in the world is that woman thinking. She is walking arm in arm with that man, and he is not leading her in the direction of her car," Tilly said in a panic.

"That only means one thing. They are going to his car. Gracie, get ready to pull out just as soon as they do. With this rain, we will have to stay right behind them, or we are going to lose them," Sadie said.

"Girls, are we doing the right thing in following them? After all, she is a grown woman," JoBeth stated.

Sadie quickly said, "JoBeth, I'm not saying this man is bad, but there is a lot of people in this world that do mean things. I can't stand the thoughts of Hannah, maybe being the next victim of one of those people."

Tilly leaned toward the car door, ready to get out. Sadie swiftly grabbed her and said, "Tilly, stop, it's all right. We will stay right up with them, and then we will do what we have to do when the time comes. If we get out now and make a scene, Hannah may never forgive us. He might turn out to be the knight in shining armor in her life. We have to wait this out no matter how worried we are." Sadie said, trying to convince herself that she was making the right decision.

"She's right, Tilly," Gracie said. "I am going to stay right up with him. You all have to help be my eyes, though. This rain is not letting up, and it is going to make it hard, especially if we get separated at traffic lights."

"Well, they just got in his car, so get ready, Gracie," JoBeth said.

Gracie watched as he pulled from the parking place and out into the highway. Gracie was right behind him. Luck seemed to be on their side. Each traffic light turned red, making him stop. This way, Gracie was able to stay right behind him.

"What if they pull into a motel?" Tilly blurted out.

"What a thing to say, Tilly. Hannah might be love-struck right now and still hurt from that ex-husband of hers, but she isn't stupid." Sadie blurted out.

Gracie shook her head at the remark Tilly had made and then said, "Oh, honey, what it must feel like to live inside that head.

"That was a nasty thing for me to say about Hannah. Please forgive me, girls," Tilly said but then slowly questioned. "But, where are they going then?"

Everyone in the car became silent.

"Well, I guess we will soon know. He just put his right turn signal on. It looks like he is turning in that driveway. What do we do now, Sadie?" Gracie asked calmly.

"Look at the mailbox on the curb. It says, Smith. His last name is Smith. He is taking her to his house," Tilly said nervously.

"Pull slowly into the next driveway, Gracie," Sadie said, pointing in that direction.

Gracie did as Sadie asked. They watched closely as the man got out of the car, walked around to the passenger's side, and opened the door for Hannah. She quickly got out, and they both ran together, hand in hand, to the cover of the front porch to avoid the heavy rain. All eyes were on them as he opened the door, and they both walked inside.

Suddenly, everyone in the car turned and looked directly at Sadie.

Stella was the first to speak, "Sadie, what do we do now?"

"Gracie, pull out of this driveway and pull right behind his car. We are probably going to make fools out of ourselves, but I guess it is now or never." Sadie said while staring at the huge house that Hannah had just walked inside.

Gracie did, as Sadie said. Within minutes, they were all standing on the front porch with Sadie ringing the doorbell.

Suddenly, the door opened wide. Hannah stood in the doorway with a broad smile across her face.

"I figured you all would be ringing the doorbell much faster than what you did. I guess Bruce wins the bet after all," she said, laughing.

Bruce walked up behind Hannah, placed his arm around her waist, and said, "Hannah, why don't you ask your friends to come inside before they get soaked."

"What do we do now, Sadie?" Stella whispered.

"Well, I don't know what you all are going to do, but I'm going in. Bruce, may I use your powder room?" Tilly said, with an urgent look on her face.

Bruce looked puzzled but said, "Sure, let me show you where it is."

Tilly always pushed the envelope beyond the limits of Southern politeness. Therefore, her words did not shock her friends.

The rest of the girls continued to stand on the porch, looking somewhat ashamed of themselves.

Hannah smiled and said, "Come on in, and I'll introduce you to Bruce's mother."

Sadie was the first to speak, "Hannah, don't hate us for this. We...."

Hannah stopped her in mid-sentence, "We have been close friends for too many years for me to be mad. I was half expecting this from all of you. I spotted you as soon as we were seated in the restaurant. I saw your car, Gracie, pull around the restaurant and park. I told Bruce, and he thinks it is sweet to have friends that care as much as you all do. Now, get on in here before you catch a cold."

They stepped into a house that looked as though it had come right out of a Better Homes and Garden magazine. It was beautiful, with large pieces of antique furniture smartly placed in all the right places. Bouquets of flowers were placed neatly on small tables in the foyer and down the long hallways.

Bruce returned to the foyer and said, "Come on in, ladies, and make your selves at home. Mother is in the next room. I am sure she would love to meet you."

They followed closely behind Bruce and entered a large room with a fireplace in the corner. There sat a petite, gray-haired woman in a large high-back leather chair sitting close to the fireplace.

She turned to them and said, "You must be Hannah's friends. She has told Bruce about all of you, and in turn, Bruce has told me. It must be wonderful to have lifelong friends that are dear to you. Now, please, be seated and tell me all about your friendship."

They each took a seat and tried not to look embarrassed or out of place.

Tilly returned to the room and said, "Mrs. Smith, you have a beautiful home."

"Dear child, it isn't my home. Bruce has kindly taken me under his wing in the late years of my life. He is a good son."

"Mother, I do wish you wouldn't put it that way. You are my mother, and I am going to take care of you the way you took care of me when I was growing up," he said, blushing.

"Well, enough about me," Mrs. Smith said. "I want to know more about you ladies and the bond of friendship that you have."

Stella was the first to speak, "We have known each other for close to thirty years now. We all met in different ways, but our close bond has grown closer year after year."

"Yes," Sadie said while looking directly at Bruce. "But I think that after tonight we will learn to realize that we should believe in the decisions that each other makes and know that they will make the right decision."

Bruce smiled and said, "Would anyone like a cup of coffee?"

"No, thank you, I wouldn't care for any coffee," Tilly said. "I think I have had enough to last me for a few days."

The conversation seemed to flow much easier once Sadie had made the comment that she did. It is evident that Bruce was a good man and was not offended by their actions.

Sadie looked at her watch and realized they had overstayed their welcome.

"Mrs. Smith, we apologize for it being so late. You and Bruce were making us feel so welcome that we forgot all about the time. We have got to be going."

The others quickly stood and followed Sadie's lead. They said their goodbyes to Mrs.

Smith and were soon getting ready to walk out the door.

"Please, do come back," Mrs. Smith announced from the living room.

"You have a lovely mother, Bruce. I enjoyed meeting her tonight. If it is all right with you, I am going to ride back with my friends. I have a few things I need to talk to them about," Hannah said and then looked in their direction.

"Well, I think that is our little hint to go get in the car," Tilly said, laughing.

Sadie reached for Bruce's hand and softly said, "Thank you, Bruce, for being so understanding. We think of each other as family, and I sometimes guess we overstep our boundaries. When you start getting as old as we are, you get scared and start using bad judgment. You are a nice man, and I am glad that Hannah met you. I just wish the rest of us could have met you in a different circumstance."

Bruce smiled and said, "Hannah is an exceptional lady, and I can see where you all would love her and want only the best for her. I understand completely, and I hope that all of you will think of me as a close friend of yours as well."

JoBeth said, "We do, Bruce, we truly do."

They walked toward the car and got in, except for Hannah. She remained on the steps with Bruce.

"Let's see if they are going to kiss," Tilly excitedly said.

Gracie was quick to say, "Tilly, I think we have invaded Hannah's space one time too many tonight. Please take your eyes off of them and let them have their privacy."

"All right, but my goodness, you are getting bossy."

Gracie remained silent. She did not give Tilly the satisfaction of commenting.

Within minutes, Hannah came to the car with a smile on her face.

She quickly got in and said, "Slide over, Tilly, and give me some room. I want to be able to hear every sarcastic thing you have to say."

Gracie turned to Sadie and said, "Do you mind driving back for me? I don't seem to be feeling very well right now."

Sadie changed places with Gracie without saying a word.

No one questioned Gracie. They knew she would not give them a straight answer. The talk on the way back to the restaurant focused entirely on the new man in Hannah's life.

Sadie was concentrating on her driving, but she could not help but to occasionally take a quick look in Gracie's direction.

Gracie sat silently when suddenly, she touched the window button allowing it to come down a few inches. She placed her head against the window, sucked in the fresh night air, and let the sting of the falling rain hit against her face. It seemed to make her feel better.

Sadie had finally reached the restaurant. She slowly pulled into the lot and drove directly to Hannah's car.

Everyone once again had become silent, aware of the change in Gracie.

Before Hannah got out, Sadie said, "Hannah, drive on over to my house. I want everyone to spend the night with me."

No one protested. They knew it was time for girlfriend talk, and this meeting was serious. They knew the focus would be on one person.

Then Sadie put her full attention on Gracie, "Honey, I think it is time for you to tell your friends what is going on. Hannah trusted and loved us enough tonight to know that we would not do or say anything to hurt her. She didn't get mad when we blundered into her life. Now, it is time for you to trust. We have stayed silent much too long, but we know there is something terribly wrong with you. You have got to let us help you with whatever is happening in your life right now."

Gracie nodded but did not say a word. She placed her head once again against the car window. She knew she had to talk to her friends, and it had to be sooner than she had planned.

Chapter 8

One of the greatest treasures in life is having friends you can confide in.

Friends, that when you cry, they will cry with you.

Friends, that when you admit that you are scared, will comfort you,

even if they are scared for you as well.

The bright morning sun flowed in the kitchen window, making the room feel warm and cozy. Usually, everyone that enters Sadie's kitchen has smiles across their face, but not this morning. Everyone was worried about Gracie.

"When do you think she is going to get up?" Tilly asked.

"I vote to let her sleep as long as she wants," Stella said while reaching for the coffee pot.

"I wish she had felt like telling us what was going on last night," Hannah said while checking her cell phone for missed calls from Bruce.

"Good morning, everyone," JoBeth said, entering the kitchen. "Where is Gracie?"

"She is sleeping in," Sadie said. "Or she is simply trying to avoid us."

"She wouldn't do that, would she?" Tilly questioned.

"Are you kidding? She has been our little mystery woman as long as we have known her. She only allows us in the part of her life that she feels comfortable with." JoBeth said sternly.

"But you all love me, now don't you?" Gracie asked while walking into the kitchen.

"Guess JoBeth should have whispered that last statement she made about you," Tilly said, laughing.

JoBeth looked in Tilly's direction, letting her know that she had said enough. Tilly looked back with a conquering smile.

"What have you ladies got cooking in here?" Gracie questioned as if trying to take the attention away from her.

"Gracie, will you sit down, please?" Sadie asked calmly.

Gracie did as she asked, reached for a cup, and then took a deep breath. Tilly quickly poured Gracie a cup of coffee.

The room went silent, waiting for Gracie to speak. She continued to say nothing at all.

Stella nervously said, "Gracie, your silence is scaring all of us. We are concerned that you are holding something back. Please, let us help."

Gracie took a sip of coffee and then calmly said, "I have a tumor."

"You have what?" Tilly exploded.

"I have a tumor. I have been having stomach problems for several months. I didn't want to say anything about it until I found out for sure. There was so much going on in our little group that I didn't want to add to the worries."

"I wish you wouldn't put it like that, Gracie. Your health is important to us. You should know that," Sadie said while trying to stay calm and positive.

"I guess I was trying to put off telling you because I knew you would act differently around me. Now, ladies, I am going to be fine, and we just need to get on with the day."

"I suddenly don't feel very hungry," JoBeth said.

"See, that is the very reason I didn't want to say anything. It is not that big of a deal. I am going to be fine."

"All right, Gracie, then we will not worry. As long as you continue to go to the doctor and do as he says," JoBeth said.

"You can rest assure that I will do just that," Gracie said, trying to look calm.

She continued, "I think I will have just a piece of toast and a cup of coffee. I am still full from the peanut butter cookies and coffee we ate all afternoon yesterday."

Tilly forced a small laugh and then said, "I agree with you."

Gracie remained quiet as she watched the girls grab for a piece of dry toast and then go their separate ways. She could hear them whispering while walking down the hall. She knew they weren't satisfied with what she had told them, but they respected her enough not to keep asking her questions. Her thoughts went quickly back to the first time she met them. Now, that seemed like a million years ago to her.

Hannah called from the other room, "Sadie, I am going to your mailbox and get the day's newspaper. Mind if I go ahead and read it before you do?"

"Of course, I don't mind," Sadie hollered back from the kitchen.

Only Sadie and Gracie remained in the room. Sadie sat down beside Gracie and remained silent.

Gracie could not look directly into Sadie's eyes.

Finally, Sadie said, "Is it a malignant tumor?"

"Yes, it is, Sadie Sue. I'm afraid it is."

Sadie knew she had to sound positive for Gracie. She had once again called her Sadie Sue. Sadie felt sick and wished she didn't have to continue with this conversation.

"Was the diagnosis done by endoscope followed by a CT scan and endoscopic ultrasound?"

Gracie knew that Sadie had a medical background. Therefore, she couldn't sugarcoat the verdict that had been given to her by the doctor.

"Yes, Sadie, all those tests were done. An operation came up in the discussion. They have already started chemotherapy. The doctor is hoping it might help the tumor to shrink. If it does, then I will talk about an operation in my future."

"How long have you been taking chemotherapy?"

"It has been several weeks now," Gracie said.

"You've been hiding it well, Gracie."

"Not well enough. Sadie. I want the rest of my life to be happy and be the way we have been for many years. I don't want everyone looking at me and wondering how many more days, weeks, or months I have left. Please, treat me the way you always have. I don't want to be treated differently. I don't want anyone to feel sorry for me."

"What can we do to help?" Sadie asked while wiping the tears that were running down her cheek.

"Treat me as you always do. Do not look at me as if I have one foot in the grave. I know this chemo is going to kick my butt, but they are giving me medicine to help with nausea. I am going to try and fight this thing, and maybe if it is God's plan, I can conquer the big "C." If not, then I pray to God that He give me the strength to face the days ahead, and it will be over quick."

"Gracie, I am still trying to gather this all in. I can't help to have the emotions I am having right now, but I will be here for you, and I will be as strong as you are. I promise you that."

"Promise me something else."

"Oh, Gracie, please don't ask me to keep this away from the others."

"You have always been able to read me like a book."

"Not always, Gracie, not always."

"I want you to promise that for right now, we can keep this to ourselves. I don't want them to know until I am ready to tell them. I will know when it is time. Right now, I want Tilly to keep teasing me and saying little remarks, and I want Hannah to keep feeling good about what is going on in her life. I want JoBeth not to get depressed and go back to her old eating habits. I want life to stay as normal as long as it can."

"I promise, Gracie. It will be your call but know that I am here right now and don't hold anything else from me. Now, you make me that promise."

"I promise, Sadie."

Gracie stood up, hugged Sadie, and said, "I feel better already since you know." She smiled and then continued, "I had better go and check on those friends of ours. There is no telling what they are doing."

When Gracie walked from the room, Sadie felt a sick feeling start forming in the pit of her stomach. She had been a nurse for too many years. She knew stomach cancer accounted for over eleven thousand deaths in the United States annually. She knew that long-term survival is poor and that Gracie would probably lose her battle in less than a year. This was one time she wished she hadn't been a nurse. Sometimes, too much information hurts. This was definitely the time.

She raced to the bathroom, fell to her knees, and hung tightly to the commode vomiting, vigorously.

She finally was able to sit down on the cool floor of the bathroom with a wet cloth to her throat. She whispered to herself, "Get your act together for Gracie's sake."

She paused, wiped her tears from her eyes, and again whispered, "Dear God, please give Gracie strength to face what you have planned for her life. I pray that she will not suffer, and God, please help her friends to know what to do and how to help her."

She slowly stood up, looked in the mirror, and wiped her face once again. Her eyes were red, but she wouldn't have to answer the question of why. She was sure the girls had been shedding their tears as well.

She heard a soft knock on the bathroom door.

"Sadie, I think you are needed out here," Tilly said, sounding in a panic.

"I'll be out in just a minute," Sadie said, wondering what could be wrong. She wondered if Gracie had decided to tell them about her condition now instead of later. She felt a sense of relief, hoping this was it. Then she would not have to carry the sadness of knowing the secret and trying to keep it from the others. At this point, she did not know if she was strong enough to keep Gracie's promise.

As soon as she walked into the living room, she knew something had happened. She felt the sense of an approaching emotional storm. It was as if gray clouds had engulfed everyone in the room.

Her attention went directly to Hannah. She was holding the newspaper tightly to her chest. The others appeared to be comforting her.

She looked up at Sadie and said softly, "I just read Father's obituary. He is being buried today."

"Oh, honey, I am so sorry," Sadie said while reaching down to hug her.

"Where is he going to be buried, and what time?" Gracie asked quickly.

Tilly grabbed the paper from Hannah and said, "Pinewood Cemetery in Waxhaw at two o'clock."

"Let's get ready. We have plenty of time to get there," Stella said while making a beeline to the quest bedroom.

"Should we go?" Hannah asked.

"Why not? He was your father, but no one has to know that except the six of us. If you don't go, you will always regret it," Sadie said in a positive tone.

JoBeth agreed, "She's right, Hannah. You have got to go, and we are going with you."

"I was just getting to know him as the man he is now," Hannah said, with her head lowered.

Gracie pointed out, "Hannah, that is right, and you know that he didn't realize you were his daughter. You need to be thankful for the time you had to know the gentleman he was. Now, get up, dry those tears, and go get ready."

Tilly smiled and said, "It's depressing me just how bossy you and Sadie are getting in your old age. Come on, Hannah, we will go to Sadie's closet and see what we can find to wear."

Hannah stood up and looked at Sadie and Gracie. She softly said, "Sometimes you need someone to give you a little direction in your life and help you know what to do. Thank you both for helping me go in the right direction today."

Then she followed Tilly into the bedroom.

Sadie and Gracie stood alone in the room. Sadie's heart was telling her to grab Gracie, give her a sisterly hug, and tell her everything was going to be all right. She immediately felt this was not the time. How could she convince Gracie that everything was going to be all right when she felt unsure of the future herself?

Instead, she took Gracie's hand, pulled her toward her bedroom, and said, "Honey, if we don't get in there now, we aren't going to have anything left for us to wear. It's not like I am a fashion model with plenty of clothing lying around."

Gracie smiled. She was trying hard to show courage, but right now, it was hard. It was very hard. She said a silent prayer thanking God for a friend like Sadie.

Chapter 9

Experiencing   grief is something that everyone has in common.

It will affect each of us sometime in life, some more than others.

It is how we handle the grief that keeps us going,

keeps us moving on through life.

Once you lose a loved one, your entire life will change.

Life goes on, but nothing is ever the way it once was.

There was already a large group of people gathered around the gravesite. Flowers lined a path that led to the open grave and the waiting casket that held the body of Hannah's father.

Hannah and the others stayed back, observing what was taking place.

"Have you ever seen so many flowers at a funeral before?" Tilly said loudly.

"Hush, Tilly, don't talk so loud," JoBeth snapped.

Sadie commented, "He was a well-known man, and this is a way for people to show their respect."

"I know he would have enjoyed visits from people instead of flowers when he is dead." Hannah continued, "Often, when his mind didn't wander off, he would comment that he enjoyed visits from his friends and students. They didn't seem to come around as much. He would try to continue with the conversation but would drift back into that nowhere land of Alzheimer's."

Stella whispered, "I'm so glad you had several weeks to visit with him before his death."

"It touched my heart when he did drift off and speak of a Mary Jo. I guess that was the happiest time of my visit. I knew he was talking about Mother and the love he still had for her. We sat there sharing a common bond, and no one ever knew, not even him."

"Let's walk on toward the gravesite. The service is about to begin," Sadie suggested.

They began their slow walk toward the grave, but Sadie noticed Gracie was not moving. She knew that fatigue from the chemo had taken over. She turned around without anyone noticing, placed her arm around Gracie, and guided her toward the others.

Sadie whispered, "Gracie, this is one of the side effects of the chemo. Do you want me to help you back to the car?"

"No, just let me lean on you. I'll make some kind of excuse if the girls notice."

Sadie continued to hold tightly to Gracie as they slowly reached the others. They all stood closely, shoulder to shoulder, in their tight little group as they watched the minister walk toward the casket and begin the service.

"It was a day I will always remember when I first met the man I learned to love and get to know as a friend. The man that everyone knew as Kenneth Reed was a wonderful man that treated everyone special. He was the type of man that never met a stranger....."

The minister continued, but Hannah was deep in her thoughts of her father. She glanced toward the two men that sat in the family section. They both resembled her father. They had a strong jawbone and a gentle look in their eyes. She could tell that they were trying to be strong during this time. She felt a wave of emotion come over her. How strange she thought to be proud of two strangers that were her half-brothers. The brothers, which she could not acknowledge to anyone except her five best friends.

Suddenly, Sadie touched Hannah on her shoulder and said, "Honey, are you all right? You seem to be in deep thought."

"Actually, I was. I was thinking about my half-brothers over there and never getting to know them."

Sadie whispered, "That's right, Hannah. You can't ever let them know the truth. Think of what you would be stirring up. They would know that every time their father had started rambling about a Mary Jo that he wasn't talking about his little daughter but the first love of his life. Imagine how they would react. The pedestal that they have their father on would no longer exist. They would feel that in a sense, he betrayed their mother to still hold on to the love he had for your mother."

"You're right, Sadie. I want to speak to them, though, as soon as the crowd that is around them thins out."

Hannah adjusted the borrowed dress she had on, slowly walked over to Tilly, and whispered, "Tilly, I know you will tell me honestly how Sadie's dress looks on me. I know I am slightly fuller around the backside than she is, and the dress feels snug on me."

"You sure picked a fine time to ask me a question like that, but the answer is you look fine. The summer sweater you have on covers the fat part you are talking about," Tilly said as if she had paid Hannah a compliment.

"Thanks, but next time you don't have to be so brutally honest," Hannah said while adjusting the back part of the dress once again.

Hannah turned to her friends and said, "I will be right back."

Sadie took a deep breath and stated, "Remember, if you make the wrong decision, you will forever change many lives, including your own."

Hannah nodded and continued walking toward the crowd that still circled the Reed brothers.

Hannah got as close as she could and then waited for her turn to speak to them.

Suddenly, Derrick looked in her direction and smiled. He touched his brother on the arm and said, "William, I want you to meet someone that visited Father many times."

They both walked closer to Hannah. Her heart began to beat rapidly. She was within inches of both her newfound brothers. She could see in their face that she actually looked like them. She wondered if they would notice this as well.

Derrick reached for her hand and gently shook it, "I want to thank you for all your visits with Father. The nurse told me that you brightened his day with your visits." He looked toward his brother and continued, "I would like for you to meet my brother, William."

Hannah reached for William's hand and said, "Hello, my name is Hannah. I want you both to know I enjoyed the visits with Mr. Reed as much as he did. He was a very nice man. He talked of you both often. He certainly loved you very much."

William continued to hold her hand softly and said, "It is as if I should know you. Have we met before?"

"No, I don't think so. Your father was my son's teacher many years ago. He made a big impression in his life at a time he needed redirecting. I have always been thankful for that."

William continued to look deep into Hannah's eyes.

She slowly pulled her hand from his and said, "I have that type of face that everyone thinks they know. I guess you call it a familiar face."

Suddenly, someone came toward William and Derrick to pay their respects. Hannah chose this opportunity to walk away from them quietly.

She rushed toward the girls and said, "We need to go, and we need to go right now."

Sadie asked, "Hannah, did you do something you are going to regret?"

"No, I promise I didn't do or say anything wrong, but William looked at me as if he saw right through me. It seemed like he knew the truth, or at least knew something was different about me."

Stella whispered, "Hannah, I swear you three look alike. I saw that right off. Maybe he sees the resemblance as well."

They walked directly to the car. Hannah opened the car door and turned around one more time to try to catch a glimpse of her brothers. She knew this would be the last time she would ever see the Reed brothers again.

It wasn't hard for her to see them. William was staring right in her direction. She quickly turned her head away from him and got in the car.

Sadie slowly helped Gracie into the car without the others noticing the individual attention she was paying to her.

Once inside, Tilly questioned, "Girls, I am so hungry. Could we go to Midway for an early supper?"

Sadie looked toward Gracie for a reaction.

Gracie said slowly, "I think that sounds great, Tilly. A good meal would do us all good. That is if Hannah is up to going."

The others agreed, even JoBeth.

As they pulled away from the cemetery, Hannah turned to take one final look.

As she wiped the tears from her eyes, she said, "Thank you all for standing by me today. This is a chapter in my life I can consider finished. I finally get to say I knew my father and had several long talks with him. I even met my brothers. I know it is going to sound corny, but I feel complete now."

Ida quickly said hello to the girls, seated them at a table, and took their orders.

"JoBeth, I am glad to see that you are sticking to your promise of eating right," Stella commented.

"Stella is right. We are all proud of you," Hannah said, smiling.

JoBeth admitted, "I made you all a promise that I am going to keep. After all, I want to live to be a very old woman sitting right here at this table with all of you. I know the only way I can do that is to realize what I was doing to my body."

Sadie glanced over at Gracie to see how she was going to react to JoBeth's comment. Gracie looked at Sadie and smiled, letting her know it was all right.

Suddenly, Hannah's cell phone rang. Sadie took a deep breath, knowing the subject of growing old with the group would not come up again for a while.

Hannah grabbed her cell phone from her pocketbook and quickly excused herself from the table.

"I bet I know who that call is from," Tilly announced.

"Yes, our new friend Bruce Smith," Stella said.

Hannah shortly returned to the table and announced, "That was Bruce. He asked me if I would like to go to the movies tonight. This time he wants to pick me up at my front door."

She looked around the table and then continued, "Now, are all of you going to be hiding in my shrubbery tonight waiting for him to come?"

Gracie glanced at the others and said, "It is my turn to speak for all of us. No, we are not going to hide in your shrubbery, follow you to the movies, nor sit in the back of the theater, munching on popcorn while keeping an eye on you and Bruce. Enjoy tonight, knowing that we definitely approve of him. Remember that tomorrow, we want all details of the date."

Hannah giggled. A pretty pink color spread across her face. She was blushing.

Sadie looked at Gracie and realized this was the most she had said all day. She hoped this meant that she was finally feeling better.

Ida walked toward the table with her large tray, smiled, and said, "Here is your food, ladiesSorry, it took so long. The cook seems to be in a bad mood today, and he is taking it out on everybody but mostly me."

"Do I need to go and have a little talk with him?" Tilly asked as she started to get up from the table.

Ida laughed and said, "No, Tilly, but thank you anyway. Now, enjoy your meal, and I will check on you later."

"You're something else, Tilly. Do you know that?" Stella asked.

"What do you mean by that?"

"She is simply saying, Tilly, that you always surprise us. Sometimes you are so sweet, and other times, well, we don't know what you are." Sadie said, laughing.

Tilly smiled, enjoying the attention she was getting from the girls.

Stella, sounding anxious, said, "Before we ask the blessing and begin eating, I need to say something."

Everyone at the table put their full attention on Stella.

She slowly continued, "I have a problem, and I need some advice. I don't want to discuss it here, and I really don't want to discuss it at all today. Sadie, can we meet at your house sometime tomorrow?"

Sadie looked at Gracie. She knew that early morning wasn't a good time for people taking chemo treatments.

"Stella, can we meet after lunch at around two o'clock?" Sadie paused for a few seconds and then continued. "Are you sure it is something that can wait until tomorrow?"

"Yes, tomorrow at two will be fine. Can I count on all of you being at Sadie's?"

Each one nodded, including Gracie.

Sadie sat silently, thinking to herself. She once again felt that sick feeling in the pit of her stomach. What crisis could possibly happen in this group now?

Chapter 10

We were all born with free will and the inclination to sin against God.
Therefore,
we all need discipline so we can learn how
to bring our desires in line with the Lord's plan
and purpose for our lives.

Sadie had opened her home to not only JoBeth but Gracie as well. She did not feel comfortable with Gracie being at home by herself. Sadie had suggested to Gracie to stay a few days with her, and she did willingly.

When Stella, Tilly, and Hannah arrived at Sadie's house, they were quickly ushered aside by JoBeth, who filled them in on Gracie's overnight stay.

Stella was the first to ask, "Sadie, why did Gracie spend the night with you? Is she sicker than what she told us?"

Gracie entered the room, smiling, "I heard that, Stella. Don't you think that sometimes this old woman gets lonely in that great big house of mine? Now, we are all interested and concerned with what you have got to tell us."

Agreeing, Tilly said, "That's right. I could barely sleep last night, wondering what this could be all about."

"Hannah, why don't you tell us about your date with Bruce first," Stella said as if trying to take the attention away from her and place it on Hannah.

"Oh, no, you don't. Now start talking, Stella. There will be time for me to share information about last night, but right now, the spotlight is on you."

Everyone found a seat in the living room, and Sadie brought in homemade chocolate chip cookies and a large pot of coffee.

She placed everything on the coffee table, found her a seat beside Gracie, and then said, "Stella, we are all ears."

"Oh, it's nothing. I don't even think I'll bring it up now. Let's talk about Hannah and her new man."

Tilly couldn't hold back any longer, "Don't waste our time on silly chitchat, and just tell us what is going on. You didn't get us all over here to talk about Hannah. So spit it out."

Suddenly, Stella's face matched the red of her hair. This was a definite giveaway when she got mad.

She looked Tilly squarely in the eyes and almost shouted, "My husband is dating his secretary. It appears she is taking care of more than just his records, letters, and dictation. Now, I have said it."

"What do you mean dating? Isn't that a stupid way of saying he is having an affair?" Tilly blurted out.

"You're getting on my last nerve, Tilly," Stella shouted.

"Girls, stop. Tilly, put a cookie in your mouth, please." Sadie said, trying to convince Tilly to stay quiet.

Sadie went to Stella, put her arms around her, and said, "Honey, how do you know this is going on?"

Stella calmly said, "The wife is always the first to know."

Hannah spoke up. "That's true, or it certainly was in my case with Gordon. The problem with him was he really didn't try to hide it or deny it."

"Sounds just plain stupid to me," Tilly whispered under her breath.

JoBeth reached for the cookie plate, placed it right at Tilly, and said, "Have another cookie, Tilly."

Tilly reached for the plate, took another cookie, and placed the plate back on the table. She gave JoBeth one of her looks but didn't say a word. She had finally gotten the hint not to say anything else negative about the situation.

"What are you going to do about this?" Gracie asked.

"I don't know. I guess I have to get proof, and then I will decide exactly what to do. That is where I need the help of each of you. That is if you are willing to do something that is really off the wall."

"Off the wall sounds exactly what we all need in our lives right now," Gracie said, sounding almost excited.

Sadie thought. Yes, this could be a distraction from the chemo for Gracie.

"Tell us exactly what you want us to do," Sadie said, sounding in favor of helping.

"Trace says he has to go out of town for the weekend on a business trip. Oh, he made such a big drama out of it all. He kept on and on saying how bad he wanted to take me, but the wives weren't to attend. He said it was an executive decision made from the very top. It was going to be all business this weekend and absolutely no fun. Oh, he even said his job might depend on decisions that were going to be made on this business trip." She took a deep breath and continued, "He even said that I could take one of his charge cards and just shop all weekend to make up for not being able to go."

"Which charge card can we use this weekend?" Tilly asked.

Sadie gave Tilly another hush look. Then she once again turned her attention to Stella. "Do you know where he is going?"

"Yes, I was able to get that much out of him. He is going to Myrtle Beach, South Carolina. He said that right now, he didn't know which hotel the men had chosen for the weekend. He had volunteered to drive, and they were going to meet at the office at seven o'clock Friday night and leave from there. I think he said that in case I was determined to try to go with him. This way, he has an excuse that his coworkers are riding with him, and so there would be no way that I could."

"Yes, it sounds like he has it all planned out," JoBeth said.

"I want to follow him somehow, but he has my weekend all planned out for me. He brought home papers from work about a big case that he wants me to study over for him. Then he said he wanted me to go to the country club Saturday and plan some events with the board members there. He will know if I don't attend that meeting. "

Gracie turned to Sadie and questioned, "What do we do?"

Sadie stood up and started pacing back and forth. The girls were sure she was going to wear a hole in the carpet with all that pacing. No one said a word, including Tilly. All eyes continued to stay on Sadie.

Suddenly, she stood very still and said, "I've got an idea. I have a phone call to make. I will be right back."

"Got a question, Stella, if you don't mind me asking," Tilly said.

"Just, don't let it be a sarcastic question, Tilly, please. I am in no mood."

"How do you know he is taking his secretary off for the weekend?"

"Yes," Hannah joined in. "How do you know who it is?"

"I finally figured out his email password. I went into his deleted mail and found out all about their little affair. It appears they have been meeting at hotels during their lunch hour. I am also excellent listening at doors when he is on the telephone with her."

"I'm sorry, Stella. I really am," Tilly said, honestly.

"I might as well admit everything. This is not his first, but she is the only one that he has wanted to take out of town for a weekend. I'm afraid he's getting serious with this one. The others have been just one-night stands."

"You're taking this much better than I would," JoBeth said.

"Not really. I've had time to cry it all out. I guess I am just getting fighting mad right now. I've had time to think about what he might do. If Trace divorces me, he will have it all planned out. I know he will leave me with nothing. I worked putting him through law school, and then I quit working. He wanted it that way. He said I would stay home, keep the house in order, and plan parties for his clients. I was to be his model wife, and a wife of a high-profile lawyer never works. It would make him look bad, or so he said. Therefore, I became his little do as I say wife and lived under his rule and thumb."

"You said that he had several one-night stands. How long has this been going on?" Gracie asked.

"I guess close to five years now."

"This makes me sick, Stella. Why did you keep this from us? We could have been giving you moral support. We could have done something to help you. Why, honey, you are an angel facing all this by yourself and holding it all in for all these years." Hannah said, almost in tears.

Stella got up and walked toward the window so she wouldn't have to face them.

She calmly said, "My dear friends, whatever I may or may not be, I'm definitely not an angel. I will leave it at that."

Tilly lashed out, "You mean we are worried sick about you, and now you let the cat out of the bag? Or should I say the man out of the bag?"

Stella turned back around to the group to speak. Sadie, while walking back into the room, didn't give her time.

"You aren't going to tell us what we don't want to hear, are you, Stella?" Sadie asked.

"I was wondering where all that hip action came into play when we were at Dr. Robert's office. Remember that, girls?" Tilly asked.

The room became silent, and then Tilly let the words fly again, "Do you have a man, Stella? If you do, you are no better than he is."

No one stopped Tilly from talking. She was asking all the questions they had wanted to but just didn't have the nerve to ask right now.

"No, I don't have a man on the side in my life, but I have to admit I have given it some thought. I figured if he knew I was seeing someone, he might change his mind and see me in a different light. I have flirted in some situations, but it never went any further than flirtation."

"Two wrongs certainly don't make a right. That is an old saying, and there is a reason for it. Do you think that in God's eyes, it would be all right for you to do the same wrong Trace is doing?" Sadie said without hesitation.

"No, I know that, Sadie. I had just gotten to the point I felt like Trace thought I was ugly and wasn't attractive to him or any other man. I wanted to prove to him I was."

"It's nothing that you have done to make him go looking around for greener pastures. Some men are like that. You were just one of the unlucky women that fell in love with the creep." Tilly said, trying to make Stella feel better.

"Honey, you have achieved great things on your own, not through him. You have your law degree. You earned that before you knew him. Until you acknowledge that, you will always live in his shadow." Sadie assured her.

Tilly quickly changed the subject, "Sadie, what are you holding in your hands?"

Sadie waved a piece of paper in the air, "You might sort of say this is your passport to Myrtle Beach, Stella. This is what is going to get you out of all the things he plans for you to do this weekend. He made those plans so he would know every step you took."

"What is it, Sadie?" Stella quickly asked.

"I called Safe Way Tour to see if they had a trip planned for this weekend. Well, lucky for us, they do, and it is leaving out Friday evening at six o'clock."

Hannah looked concerned, "Sadie, how is that going to help Stella?"

"Stella, you are going to call Trace and tell him that we are going on that trip. It is a weekend trip that is going to tour Tennessee. Of course, we aren't going to take it, but it will cover your tracks if he calls them and ask about the trip."

"What if he calls and asks if I am on the list to take the trip?"

"They will not give him an answer because it is against the rules to divulge any person that has signed up for any trip. Therefore, we have that covered. You call him now and tell him that we as a group are going, and so he doesn't have to worry about you being all by yourself at home this weekend."

Tilly jumped up and handed Stella the phone.

Stella didn't waste any time getting him on the other end of the line. The girls remained silent while she talked to Trace, telling him all about her new plans.

She stayed very calm, "Yes, Trace. This way, I won't be lonesome. It will be fun. I just hate you will be having a long working weekend while I am off having fun with my friends."

She turned and gave them a wink as she continued talking to him, "Oh yes, Trace, I am sure. It will be a great trip. We will be touring different places in Tennessee. Well, we will talk more about it when you get home."

She paused while Trace talked. "Oh, so you're going to be late tonight? Trace, you are working much too hard lately. I will wait up for you."

She again paused to listen to Trace. "Are you sure? All right then. I will see you in the morning. Love you, dear."

She handed the phone back to Tilly without saying a word. Tilly placed it back on the receiver and remained silent.

"Well, the silence of you all lets me know that you are aware of what he was saying on the other end of the phone. He is working late, or so he says, and there is no need for me to wait up for him. It is the same old storyline that he has been pushing to me for a very long time. He sure is one hard-working man."

Stella couldn't hold back any longer. She let the tears that she had been holding back all afternoon roll down her cheeks. She didn't want to act like the brave woman she had been portraying all this time. She was scared, and she wasn't going to pretend she wasn't any longer.

Sadie handed her some tissue and said, "Dry up, young lady, we have some planning to do. There is no way he is going to dump you and take the money with him. You have earned every cent he has put in the bank, and if he leaves, half of it will be yours. Now, everyone, pour you another cup of coffee, or I will bring in some ice tea, and let's put our heads together. We have some planning to do."

Gracie made eye contact with Sadie and then said, "I think I would like to have a glass of ice tea, Sadie. I'll help you get it."

She looked around at the others and said, "Anyone else care for a glass of tea?"

"I would," Tilly quickly said and started to get up.

Gracie whispered to Tilly, "You stay here with Stella. I think she needs some encouraging words."

Tilly looked strangely at Gracie. No one had ever told her to give someone encouraging words before now. She smiled, took this as a compliment, and sat down beside Stella.

Gracie followed Sadie into the kitchen. She looked around to make sure no one else was in hearing distance of what she was about to say.

Then she whispered, "Sadie, I have a chemo treatment in the morning. Do you think that I will feel strong enough to go on this little trip by Friday afternoon?"

"I hope so, Gracie. I am going to drive you for your treatment and then bring you right back here. You can go straight to bed and rest as much as you need. I'll take care of you."

Sadie continued, "Have you considered telling the others?"

"I'm not ready right now. I will, Sadie, I promise, and it won't be much longer. I have some other things I have got to get off my chest as well."

"Gracie, you told me that you would not hold back anything else about your health to me. You promised." Sadie said sternly.

"It's not about my health, Sadie, but I'm not ready to tell you or anybody else what it is right now."

Sadie walked to the cabinet and removed several glasses for the girls. She proceeded to fill them with ice. She acted as if Gracie hadn't made the last comment to her. There wasn't any use in trying to talk to her about it any longer.

Changing the subject, Sadie slowly said, "Gracie, can you carry the pitcher of tea for me?"

Gracie grabbed for the tea pitcher and followed Sadie back into the living room, where the girls were waiting anxiously.

Tilly helped fill the glasses with tea and then sat back down beside Stella. They were all waiting on Sadie to tell them just how they were going to go about catching Trace in the act of cheating.

Stella said, "Maybe I am paranoid, but it seemed he was suspicious when I was telling him about our weekend."

JoBeth shrugged, "Maybe he is feeling guilty."

Hannah suggested, "No, it's that he had it all planned out for you, and you did something different. You made your own plans. I'm telling you, I have been there and done it. Every time I went against what Gordon had planned or suggested, he would act strangely. The fact was that he didn't feel in control for a split second, and he didn't like it."

"I am sure you are right," Stella agreed.

Once again, the room went silent, and they waited for Sadie to tell them what they needed to do.

"All right, ladies, feel free to jump in at any time with suggestions," Sadie said, smiling.

That seemed to change the entire mood of the room. They started laughing, and this encouraged Sadie to begin.

"First, Stella, do you know where and when Trace is picking up this secretary of his?"

"Yes, he is picking her up in the office parking lot at seven o'clock. I guess he doesn't want his car spotted at her house."

"That gives everyone a chance to meet here, drive to a spot where we can't be seen, and then follow them to the beach," Sadie said with confidence.

"We have got to have another vehicle. So, I will take care of that," Gracie said, getting into the act.

"This sounds like a stakeout to me," Tilly said, laughing.

Sadie agreed, "I guess in a sense, it's going to be a stakeout. We are going to have to be very careful that he doesn't see us until he has her in his car. It's not going to be easy, but we will try. If he does catch us in the act of following him, just what is he going to say? We are in a win-win situation, regardless of what happens."

Sadie quickly writes on a piece of paper and hands it to Stella.

"Here is the name of the tour bus we are supposed to be taking and the destination. Now, when Trace talks to you about it, you will be prepared. Trust me, he will question you. I have even written down some of the places the tour guide said they are going to visit. It sounds like it would be fun."

"Let's just plan a trip after all this is over," JoBeth suggested.

Sadie took a quick look at Gracie's reaction to JoBeth's comment. Gracie had a look of gloom come across her face. It would be so much easier if Gracie would just tell the others how bad her condition was. Why was she holding back?

Out of the blue, Tilly said, "Well, Hannah, how was the movie last night with Bruce?"

Hannah sort of giggled and said, "The movie was great, and so was the person I had with me."

"Did you go see his mother again?" JoBeth asked.

"No, I didn't go back to his house. I invited him back to mine for coffee."

"You what? Well, I hope that all he got was coffee," Tilly blurted.

"I knew that was coming," Hannah said, laughing. "Rest assured, Tilly, that it was all very honorable. He is a true gentleman and doesn't try to take advantage of this Southern lady."

Gracie softly said, "Hannah, it sounds like you are enjoying his company, and that is good. Life is much too short not to enjoy it. You can enjoy life and still keep your honor and your beliefs. Just remember that, and don't worry about what others think."

"Well, my dear Gracie, I wasn't trying to imply that Hannah would let him take advantage of her," Tilly said as if she had to defend herself.

"Of course, you weren't. You were concerned and voiced your opinion. You just have a strange way of stating things at times, but you wouldn't be our Tilly if you were any different. Stay the way you are, Tilly, never change," Gracie said, sounding a little sentimental.

Sadie could see the look that the other girls were giving Gracie. She could see it in their eyes. They knew Gracie was holding something back from them.

JoBeth calmly said, "Girls, I have to go to a therapy session tomorrow. Who would like to go with me?"

Stella and Tilly quickly said they wanted to go.

Tilly teased, "Yes, Stella wants to go so she can stare at Dr. Roberts, and I will go to make sure she doesn't flirt with him."

Hannah joined in, "Well, I guess I need to go and take care of all of you. Gracie, are you and Sadie coming?"

"It sounds like you all have everything under control. I need to make some arrangements for our transportation for Friday, and I really need Sadie to help me," Gracie said, being quick with her statement.

JoBeth looked at Sadie and said, "Do you think you can trust me if I go from the session to home? I know I am in control enough to stay by myself, but Sadie, I want you to know it, also. I want you all to be able to trust me enough to know I will be making the right decisions from now on."

Sadie smiled and said, "We trust you, JoBeth. You are definitely on the road to recovery."

Sadie felt a feeling of relief. Now, she could take Gracie to her chemo treatment, bring her back home, help her to bed, and the others wouldn't have to know what she was going through right now.

Sadie glanced toward Gracie and smiled. Gracie smiled back, knowing her secret would be safe for at least a few more days.

Chapter 11

Freeing yourself from the secrets of your past
can create a feeling of
inner peace,
secured hope,
and solid faith.
You are able to face what God has planned for you –
even if it is death.

The next few days went quickly for the entire group of the Southern Belle Breakfast Club.

Stella remained concerned the entire time that Trace was somehow going to find out she had lied about the trip. She was always on the phone with one of her friends, trying to draw strength from the encouraging words they would give her.

JoBeth had her session with her therapy group. It was another success, making her feel stronger and more secure about herself.

Gracie had endured another round of chemo, but this time Sadie was by her side the entire time. Having someone to be there with her enabled her to feel more comfortable about everything. Sadie had quickly driven her back home and helped her to bed. She had slept for several hours and woke to a bowl of warm chicken soup that Sadie had waiting for her. She waited on her hand and foot allowing Gracie complete bed rest.

Early Friday morning, Gracie was out of bed, making plans on the phone with the Rent A Car agent. She had arranged for the agency to bring the vehicle straight to Sadie's by three o'clock sharp. She smiled, knowing that she would be able to make the trip with them after all.

"Well, just look at you," Sadie said while coming into the room where Gracie was sitting with pen and paper in her hand.

"Good morning, sleepyhead. It's about time you got up. We have a big day and an even bigger weekend ahead of us," Gracie said, smiling.

"Are you sure you are up to this?"

"I wouldn't miss this for the world. I have us a vehicle coming, and here is a list of things I know we are going to need." Gracie said as she handed Sadie the paper.

"There is a lot on this list. You have put down wigs, sunglasses, binoculars, and food. It looks like you have it all covered."

"Yes, I do, and I have already arranged for that to be brought over by a delivery boy."

"A delivery boy, how did you arrange that?" Sadie said with a puzzled look on her face.

"Sadie, you are always taking care of things. Now, don't ask questions, and let me help you out with some of the little details you always do."

Sadie was relieved to see her smiling and feeling good. So, she decided not to ask any questions.

"Well, do you think that I can talk you into letting me pack for the both of us?" Sadie said, teasing.

"That can certainly be your job. I never liked to pack a suitcase."

Sadie reached for a throw pillow from the couch and walked toward Gracie.

"Here, honey, lie down, place this under your head and rest while I bring you a hot bowl of oatmeal. You don't need to eat anything that might upset your stomach. You have had very little nausea since the chemo. I'm packing you cheese and crackers to munch on if you start feeling sick while we are on the road."

Gracie smiled and said, "Yes, Doctor Sadie."

"I am serious, Gracie. If at any time during this weekend you get to feeling sick, I want you to promise me that you will let me know. I will turn that car around so fast it will make all of our heads spin. You don't need to be pushing yourself while you are taking these treatments. That is very important for you to remember."

Gracie nodded, laid down on the couch, and placed the pillow under her head just as Sadie had instructed.

Sadie smiled and walked toward the kitchen to get the oatmeal.

Gracie looked around the room. She caught a glimpse of a picture frame that held a picture of all the girls. She got up, went straight to the picture, and brought it back to the couch. She placed it on the coffee table and laid back down. She stared at the picture, remembering the event as if it were yesterday. They had been at the lake enjoying a picnic. Tilly had asked a total stranger to take a picture of the group. He had happily agreed, and soon he had taken several photos of them. This was their favorite picture. So, Sadie had purchased them all a unique frame, had several copies made, and then gave them each the special gift to remember that day. She chuckled as she continued to remember that Tilly had accidentally walked off the end of the pier getting completely soaked. It had indeed been a fun day for them.

Her laughter soon turned into tears. She reached for the picture and held it tightly in her hands.

She softly prayed, "Dear God, I'm scared. I am scared of what I know I am going to have to face. You know all our thoughts and feelings, and so there is no need for me not to admit it. Please give me the strength to face what you have planned for me while on this earth. Please be with my friends, dear God. Some of them aren't very strong when it comes to facing facts. I've done wrong in the past, God, and I don't feel worthy ...."

Sadie came back into the room with the hot bowl of oatmeal.

"I thought I heard you talking. Were you on the phone with one of the girls?" Sadie asked.

"No, I haven't called them yet." She paused and then continued, "That smells good, Sadie. Have I thanked you for everything you have done for me?"

She placed the tray with the oatmeal on Gracie's lap and said, "Seeing you feeling better is all the thanks I need. Now, eat up before your meal gets cold."

At three o'clock, there was a knock on Sadie's front door. Gracie went to the door, and within minutes, she was holding the keys to a minivan. The Rent a Car service was right on time.

The next knock on the door was a man holding a large package. Sadie watched as she saw Gracie showing him where to place it. Then she handed him some money, and he quickly left.

"You have gotten everything under control," Sadie said.

"I put you and JoBeth down as the drivers for the minivan. Was that all right? I don't think I am going to be able to drive."

"Gracie, of course, it is all right. I was hoping you would not attempt to drive. We will carry several pillows, and then if you want to stretch out in the back, it will make the ride much easier for you. I will tell the girls the pillows are for anyone that gets tired or sleepy. That way, they won't ask you any questions."

Suddenly, the phone rang. Sadie picked up to say hello, but before she got the words out, she knew there was trouble on the other end.

"Sadie, this is Stella. We have got a problem, and I don't know what to do."

"Calm down, Stella, and tell me what is going on."

"Trace is demanding to take me to meet the tour bus. I keep telling him that we want to meet at your house and go together, but he is not buying it. He said that he wants to take me himself because he will not get to see me all weekend. He wants to spend every minute with me before he goes. What do you think is up with him?"

"It sounds like he is so paranoid that you are going to find out about him that he wants to make sure he puts you on the bus going in the opposite direction of him.

Now, Stella, calm down. You give him the directions to Safe Way Tour and let him drive you there, but make sure he knows that we will be coming back Monday and that I will bring you home."

"What am I going to do when I get there?"

"When you get there, don't look for us, just go toward the bus and stand there. I will figure something out."

"I don't know if I can pull this off."

"Stella, listen to me. You are going to do this, and we are all going to help you. Now, get off the phone and get packed. Then call Trace at work and tell him you are pleased he wants to drive you there, and it is so sweet of him. Play him like he is playing you. One thing, when you are about ten minutes away from Safe Way Tour, call me on your cell phone, and I will know when to start my plan of action."

"What plan is that, Sadie?"

"Don't ask, Stella. The least you know might be the best. Then you can play right along without getting nervous. You just get there without Trace becoming suspicious, and let me do the rest of the work."

"All right, I will do as you say."

"All right, honey, just remember you are not the villain in this situation, and it is all going to work out."

Sadie said goodbye and hung the phone up before Stella could ask any more questions. The fact was Sadie did not exactly know what she was going to do, but she knew the plans had to be quickly changed and new arrangements made.

Gracie smiled and said, "Sounds like someone has their hands full once again. Do you have a game plan?"

"Well, we need to call the girls and get them over here earlier. We have to get to Safe Way Tour before Stella and Trace does. Then I will have to figure something out. I'll start making those calls now."

Within five minutes, Sadie had called all the girls, and they were on their way over. She then went and got her and Gracie's suitcase and placed it beside the front door. She rushed into the kitchen and packed enough cheese and crackers for everyone. At least that part was completed.

Sadie started pacing back and forth. She was not entirely sure if she could carry off what she had in mind, but she was going to try.

Within twenty minutes, the girls were walking up Sadie's sidewalk with suitcases in hand.

Sadie met them at the door with Gracie right behind her.

She pointed to the minivan and said, "No time to lose, girls. Take your suitcases and get on in. We've got a lot of planning to do."

"A minivan, oh, this is going to be fun," Tilly said while jumping in the back.

Sadie got on the driver's side and then turned to JoBeth.

"JoBeth, can you and I take turns driving if needed?"

"Of course, you let me know when you are ready to switch."

Hannah jumped into the passenger seat and said, "I once carpooled in a minivan. That certainly was tons of years ago."

"Oh dear, let's not go down memory lane, Hannah," Tilly said.

"Wasn't going to go there, Tilly, so set back and enjoy the ride," Hannah said, laughing.

Gracie could not help but giggle. Hannah had grown so much in personality since she had met Bruce Smith. He was certainly good for her.

Sadie drove slightly over the speed limit but making sure she was safe enough not to get a ticket.

"Girls, I explained on the phone to each of you why there was a change in plans, but I didn't tell you what the new plans were going to be. Frankly, I don't know myself right now," Sadie said, honestly.

"Well, you better come up with something quick cause there is the Safe Way Tour building on the right," Hannah said, pointing.

"Good eye, Hannah. Now I see why you jumped upfront," Tilly said.

Sadie pulled into the parking lot and then stopped.

Suddenly, Sadie's cell phone rang. She looked at the caller ID to see who was calling.

"It's Stella. I told her to call about ten minutes before they got here. I thought we would have more time."

"Maybe Trace is trying to get rid of Stella so he can go and pick up his bimbo earlier than planned," Tilly remarked.

Sadie answered the cell, "Hello Stella, so you are almost here? So, listen as I talk and just smile as if everything is all right. You only need to say okay, or that is right when needed. Now, when you get here, go straight to the bus, and I will come to your side. Hand me your suitcase and then continue to stand at the door of the bus. If other people are getting on, let them all pass. If the driver happens to ask you for your ticket, tell him that your friend has it. Hopefully, Trace will drop you off and leave, but something tells me he will not do that. I sure hope you are smiling while I am talking to you because I am sure Trace is watching your reaction as I talk."

Sadie paused while Stella calmly said, "That's right."

"I thought so. Now, if he walks you to the bus, you talk to him and keep him preoccupied as much as you can. It's going to work. Everything is going to be all right. We will see you in a few minutes."

Sadie closed her cell phone and then said, "She is so nervous, bless her heart."

"I could wring his neck," Tilly said angrily.

"I think we all could help you do just that," Gracie said.

Sadie pulled the minivan around the side of the building and said, "Gracie, you stay here. The rest of you come with me."

They swiftly got out. Then Sadie opened the side door and whispered, "Gracie, I know you said that you weren't going to drive, but you might have to do just that. Do you think that if it comes down to it that you could follow the bus for a little way?"

"Right now, I could do anything. That Trace has me so mad. I guess getting mad is good for me."

"I think I have parked where you can see us. You can use those binoculars if needed. Now, if I drop my pocketbook on the ground, that will be a sign letting you know that you have to follow the bus. For how long, I don't know. I'm not telling the others, but I don't know how this is going to go."

"You can pull this off, Sadie. Now get going before Trace pulls up. I am completely all right. I promise."

Sadie nodded and then walked toward the others. She smiled to try to reassure them, and then she headed toward the bus. They followed closely behind her.

People were already getting on the bus. Now, she had to talk to the bus driver. She motioned for the girls to stop and then pointed toward the side of the bus. They did as Sadie motioned for them to do and stood as if they were robots. They didn't know what they were to do next, but they were undoubtedly following Sadie's instructions to the letter.

Sadie got in line and stepped onto the bus. They watched as she stopped and started talking to the driver.

Tilly happily pointed out, "It's a woman driver. Maybe she will cooperate with whatever Sadie is asking her to do."

"What is Sadie asking her?" Hannah asked.

"Hannah, I don't know what she's asking her. We will just leave that to Sadie. She will come up with something; she always does." Tilly said.

They watched as the driver, along with Sadie, got off the bus and walked away from everyone. Sadie seemed to be talking a mile a minute, but the girls could not hear anything.

"Do you think it is working?" JoBeth asked in a nervous voice.

"Well, it must be. Look, Sadie just hugged her, and the driver is smiling," Tilly pointed out.

Then it seemed as if out of nowhere, Stella walked up behind them. Trace was right by her side, carrying her suitcase.

"Hello everyone, I was scared I was going to be late," she said, sounding nervous.

Sadie whispered to the driver and then walked toward Stella.

"Hello, you two. Have you decided to go on the trip with us, Trace? That would be such fun. I am sure Stella would love that."

Trace seemed to lose that confident air about him he always had but answered, "I wish I could, but I have a dull business trip I have to attend this weekend. I just had to drive Stella here, though. This way, it won't make my weekend seem so long."

"Now, aren't you sweet," Sadie said, trying to sound convincing.

"Tilly, tell Trace all about the places we are going while I take Stella's suitcase around to the side of the baggage holder of the bus," Sadie said.

"I can do that," Trace said while reaching for the suitcase.

Suddenly, Hannah questioned, "Trace, is that a new BMW I saw you driving? Why I think they are just the coolest cars coming off the assembly line now."

Instantly, it seemed as if Trace had forgotten all about the suitcase. All attention was on his car.

"Can you show me the inside of your car? I bet you have the complete leather package. Yes, I can tell you are the type of man that would only have the best," Hannah giggled in a flirting way.

Trace was putty in Hannah's hand. She knew it and loved every minute of it. As he escorted her toward the car, Sadie grabbed Stella's suitcase and raced toward the minivan. She opened the door and threw it into the back.

"New plan Gracie, you don't have to watch for me to drop my pocketbook on the ground. It is already set. The bus driver is going to let us get on the bus as if we are taking the trip. She will drive down the road and then stop. You follow behind the bus. As soon as she lets us off, we will jump right in, and I will start driving again."

Gracie nodded.

"Are you feeling all right?" Sadie asked, hoping Gracie's answer was going to be what she wanted to hear.

"I am doing just fine. I've got this end completely covered. You go and take care of that end," she ordered.

Sadie ran back toward the bus making sure that Trace didn't see which way she had come. She did not need to worry. He was utterly engrossed in showing Hannah his new car.

Sadie raced to the group, took a deep breath, and said, "Girls, all I can say is do as I do, and all this will soon be over. Shortly, we will be in the minivan laughing at how easy it was to fool Trace."

"I hope so, but somehow I have my suspicion it's not going to be that easy," Stella admitted.

The bus driver walked toward Sadie and whispered, "Be the last ones on and stay right at the front of the bus. Agree with everything I say, and it will be all right."

She looked at Stella and said, "So, you must be Stella and that bum over there, showing off his car is your so-called husband?"

Stella nodded.

The bus driver pointed toward Trace and said, "I had one of those before, the man, not the car. I got rid of him, and it was the best thing I have ever done in my life. I'm not saying it was easy. I finally became my own person when I told him I wasn't going to take any more of his crap. Yes, the best thing I ever did was kick my old man to the curb."

She took a quick look in the direction of Trace once again, shook her head, and then got on the bus.

Finally, Hannah took Trace by the arm and walked him back toward the group.

"Interesting car, Stella, very interesting," Hannah said while winking at Stella but making sure Trace didn't see her.

Trace smiled the smile of a man that thought he was on top of the world.

Sadie took a deep breath as the last woman got on the bus.

She turned to Stella and said, "Well, you better kiss your sweet hubby bye. If we don't get on this bus, we are going to miss a great trip to Tennessee."

Stella turned to Trace and said, "Oh honey, I do so hate to go off, knowing I am going to have a wonderful weekend, and you have to work. All you have to do is just say the word, and I will grab my suitcase and come with you. You don't have to worry about that job of yours."

Trace gave her a quick hug, a kiss on the cheek, and said, "No, you go on and enjoy yourself. I'll struggle through this weekend. It will be all right. Remember, I am doing this for us. Maybe it will even get me more clients."

He gave her a gentle push toward the door of the bus.

"That's right, Stella, listen to your husband," Tilly said as she reached for Stella's hand and pulled her onto the bus.

Then she whispered softly in Stella's ear, "Oh man, I just love a liar with imagination, and your husband is full of it."

Sadie motioned Hannah and JoBeth to follow their lead.

As they got on, the driver said, "Stay right at the front. I have already asked the ladies to make room for you in the first three seats."

The driver shut the door and started the engine to the large bus.

Trace continued to stand motionless, making sure that Stella was going to stay on the bus.

The driver slowly pulled from the parking lot and onto the main road. The strangers sitting on the front rows turned their heads to watch Trace.

"That man of yours is determined to watch us pull away," one of them stated.

Stella was shocked at her remark but nervously said, "Yes, I wish he would just go, get in the car and drive away."

Quickly, the driver picked up her microphone and began her speech, "All right, ladies, I have something I need to announce. We rather have a situation here, and I need your help. First, I could easily lose my job, but we have a young lady on this bus that needs our help."

Everyone inside the bus went utterly silent. The only noise that was heard was coming from the engine of the bus.

She continued, "I need to let these five ladies ride the bus for a few miles and then let them off. One of them is attempting to get away from her abusive husband. Now, I need a show of hands that will promise me that this situation will not leave this bus. We need to keep this secret to ourselves. If it ever gets back that I stopped and let anyone off, I will lose my job. Many of you have been on trips before with me as the driver. I am getting to know some of you, like family, and you know that I wouldn't do anything to jeopardize my job unless I knew it was important. Now, what is the vote?" Someone from the back stood up and said, "We don't have to take a vote. You let those women off anytime you need to."

Suddenly, everyone on the bus started to clap and give their approval. Stella stood up, turned to the large group, and threw them a kiss.

"Thank you all so much," she said. "You can never imagine what this means to me."

"There you have it, ladies. You have all their votes. I can let you off and feel comfortable about not losing my job," the driver said, looking relieved.

A woman from the back hollowed out, "The bum is right behind us. He is sticking like glue."

The driver once again picked up her microphone and said, "Ladies, I am going to slow this sucker down as much as I can. Maybe he will get tired of getting diesel fuel fumes on that new BMW of his and pass us."

She slowed the big bus to almost a crawl. Trace slowly passed and then sped away as if this had angered him.

Everyone stood to watch as Trace quickly left their view. Then once again, the bus exploded with their applause.

The driver immediately spoke in the microphone, "Houston, we have lift off."

The bus was filled with laughter from all the women aboard.

Stella looked at Sadie, and tears filled her eyes, "We've done it. I have won this battle against him. We outplayed him."

Sadie said, "You sure have Stella, and this is only the beginning."

The driver slowed to a complete stop and then said, "It's the end of the road for you, ladies. Good luck, and I hope that everything works out the way you want it to. I am sorry, but I can't take you back."

"You have already done enough. You have actually gone out of your way to help us. We have someone that will pick us up. She should be following behind the bus as we speak." Sadie assured her.

Stella once again turned to the women on the bus and said, "Thank you all once again."

They quickly got off the bus and stood at the side of the road. They could hear shouts coming from the bus, "Power to the women, power to the women."

Tilly cheerfully said, "They sure would be a great group to go on a trip with."

The girls nodded and then laughed, but Sadie wasn't laughing.

"Quick girls, follow me. We got a problem. We got a big problem."

Sadie ran toward the ditch, up a large bank, and into the dense underbrush. The girls tried to follow close behind, but the thick vines were wrapping around their ankles.

"Get down on the ground," Sadie commanded.

"I'm already on the ground, Sadie, but it's not by choice," Tilly said, trying to unwind the vines from around her ankles.

Stella nervously asked, "What is going on, Sadie?"

"Well, for one thing, Gracie was supposed to be behind the bus to pick us up. I guess when she saw that Trace was following us, she lagged behind, but the problem is Trace."

"What do you mean?" JoBeth questioned.

"He turned around somewhere down the road. I caught a glimpse of that bright shiny new car headed back this way. I can't figure out what he has in that brain of his."

Stella quickly reached for her ringing cell phone and said, "Well, I guess we are going to find out. This is Trace on the phone."

Sadie grabbed her phone before Stella could answer and said, "Stella, you are on your own. I can't tell you what to say because I don't know what he is going to ask. You are smart, Stella, play him." Then, she slowly handed Stella back her phone.

Stella placed the phone to her ear, and calmly said, "Hello darling, miss me already?"

She paused to listen to what Trace had to say and then said, "Oh Trace, that is so sweet of you, but there is no need for that. Actually, the bus driver can't stop for anyone once they have pulled out of the lot. So, you just keep my makeup case, and I will use the girl cosmetics this weekend."

She paused again to listen to Trace tell more lies. She smiled at the girls to let them know she had everything under control.

She continued, "You try not to work too hard this weekend, honey, and I will see you sometime Monday. As I told you earlier, I will have Sadie or one of the girls drop me off at home. Monday night, we can tell one another all about our weekend. Love you."

She closed her cell phone, took a deep breath, and said, "I can't believe I left my makeup case in the car."

"I can't believe the jerk actually wanted to get it to you," Tilly said without hesitation.

"He had turned around and was going to get in behind the bus, blink his lights and get the driver to pull over. What would have happened if he couldn't have gotten me on the phone and attempted to do that anyway?" Stella asked.

"Well, we don't have to worry about that now, but I wonder where he is. I know he passed here, but I haven't seen him go back down the road. So, we need to stay low until Gracie calls me on the cell phone." Sadie said, trying to keep the others calm.

"It's getting dark fast, Sadie. "I'm scared," whispered Tilly.

"You wouldn't be so scared if you didn't have so much devil in you," JoBeth teased.

"Hush, girls!" Sadie said. "We need to listen out for Gracie. Also, keep a lookout for Trace driving back down the road. He is running late to pick up his woman. He will probably fly by here any minute like something is after him."

They quietly continued to lay on their stomachs like scared rabbits hiding from a hunter. It was getting darker and darker. All they could hear was the wind blowing in the branches of the trees.

Suddenly, Hannah pointed and said, "Look, there is a kitty cat. Meow, come here, baby."

"Shut up, Hannah. That's no cat. That's a raccoon." Tilly screamed, jumped up, and ran to get beside Sadie.

Without hesitation, Sadie reached for a rock and directed it toward the raccoon. It scurried away as fast as it could.

"Calm down, Tilly. It's as scared of us as we are of it." Stella said, almost laughing.

They couldn't hold back any longer. They all looked at one another and started laughing right out loud.

"Did any of you ever dream that we would be lying on our stomach, hiding in bushes and facing down a raccoon at our age?" Sadie said, rolling on the ground.

"Well, speak for yourselves because I'm not old," Hannah giggled.

"Well, then you are young and blind because the rest of us could see well enough to know the difference between a cat and a raccoon." Tilly clarified.

"Well, I can see this is going to follow me to my grave," fumed Hannah.

Sadie continued to laugh and said, "Yes, Hannah, I'm afraid it is."

"Listen, I think that was your cell phone, Sadie," JoBeth said.

Sadie reached into her pocket, pulled out her phone, and quickly said, "Oh Gracie, we have been worried about you. We are hiding on a high bank on the side of the road. You won't be able to see us because there are so much underbrush and foliage. We will watch for your lights. Can you put on the emergency blinkers? We will look for lights blinking and then come out. We are on the right side of the road. We will be easy to see once we are out of this mess of vines and woods."

She listened to what Gracie was saying and then said, "All right, honey, we will be watching."

She closed her cell phone and then said, "Let's get closer to the road. I am sure Trace has gone by now, and we missed him. Gracie explained that she was staying as far behind Trace as she could, but she got scared that he would notice her following him. So, she pulled over into a store parking lot and waited for a while. Then as she started to pull back out, she saw Trace pass by. She pulled around the back of the store and stayed there until she felt safe to come out. She tried to call us, but she didn't have service on her phone. Anyway, she is on her way now."

"I bet that is her coming now. You told her to put on her emergency lights. That was a good idea," said Stella.

"Let's go, girls. I am ready to get in that minivan and continue on this adventure," Tilly said.

'This isn't an adventure for me, Tilly." Stella said sternly.

"Sorry, honey. I realize that was a poor choice of words," apologized Tilly.

They quickly made their way back down the bank and waited for Gracie to come to a complete stop.

Sadie rushed to the driver's side and opened the door. She could tell by looking at Gracie that she was not feeling well. Sadie carefully helped her out of the van hoping the others would not notice. Tilly had the sliding door opened wide, waiting for Gracie to get inside.

Tilly took the pillows, placed them on the back seat, and said, "Gracie, come and lay down while we tell you what went on with us."

Gracie followed her instructions and then slowly said, "I am anxious to hear everything."

Tilly did not like the washed-out look on Gracie's face, but she was not going to let her know it. She had noticed the special attention that Sadie had been giving to Gracie. She loved her friend enough to know when to ask and when not to ask questions.

Tilly lowered her voice to almost a whisper. "We saw a cat tonight that turned out to be a fighting mad raccoon."

Hannah whined from the passenger seat of the van, "I heard that. Yep, I see I will never live that one down."

Sadie adjusted her seat, buckled her seat belt, turned to face everybody, and said, "Well, ladies, thanks to Gracie, we are safe and sound. Now, we have to catch up with Trace, but we can do that. We are a team, ladies, and together we can do anything. We're definitely stronger together than we are one."

"Yes, we are, Sadie. That we are!" Hannah said loudly.

Sadie watched as Tilly took a blanket and wrapped it around Gracie. She knew that she did not have to hide the secret from Tilly any longer. It was clear to her that she knew that Gracie was much sicker than she led them to believe. Just how much she did know, Sadie was not sure.

She took a deep breath and pulled back onto the dark highway. She would face Tilly's questions when the time came, but she was not going to break the promise she had made with Gracie. Southern women always keep their promises, especially a promise made to a dear friend.

Chapter 12

It is impossible to live your entire life without having
    some kind of secret,
    some kind of failure,
    or
    some kind of regret.
It is how you deal with these events
that gives you your self-respect back
without
apologies or excuses.

Sadie pulled slowly into the parking lot of the law office. There sat a little red mustang that Stella quickly acknowledged as the car of the *other* woman.

"I feel like getting out and keying her car," Stella ranted.

"What point would that prove? There are probably cameras all over the place looking at us as we drive through. We know that they are definitely on the road and are on the way to

Myrtle Beach. So stay calm, and let's start looking for that car of his," Sadie said, trying to calm Stella.

Stella started laughing so hard that she had to hold her stomach.

"What in the world is wrong? Are you having a fit, Stella?" Tilly asked nervously.

"I forgot to tell you all what I did to his new car. I kicked the tail light out on the right side. I knew that way when it got dark; we could spot him ahead of us without getting right behind him."

"You are one hot detective, Stella. That is smart thinking on your part," bragged JoBeth.

"I didn't notice it being broken when he was showing off the car to me this afternoon. I guess I was too nervous," Hannah admitted.

"I just about didn't get away with it. I did it early this morning when he was in the shower. I hoped he would not notice until this afternoon, and in that way, he wouldn't be able to get it fixed until Monday. Well, he is so in love with that car that I should have known he would have noticed right away. I watched from the window as he pulled the car from the garage, stopped, and went to the paper box. On the way back toward the car, he gave it one quick look around and saw the busted tail light. He was so funny. He took the newspaper, slammed it down on the ground, and looked around as if it had just happened, and he was going to find out who did it. I had to look away because I was laughing so hard."

She paused, giggled a bit more, and continued, "Well, he bounced back into the house and started swearing loudly. I pretended to act as if I didn't know what was going on. He kept saying he bet the gardener hit the car when he was putting the lawn equipment away. I didn't go to his defense, so he will probably be hiring a new gardener."

"I'm surprised he didn't have it fixed today," Hannah added.

"Oh, he tried but couldn't get anyone to do it on such short notice. Therefore, there is another score for us, ladies. If we can ever make up the time we lost, he will be easily sited."

"We'll catch up with him, and it won't take us long. He wasn't that much ahead of us. I figure we are probably about five to six miles behind him. I am going just a little above the speed limit. I am sure he is obeying all the laws of the road. He wouldn't want to be pulled with *her* in the car with him," Sadie said as she continued to keep her eyes glued to the road.

"I'm getting a little hungry," Hannah said. "I just know you packed us some food somewhere in this van, Sadie."

"Yes," Gracie said as she passed the large basket toward JoBeth. "Grab out what you need and pass it on to Hannah. The cheese and crackers are coming in handy, Sadie. It's truly hitting the spot."

Sadie smiled to herself. She knew that right now, Gracie was feeling better, and that gave her a feeling of relief.

Tilly reached into the little cooler and pulled out a coke. "Who wants something to drink?"

Everyone seemed to be thirsty, so she passed each one a soda.

"We are having a regular little picnic in a minivan," Tilly said, laughing.

Without warning, Hannah gave out a yell, "Up ahead is a car with a tail light out. We have done it. We have caught up with him."

"We sure have, girls," Sadie said, beaming. "Gracie, do you think it is time to pull out that box you got ready for us?"

"I think we had better prepare for whatever might happen. Here girls, pick out the color you want," Gracie said as she opened a box filled with wigs, big-rimmed sunglasses, and oversized clothes.

Stella grabbed the red wig and said, "I want this one."

"Your hair is already red. Why in the world would you pick out a red wig?" Tilly asked while grabbing the wig from Stella's hand.

Each one took a wig except for Sadie and Gracie.

Gracie said, "He has never seen me. I don't need a wig, but the fact is, if it comes down to it,

I will just get down on the floor and cover up with this blanket."

"I hope it will not come to that, but he doesn't need to see six of us in this van. So, at least two more of you will need to hide with Gracie. Stella, you are one that needs to hide." Sadie insisted.

"By the way, Stella, have you ever met this woman, and do you know her name?" Tilly questioned.

Stella didn't answer immediately but finally said, "Yes, I've met her at a dinner party I had for the lawyers of the law firm. Trace insisted that I invite all their secretaries. I didn't think much about it at that time. During dinner, between the main course and dessert, I noticed right off that something was fishy between Trace and Miss Melody."

"Now, let me see if I can look in my crystal ball and see Miss Melody." Tilly pretended she was holding a crystal ball and was playing as if she was a fortuneteller. "I can see this young girl. She is in a strapless black dress that has a split up to her thigh, but wait, the split seems to be only on the right side of her dress. She is a young woman with big red lips that seems to have had botox injections many times to give her that full effect."

Everyone, including Stella, laughed.

Tilly continued, "Wait, I see more in my crystal ball. She has recently had a boob job, going from size thirty-two A cup to a thirty-eight D cup. This appears to have come from a Christmas bonus she received."

"Well," Stella said, "You are probably correct about that. Doesn't take a crystal ball to figure out she is getting money from *my* husband."

"Well, let's put a stop to it," JoBeth said, sounding tuff and brave. "Let's just all go and pay her a little visit come Monday night or call her from an unlisted number, letting her know that someone knows she is running around with a married man."

"I know you all are trying to cheer me up, and it is working. First, before I threaten her, I need to find out if Trace is using her for a mid-life crisis or if he is falling in love with her. See, the last part scares me to death. I still love him. I can't help it. Maybe this weekend will take some of the love away, but so far, the love is still strong."

"Oh my goodness, I don't want to change the subject, but I have to go to the bathroom. I need to wet real bad. All those sodas have gone straight to my bladder. Look, there is a gas station coming up on our right," Tilly said anxiously.

"No way, Tilly. We can't stop now. We might not be able to catch up with him again. He might even pull into a hotel instead of going straight to the beach. We would never know the difference," Sadie said sternly.

"Whatever!" Tilly said, waving her hand for Sadie to continue driving.

Hannah spoke up, "Well, I have to admit, Tilly is not the only one that needs to go to the bathroom."

"Well, I am sorry, girls. Sadie and I tried to bring everything we thought we might need, but that is something we didn't consider." Gracie said, apologizing.

"The only thing I know to do is hope that Trace needs to stop at a bathroom and then try to figure something out then," Sadie said, trying to come up with an idea.

Stella shook her head and said, "They will never stop unless she has the urge. She has the bladder of a sixteen-year-old, and he will hold it in as long as he can so she won't realize he is a leaky faucet."

Tilly whined, "Don't make me laugh, Stella. I can't take the pressure."

"Calm down, ladies," Sadie said, " I promise if he stops, we are stopping right with them. Who else in here needs to go to the bathroom?"

JoBeth slowly raised her hand as if she was ashamed to admit she needed the bathroom as well.

Tilly laughed, "I knew Hannah, and I wasn't the only one."

"The problem is that Trace knows exactly what five of us looks like. The only thing going for us is that his little friend doesn't have a clue we even exist. Now, make sure you three have on wigs just in case Trace would glance your way, then he wouldn't recognize you. I will slip on a wig and set tight. Stella and Gracie will hide in the back. We can do this, ladies."

" Look, Sadie," Hannah said, pointing toward the cars ahead of them. "It looks like he is pulling into that gas station."

Sadie gripped the steering wheel so tightly her fingers felt as if they were going to fall off. She turned her turn signal on and proceeded to pull into the gas station. She slowed down to see where Trace was going to park the car.

"Great, he is going to pump some gas. Now, I am going to pull around to the other side. You three jump out as fast as you can, get to that bathroom and get back in this car in case he decides to go into the store."

"He will be in there, girls. I can promise you. One thing I know for sure about my husband is that by now, his eyeballs are floating, and he needs to go to the bathroom badly," Stella said as if she almost felt sorry for him.

Sadie drove as far from the gas pumps as she could toward the other side of the store and stopped the van.

Just as Stella had predicted, Trace hurriedly got out of the car and went straight into the gas station.

"I told you he would go straight inside. He's headed to the bathroom," Stella said.

"Hold on, girls. You can't go in until he comes out." Sadie instructed.

Tilly, Hannah, and JoBeth sat patiently but eager to get out. They watched carefully to see when Trace would head back toward the gas pumps.

"There he goes," Sadie said. "Now, go as fast as you can."

Tilly reached for her pocketbook, but Stella grabbed it quickly from her and said, "No way, Tilly. You are not buying anything in that store."

"Yes, Ma'am!" Tilly said sharply.

Sadie watched as the three took off in a dash toward the entrance of the store.

"I can't believe that Tilly at times," Stella said as she crawled into the back seat to hide with Gracie.

Sadie quickly put her wig on, adjusting it to make sure it was on correctly.

She looked in the mirror and said, "Look, I might consider becoming a blond."

Gracie placed her head slightly above the seat and said, "Forget it, Sadie. It doesn't do you justice."

Sadie quit admiring herself in the mirror and said, "We have problems. Trace's little friend is getting out of the car and is heading straight into the store. She doesn't have her pocketbook, so she certainly isn't going in to buy herself some bubble gum. She is going to the bathroom."

"Well, then I guess we need to hold on to the hope that only one person at a time can get into the bathroom. We know that our three would have gone in at the same time, trying to stay hidden. That would mean that Melody would have to wait until they come out." Stella said, trying to stay calm.

Gracie reached for the box that held all the necessary items they would need for the weekend. She carefully removed a camera.

"If possible, I am going to take a picture of Trace and his friend. Stella, you need all the evidence you can get if you decide to do something about this weekend."

"I know, Gracie. I was thinking about that earlier." Stella said sadly.

Suddenly, a cell phone inside the minivan started to ring.

Stella grabbed her phone, "I can't believe it. Trace is calling me while he is pumping the gas."

"Of course, the girlfriend is in the store using the bathroom. What a perfect time to call the wife," fumed Sadie.

"Quickly, tell me, girls. Should we be in Tennessee by now?" Stella asked.

"No!" Sadie and Gracie both answered.

Stella opened her cell phone and said calmly, "Hello, honey."

She waited for Trace to talk. He seemed to have a lot to say.

Finally, it was Stella's turn. "No, we aren't in Tennessee yet. We stopped for a quick meal, and it took a lot longer than was planned. I guess we are still at least an hour or two away from the hotel."

She glanced toward Sadie to see if she might have said anything wrong. Sadie smiled to reassure her.

Gracie quietly got Sadie's and Stella's attention and pointed toward Trace. Melody was walking straight toward the car.

Stella continued to talk, trying to see how long she could keep Trace on the phone.

"Oh, honey, must you go. I miss you so much. I really wish I hadn't taken this trip. I wish there had been some way that I could have gone with you. All right. Well, I love you, and I'll see you Monday night. Trace, I said I love you. I love you, Trace."

She paused, "Trace, are you there?"

Gracie reached toward Stella's hand and removed the phone.

"Don't do this to yourself. He's not going to tell you he loves you. She is already at his side, and I got the perfect picture of the two. He is no good, Stella. The sooner you realize this, the better off you will be."

Stella put her head back down and covered it with the blanket. Sadie and Gracie let her cry without saying a word. Maybe now, the love for Trace was slowly leaving her heart.

Sadie watched as he walked the "other woman" to her side of the car, kissed her on the lips, and opened the door so she could get in. How gallant of him, Sadie thought. She didn't say a word. She wasn't about to tell Stella the little details she was missing while crying in a blanket.

"I can't believe this. They are getting ready to pull back out on the highway. Where in the world is the rest of our group?" Sadie said as she began to rub her hands together nervously.

Suddenly, the van door opened, and in they jumped.

"I thought you'd never come back," Sadie said as she started to drive off before they could be seated.

Hannah pointed out, "Just get us back on the highway. They are easy to point out with that kicked-out tail light."

Sadie nodded.

Stella came out from under the blanket and got back in the seat. She wiped her eyes with the sleeve of her shirt.

She could not hold back any longer and finally said, "There is no way that you didn't see her. What do you think about her?"

Tilly, without hesitation, said, "She has such pretty blond hair. I don't know why she dyes her roots black."

No one said a word, and then suddenly Stella busted out laughing. Then the rest joined in.

"Stella, honestly, the only thing that girl has over you is her youth. She is as ugly as homemade sin!" Hannah blurted.

She continued, "By the way, Sadie, there they are just two cars ahead of us. Drive the speed you are doing now, and we will be fine. He doesn't have a clue this minivan packed full of women is watching his every move."

"I want to hear everything," Stella said. "How did you end up going into the store before she did, but you came out last?"

"We go in, and the bathroom had only two stalls, and someone was already in both. We are standing patiently waiting our turn, and in walked a dyed blonde-haired person. She looks like she should be in high school cheerleader clothes. She is chewing her gum like there is no tomorrow."

Tilly paused to catch her breath and said, "Well, I'm not a bit ashamed to admit that I'm impressed with myself. I up and asked her for a stick of gum, and she pulls a stick out of her pocket and hands it to me."

"You have got to be kidding," Sadie said.

"Nope! Then she starts babbling on about going to the beach with a rich old dude that owns a BMW and is her boss."

Stella shakes her head.

Hannah hastily said, "We aren't kidding. She really did. I didn't think she was ever going to shut up. Then we are in line to be next, and she jumps ahead of us as if she owns the entire bathroom. That is exactly why she came out before we did."

"She is using Trace," Stella said.

"Stella, get a grip," JoBeth blurted out. "Who is using whom? Your husband is just two or three cars ahead of us with a dumb bleached blond in her early twenties and headed to the beach for a weekend. You are feeling sorry for him. I don't believe you."

"I can't think about that right now. If I do, I'll go crazy. I'll think about that tomorrow." Stella said in a dramatic voice.

"I do declare, Miss Stella. Now you are going to play a Miss Scarlette O'Hara on us. That is words right out of Gone with the Wind," Tilly implied.

"Hush, girls. Leave Stella alone," Gracie said from the back of the van.

JoBeth and Tilly instantly quit fussing at Stella.

Stella took a deep breath and said, "Thank you, Gracie."

Gracie whispered, "Stella, actually, they're right. You have some decisions to make, and you have to start making them with your brain, not your heart. There is no use in being a doormat for the rest of your life. Now, I have said my peace, and it is directly to you, not in front of all the others."

Stella touched Gracie on the hand and said, "Thank you again. I needed that."

Hannah turned to Sadie and asked, "Sadie, how much further is it to Myrtle Beach?"

"We have about another hour, and then it depends on where he is going to stay. Why are you asking?"

Hannah shrugged her shoulders, sat silently for a few minutes, and then said, "Gracie, why in the world did you rent a minivan with bucket seats? The trouble with bucket seats is that not everybody has the same bucket."

"Hannah, just slide back here. We will trade seats." Tilly suggested.

"Are you saying I am fat, Tilly?" Hannah questioned.

"Hannah, you're the one that said your bucket doesn't fit that seat. That is the way you put it. I didn't."

"Gracie, didn't she say I was fat?" Hannah asked.

"Oh, dear," Gracie said and sighed. "I just rented the van. I didn't choose what seats. Don't get me involved in this. Just consider me asleep back here."

Sadie started laughing and said, "I can't believe all of you. It seems we jump from one subject to another without giving it a second thought."

"We always know what the other is talking about, though, and that is what counts," JoBeth said.

No one said a word, but they silently knew in their hearts that JoBeth was correct.

Sadie kept her eyes straight ahead. Between watching the traffic and making sure she stayed at least three cars behind Trace, she was getting tired. The next hour slowly went by.

"Well, up ahead is the sign showing we are at Myrtle Beach. Now, everyone keep a close eye on him. There is no telling which hotel he will be checking in at," said Sadie.

"I can tell you right now it will be the best on the strip, and it will be oceanfront. He will probably stay at Tropical Breeze and has rented the penthouse." Gracie said calmly.

"It sounds like you have borrowed Tilly's crystal ball," Stella said, sounding puzzled.

"Just an educated guess, you might say," Gracie replied.

"Well, we will see shortly. He has his turn signals on, and he is definitively getting on

Ocean Boulevard. Now, this is where it gets tricky, ladies. He will start looking around to make sure no one he knows is staying at the same hotel. It's dark, and that is in his favor as well as ours." Sadie said.

Stella sat quietly, trying to hide the tears that were beginning to form in her eyes.

"Hannah, please quit smacking that chewing gum." JoBeth pleaded. "It is getting on my last nerve."

"I can't help it. When I get nervous, I smack my gum." Hannah said, apologizing.

"Then take the gum out," JoBeth sharply said.

Hannah took a tissue, placed the gum inside, rolled the tissue up, and threw it toward JoBeth.

"Now, are you happy?" Hannah asked.

JoBeth nodded.

"Gracie, you are a mind reader. He is turning into Tropical Breeze. Look how slow he is pulling in. Yep, now he is scoping out the parking lot, making sure he doesn't know any of the vehicles that are parked there." Sadie said, almost laughing at the actions of Trace.

Hannah pointed to another hotel and said, "Pull into that hotel lot. We can watch him from there. He won't be able to see us."

Sadie did as Hannah had instructed.

"Now, I can tell you what he is going to do next," Tilly said eagerly. "He is going to back his

211

car into a parking spot so no one will be able to see his tag showing that he is from North Carolina. I don't need my crystal ball for that. I have seen it on television."

"Good gosh, you're right. He is doing just that." Hannah shouted.

"Told you," Tilly said, with a confident look on her face.

Gracie grabbed the camera, rolled the window down, and aimed directly toward the couple, "Smile, Trace, you're on Candid Camera."

"That is one expensive-looking camera, but are you sure it got their picture?" Stella asked.

"I'm sure Stella, and there will be plenty more. We will get as many as you need this weekend."

"Well, girls, we could sit right here waiting, but everyone in this van knows they will not be out anymore tonight. I'm not trying to hurt you, Stella, but they both came here for a reason, and it wasn't to sightsee." Sadie said, being brutally honest.

Stella's lip quivered, "I know."

"We need to try and find a place to stay. They won't be out until probable lunchtime tomorrow," said Tilly.

"Sadie, head to Garden City. I have already gotten us a house on the beach for the weekend," Gracie said casually.

"A house on the beach sounds great to me," said Tilly, sounding like a young girl who was at the beach for the first time in her life.

"We need to discuss all the money that you have spent on this undercover work we are doing this weekend. Then we will split it all equally," suggested Sadie.

The rest of the girls nodded.

"No, this is on me, and don't bring it up again," Gracie said sternly.

Again, they knew there would be no reason to attempt to argue with her. Therefore, they smiled and thanked her.

Sadie pulled out of the lot, with Stella giving a quick glance over her shoulder at the motel.

"Don't try to visualize what is going on in that room, Stella. It will only make you feel worse," whispered Gracie.

"I would like to find out what room they are in, knock on the door, and just stand there when he opens it. I wouldn't say a word. I would just stare him down."

Gracie took Stella's hand in hers and said, "Then what would you do? If you still love him after this and want your marriage to work, then face him without her being there. You deserve to hear what he has to say without the threat of him closing the door in your face and then crawling in her arms."

"Why can't I be as wise as you, Gracie?"

"Oh, Stella, I am far from wise. I have so many questions going through my mind right now and no answers in sight. I just know in my heart what I would do if I were in your shoes."

Stella softly whispered back to Gracie, "What questions, Gracie? You know we are here for you, but you have to let us into your life. We are always here to help one another."

"I know, sweet pea. I know." Gracie said as she patted Stella on her hand.

"Gracie," Sadie called from the front. "Where do I go from here? We are in Garden City."

"Go to the end of this road and turn left. It is the third house. I'll point it out when you get closer."

Sadie followed her directions and, within minutes, was pulling into a paved driveway. The outside of the house was breathtaking. This was definitely not an ordinary beach house.

They hurriedly gathered their suitcases and went inside.

"Goodness, Gracie. This is beautiful," Tilly said as she went from room to room.

The rooms were huge and fully furnished with lavished furniture. It was apparent that a professional decorator was responsible for the look.

Tilly opened the French doors, leading out to the balcony that overlooked the ocean.

"This is beautiful," Tilly yelled as she walked on the balcony. "I feel like an important person in this house. Quick, come and look at the moon. It is full tonight."

They walked onto the balcony with Tilly.

Gracie calmly said, "It is beautiful, isn't it? I love the beach. God's love is like this ocean. You can see its beginning but not its end. God's love is never-ending."

Everyone became silent as each pondered Gracie's remark and her sudden state of overpowering calmness.

There was a long pause, and they knew there was more that should be spoken. Would Gracie continue?

Instead, Gracie turned and walked back into the beach house, stopped, slowly turned to them, and said, "I'm tired and sleepy. Choose the room you want, and by the way, the refrigerator is stocked, and so are the cabinets. So, I guess we need to make ourselves at home."

She smiled and went straight into a bedroom and closed the door behind her.

All eyes turned directly to Sadie.

"Don't look at me. I don't know how she got this house rented, and I know she is not going to tell us. All I know is that I am beat. I am going to bed. I feel like I have been running a foot race, and I came in last. Good night and I love each one of you."

She walked back into the house, found her a bedroom, and closed the door swiftly behind her. She leaned against the bedroom door with tears running down her cheek. She had once again escaped the questions that would have probably popped up about Gracie's health. Earlier, she had seen in Gracie's face and eyes that she was getting worse. The chemo was not doing what she had prayed; it would do. She also realized that Gracie knew it was not helping. She was slowly and in her own way facing the fact that she was dying. Sadie knew that the days of Gracie's silence were growing shorter. She would soon tell the others. She felt as a group that they could help Gracie cope.

Tilly, JoBeth, Hannah, and Stella each made themselves comfortable on the balcony and talked into the early hours of the morning. The talk was certainly about Trace, but the main subject was the way Gracie had remained a mystery to them during the long years of their friendship. They felt she was holding something back from them, but just what, they were unsure.

Chapter 13

Do not compare your life to others,
Or wish you could walk in their shoes.
You have no idea what their journey is all
about.

Sadie woke to the morning sun beaming into the bedroom window. She looked around the room, realizing suddenly where she was. It had been a long night for her. Once in bed, her thoughts and concerns about Gracie would not leave her mind. She had tossed and turned, finally falling into a sound sleep around four o'clock in the morning.

She rolled over in an attempt to doze back off to sleep, but in less than five minutes, she realized this was in vain.

She got up, dressed, and went into the kitchen. She could smell the coffee, letting her know that someone else was out of bed.

She looked around the room but did not see anyone. She poured herself a cup of coffee and made her way toward the balcony.

As she got closer, she saw Gracie stretched out in a lounge chair with the cell phone to her ear. She appeared to be in a deep conversation with someone.

Sadie debated whether to give Gracie her privacy or not. She made her mind up quickly. She opened the French doors and immediately felt the breeze from the ocean. The warm morning sun felt good against her skin.

Gracie turned to see who was joining her but continued the phone conversation.

She spoke softly into the phone, "We will discuss that when I get back in town. I will be home Monday afternoon. I will be back in contact with you the first of the week. Thank you for your help." She then calmly placed her cell phone back into her robe pocket.

She smiled at Sadie but did not give any clues about whom she was talking with on the phone.

Sadie walked to the railing of the balcony and leaned over, looking out across the beach. Finally, she could not hold the question any longer.

Without giving Gracie eye contact, she asked, "Do you want to share with me who you were talking with?"

Gracie hesitated and then said, "Just someone that is doing a little bit of work for me."

Sadie didn't continue to question.

Instead, she said, "Beautiful day, isn't it, Gracie?"

Gracie nodded but stayed completely silent.

The only sounds heard were the lapping of the ocean waves breaking against the shore and the sea quills overhead.

Eventually, Gracie calmly said, "Sadie, I think we should have a picnic on the beach tonight. We could make a small fire and roast wieners. We already have everything we need for a picnic waiting for us in the refrigerator. I cannot remember the last time I roasted a wiener over an open fire."

Sadie felt Gracie really wanted to say something else but was scared to get to the point. She decided to let her continue to talk without interruption.

"Sadie," Gracie said. "Do you remember a long time ago when I asked you did God answer prayers? You told me that you felt He did, but in His own way and time."

"I remember Gracie."

"If God doesn't answer your prayer the way you would like, what does one do then?"

"We pray that He will give us the strength to face the path He has planned for us."

There was silence between the two once again. Sadie prayed silently that she had said the words that Gracie needed to hear at this time.

"I need to talk to everyone tonight. It is time everyone hears the truth."

Sadie nodded. She didn't have to ask Gracie any more questions. She knew what the afternoon was going to bring.

She walked toward Gracie, reached down, and kissed her softly on the top of her head. Gracie looked up and smiled.

"For all the years that I have known you, I have noticed one thing. Gracie, you smile, but your smile never reaches your eyes. You have sad eyes, and I have always wondered why. Has there ever been a time that I could have made those eyes light up with happiness?"

Gracie reached for Sadie's hand, held it tightly, and said, "Let's keep this to ourselves until tonight. I want a few more hours to be treated normally."

She slowly rose from the chair, continued to hold Sadie's hand, and said, "Let's go and get those sleepy heads up and get this day started. We need to go and see what that Trace is up to this morning."

Once again, Gracie had not answered a question that Sadie much needed to hear.

The girls sat patiently, waiting for Trace to come out of the hotel. They had already been parked there for three hours.

Tilly slipped off her shoes and wiggled her toes, hoping the feeling would quickly return.

Then she said, sounding bored, "How much longer are we going to stay here? Someone will notice a van sitting at the same spot for several hours and send a police officer out to talk with us. Then what are we going to say?"

"Sadie, what should I do at this point?" Stella questioned.

Sadie looked at the hotel, staring as if she were in deep thought. She had no idea of what to do except to wait and watch for them to come out.

"Trace doesn't have a clue of what I look like even after all these years," Gracie said. "I have an idea. Someone get the camera and place it in one of those big canvas bags."

Tilly did as she asked and handed her the bag.

Gracie opened the van door, got out, and said, "Don't go away. I'll be right back."

They watched as she walked into the hotel parking lot and went through the side door of the building.

"What if she gets caught?" Hannah asked nervously.

"Get caught doing what? Trace does not know her from Adam. If security stops her, she can play as if she is lost. Trust me, Gracie can figure out anything," Sadie said, thinking of the way she had kept her illness from all of them.

"It's just that all this is making me nervous. I sure am glad that real Southern women don't sweat," Hannah said anxiously.

"Did I hear you correctly? Did you say Southern women don't sweat?" Tilly questioned, with an odd look on her face.

Hannah nodded.

Tilly laughed and then sarcastically said, "I think that is the dumbest thing I have heard you say in several days."

"Please don't start teasing one another. Let's all just keep a watch out for Gracie." Sadie pleaded.

"Who's teasing? I was stating a fact to Hannah," Tilly said, almost pouting.

Hannah ignored Tilly completely and reached inside her pocketbook for her cell phone.

She punched in the numbers and was soon talking to Bruce.

"Hello, Bruce. How is your weekend?" Hannah said, smiling,

The conversation was short but sweet. She placed her phone back into her pocketbook and then gave out a big yawn.

They all waited for her to say something, but she stayed silent. This made Hannah feel as though she had the advantage over Tilly. She enjoyed this feeling and was determined to make it last.

Tilly could not stand it any longer. "Well, how is he doing?"

"He's doing great, Tilly. Thank you for asking," Hannah said with a conquering look on her face.

Tilly shrugged her shoulders, turned her head, and stared out the window in hopes of seeing Gracie on her way back.

"Hannah, did you tell Bruce about the situation with Trace and me?" Stella questioned.

"Oh my no, honey, I would never do that. I told him before we left that I would be enjoying a nice beach weekend with my friends. I didn't lie to him. I just didn't fill in the details."

"Thank you for that," Stella said, sounding relieved.

JoBeth said, "Stella, you should know after all these years that what we talk about or discuss around the breakfast table stays at the breakfast table. It does not go any further. We know that we can share our fears, problems, and secrets with one another, and it will not leave the room. We have our own little Southern Belle Breakfast Club, and we stick together no matter what."

Stella smiled and said, "I know. I guess I needed to be reassured."

Reflecting back, Sadie said, "We certainly have had some big secrets to keep among ourselves over the years."

"Yes, and something tells me that after this weekend, we will have even more to deal with," Tilly remarked.

"Are you talking about Trace and me?" Stella asked.

"No, actually, I was talking about Gracie. Here she comes now, and she isn't walking as fast as she did when she left before."

Tilly suddenly jumped from the van to meet her. She grabbed for the canvas bag that was holding the camera. Then she placed her arm around Gracie and helped her into the minivan.

"Well, ladies, I got a picture of the two lovebirds, but if you don't mind, I am going just to lay back here and rest a little during the drive back to the house. I can't wait to tell everyone but just not right now," she said as if trying to catch her breath.

Sadie started the engine, immediately pulled from the parking lot and onto the main road. Stella reached into the ice chest, pulled out a bottle of water, opened it, and passed it to Gracie.

She reached for it but didn't make any comment.

Within five minutes of their drive, Stella pointed to the right side of the road and became very excited. "Look, there's a Wal-Mart!"

"I can't understand you. We have sat in a cramped-up minivan for over three hours, trying to catch a glimpse of your husband and his bimbo. Now, we are finally headed back, and you site out a Wal-Mart," Tilly said, shaking her head in disbelief.

There were a few nervous laughs, and then once again, the van became silent.

"Good grief, girls, lighten up," Gracie called from the back. "She is just letting you know there are other things in life. It is called a distraction. She is trying to draw her mind and attention away from Trace."

"That's right, Tilly, just what Gracie said. So quit trying to get on my nerves," Stella said, smiling.

Tilly beamed back, "All these years, I have annoyed, irritated, bugged, and yes, got on everyone's nerves in this van. Just suck it up, cupcakes, because I think I'm just too old to change."

"You certainly are too old to change," JoBeth agreed. "So, I guess we will continue to love you for what you are."

Sadie pulled into the beach house driveway and said, "Finally, we are back, and everyone can take a much-needed rest."

They each started to get out. Tilly once again grabbed for the bag with the camera in it. Stella held the door for Gracie to get out, with JoBeth reaching for her arm to help her toward the beach house. Sadie lagged behind, watching as they took over. Yes, it was evident that they knew something. Their silence was showing just how much they did know.

"I think I will go and lie down for a while," Gracie said while heading to her bedroom. "Later, can we have a picnic on the beach?"

Sadie nodded and said, "That sounds great to me, and I am sure the others would love it. I know exactly what we could fix. So, you go rest, and I will take care of everything."

The others nodded and then went their separate ways. Sadie was thankful for this. No questions meant no lies at this time.

Gracie smiled a weak smile, turned, and went into her room, closing the door behind her.

It was early evening, and Gracie had slept all afternoon. They had tiptoed around, making sure they did not wake her.

They had gotten everything ready for the picnic that Gracie had suggested to Sadie. It had all been placed in a basket with two blankets that would be needed on the beach.

Sadie placed a box of matches in her pocket and then went to make sure there was enough wood in the wood box that they could use for the campfire.

Tilly followed close behind her and whispered, "Something tells me you should put tissues in the picnic basket."

Sadie didn't remark.

"You don't have to say anything, Sadie. I am sure Gracie swore you to silence until she could talk to us. Sometimes silence can let one know when something is terribly wrong."

"Thank you, Tilly," Sadie said.

JoBeth came into the room, followed by Stella and Hannah.

"Should we let Gracie continue to sleep?" Hannah questioned.

"No, we should not let her sleep the night away," Gracie said, laughing as she came into the room. "Is everyone ready for our picnic?"

"A picnic on the beach sounds like fun to me. I have never done that, and I am ...well, let's just say I am old enough to have a picnic on the beach finally." Tilly said, smiling.

"Well, what are we waiting for? Everyone grab some of the stuff we need, and let's go get our bare feet in that sand," JoBeth said, trying to sound upbeat.

They each carefully filled their arms with what they needed and headed out of the house and onto the beach. They took off their shoes and let them lay right in the sand. They found a place that was perfect but still close to the beach house. Sadie dug a small hole while Tilly placed the wood carefully inside. Hannah, JoBeth, and Stella spread the blankets out on the sand.

Gracie asked, "Did someone remember to bring matches?"

"We sure did," Sadie said as she removed them from her pocket and handed them to Gracie.

"Will you do the honors of starting our first fire on the beach?"

"I certainly will," she said as she kneeled and struck the match against the side of the box.

Soon, they had a roaring fire that would have made a boy scout proud.

"I can't believe we did it. I felt like we would end up sitting out here with flashlights and eating cold wieners in a bun," teased Stella.

"No, as we have always said, we're stronger together than we are as one," Sadie said, smiling, knowing that had always been one of their favorite things to say. She wanted to say it as many times as possible now. It seemed to make the group feel stronger, and it showed in their face.

"That's right," agreed JoBeth.

They soon had the wieners on long sticks, pointing them over the flame.

"When they are finished, I would like to ask the blessing," Stella said.

They pulled them from the sticks and placed them on a paper plate. It was time to ask the blessing.

Stella said, "Let's join hands the way we always do."

They did as she asked, and then she began, "Dear God, we thank You for this food that we are about to receive, but I want to thank you also for my friends that are gathered around this fire. Thank You, God, for bringing them into my life so many years ago.

Amen."

There was so much more Stella wanted to pray about, but she was barely able to talk without choking on the words. She wanted this night to stay as cheerful as it could, as long as it could.

Tilly spoke up, breaking the silence, "You kept it short but sweet. You must have known how hungry all of us are."

"That's right. So, let's all dig in," JoBeth said while reaching for a hot dog bun.

She continued, "Well, as you all have been able to witness, I am eating correctly. I'm not feeling guilty about the food that I am putting in my stomach."

"We have noticed, JoBeth, and we are proud of you," Gracie commented.

Sadie didn't comment. She had actually noticed JoBeth taking food from her mouth when she thought nobody was looking. It worried her, but she knew now wasn't the time to bring it to her attention.

They spent the next thirty minutes eating and making small talk. Sadie looked around and knew that everyone, including Gracie, was going through the motions of eating but not enjoying the food.

It was late in the evening now, but the full moon hung over the ocean, making it look as though it was being pulled into the water.

Gracie, not speaking, looked into the waves for what seemed to be several minutes.

Finally, she broke the silence, "What a miracle life is. God knew exactly what He was doing when He created the sand and the water."

They all sat silently, watching the moon glisten on the ocean. Sadie felt a big lump form in her throat. She wanted to show strength in front of the others when Gracie talked to them. She had to hold back the tears until she was alone. Then she could cry into her pillow as she had done every night since Gracie had told her about the cancer.

Sadie was glad the fire had started to die down to a soft glow. The others wouldn't be able to see the tears that were determined to form in her eyes.

Suddenly, Gracie broke the silence that had formed around the campfire.

"When I was a young girl, we would play a silly game called truth or dare. Have any of you played it?"

"We played it at night when I was in college. Some of the girls got really into the game," said JoBeth.

Gracie softly said, "When I played, I would always take the dare. I was never good at telling the complete truth. Not that I lied, I would just not tell everything I was supposed to."

Gracie paused as if in deep thought. No one said a word waiting for her to continue.

"I think I am ready to tell the truth now, but I don't really know where to begin," she admitted.

"The beginning is always the best place to start," Hannah said, sounding nervous.

"Yes, Hannah, I guess the beginning would be the best place to start. I know that I sometimes keep things to myself. There have been some things in my past that I wanted to hide from the world. I was so ashamed that I wouldn't admit them to anyone."

She took a deep breath and opened her mouth to speak, but the words would not seem to form.

Sadie quickly said, "Gracie, it is all right. You don't have to talk about anything that you don't want to right now."

"No, I want to continue. I will pretend that I am playing the game, and I have decided not to take the dare but tell the truth."

She once again took a deep breath, put her head down, and said, "I never told you girls, but when I was first married, I had a baby. Her name was Lindsey Grace. She was a beautiful baby that my husband and I had always dreamed of having."

Tears began to roll down her cheek, but she continued, "When she was born, I waited frantically for several minutes for her to start crying. Finally, she did, but it was not the way babies usually cry. The nurse removed her from the delivery room immediately. I knew in my heart that something was wrong. They finally rolled me into my room, and then the doctor came in. He told me that my baby would not live through the night. Well, she did. Then the next day, the doctor came in, told me without any compassion that Lindsey Grace would only live for a few days. He told me that it would be best for me to go home and leave her to die in the hospital. I would not hear of that. I wanted to take my baby home and place her in the crib my husband had made for her. Somehow, I felt that if I just got her home and in my arms, she would be all right."

Gracie reached for her bottle of water, took a sip, and then continued, "Well, they let us take her home but against the doctor's better judgment. I see now I should have stayed at the hospital with her. I was young. Still deep inside my heart, I could not accept the fact she was very sick. She never stopped crying, and it got worse and worse. After three days and nights, her breathing got very shallow. There were times I thought she was dead, but then she would take a deep breath, and then it was as if I had my baby again. I continued to think there was still hope for her. I took Lindsey Grace in my arms, placed her little head against my heart, fell to my knees on the floor, and rocked back and forth. I thought this would soothe her enough so she would stop crying. I pressed her little head into my chest too hard, and she stopped breathing. She stopped breathing right there in my arms. I killed my baby. I killed my baby!"

Gracie sat in the sand, rocking back and forth, cradling her arms as if she was holding her dead baby. Sadie jumped to Gracie's side and took her shoulders in her hands. She shook Gracie softly and then held her in her arms.

"You did not kill your baby, Gracie. I promise. Having been a nurse, I can tell you all the things that Lindsey Grace did were signs of her dying. You said she did shallow breathing, and then her breathing would come in long gaps. That is a sign of dying. When you took her in your arms and placed her to your heart, that was a mother's love. That helped her die peacefully. You let her die in a peaceful way that was intended. You lovingly held your dying child in your arms, and she went the way that God intended. You did not kill her. Believe me, Gracie, please believe me."

Gracie turned completely silent. She stopped crying as she glared into what remained of the fire. Her thoughts seemed to deliver her to another place and time.

Her lip quivered, and she said, "All these years, I have been asking God to forgive me for something I didn't do."

No one said a word. They sat in silence, letting Gracie take control of what would happen next.

Gracie stood up, placed another piece of wood on the fire, grabbed a stick, and stirred the ashes to make it once again start to blaze. She sat back down and again grew silent.

The others could see a change come over her face. After all these years, it was as if she had found inner peace.

"Would it be all right if I walk down the beach for just a few minutes? I feel like I need to be alone with God. I need to talk to Him, and

I would like for it to be just Him and me," Gracie said, smiling.

"We will be right here if you need us," said Sadie.

Gracie got up slowly and started walking down the beach. The moon allowed them to be able to watch her as she slowly walked. They watched as she stopped and then went to her knees.

Tilly quickly jumped up to go to Gracie.

"It's all right," Sadie said. "She is praying. There is no doubt in my mind she is thanking God for letting her finally realize she didn't take the life of her child."

"Yes, and she is praying for strength for what lies ahead for her," JoBeth said. "We have known that she wasn't telling us the complete truth about her illness for a long time now. We would never let Gracie know. We knew she had to tell us in her own way. We feel like it will be tonight, but I'm not sure if I can handle it."

Sadie remained quiet.

"We aren't asking you to betray her wishes. She had a reason for not telling us all at the same time. We will wait for her to tell us exactly what is going on," Stella said.

"Oh dear," Tilly said and sighed. "Bless her heart. She is coming back."

Gracie stepped out of the shadows and toward the flames of the fire. She sat down and reached for each hand of the person that sat beside her.

She turned almost as white as the color of her hair. She looked at each one and then calmly said, "I guess it is time to play the truth or dare game once again. It seems like I am the only one playing tonight. I know I didn't handle things too well. I am sorry. I should have told everyone at the same time, but I am ready now."

She frowned and then continued, "And I don't suppose I can ask you to forgive me for my silence."

She sort of coughed, squeezed the hands she was holding, and blurted out, "Girls, I am dying, and I have faced it."

"You're what? You don't know that for sure," Tilly said, trying to fight back the tears.

Gracie calmly said, "We don't live in a fairy tale. There's no happy ever after, just reality."

"Gracie, you said that you had an ulcer. We thought it was just really bad but not this bad," Hannah said, crying.

"Hannah, honey, don't cry. I have made my peace with God, and it is going to be all right. I am not scared of dying, but I am scared of living with the pain I know I will be going through. That is where I am going to need each of you. Knowing that you are all standing by me will help me fight the pain."

She continued, "Do you forgive me for not being completely honest with all of you? Sadie guessed because she was a nurse. She knows the facts, but I made her promise to let me be the one to tell the rest of you. I see now that I should not have made her promise. Sadie, can you forgive me?"

Sadie looked at her and nodded, but she could not speak. The tears were rolling down her cheeks, and she could not make them stop.

Tilly reached inside the picnic basket and brought out the box of tissues. She handed the box to Sadie, and then they seemed to be passed from one to the other.

Sadie looked at Gracie and said, "I wanted to be strong not only for you but for the others. I'm trying, but I just can't be strong right now."

"My life, since I talked with my doctor, had been stuck in the form of limbo. After tonight realizing the truth about Lindsey Grace, I have an entirely new feeling in my heart. I know I have no real future, but none of us truly know when God wants to take us home. I know that I have to live each day as if it will be my last."

"But ulcers can be treatable, Gracie. Why are you talking about dying?" Stella said, pleading.

"I have stomach cancer, Stella. I have been taking chemo now for several weeks. That is why I have been so tired. That is the reason I cannot keep up with all of you. Sadie has been covering for me, helping me walk, and taking care of me after the treatments. Each of you has been helping me in some way or the other. I cannot make any promises right now. I just want the rest of my life to be productive as long as it can."

Gracie grabbed for Tilly's hand and said, "Tilly, you are the one that is always telling us exactly what is on your mind. You do not hold back the punches. You just let them fly. I do not want you to stop teasing me or telling me exactly how you feel about things that I might say or do. I don't want this cancer to set me apart from the rest of you."

She took another deep breath and said, "I don't want to define my life as a sad woman dying of cancer. I will be a vibrant woman dying of cancer. That is the way I want to live the rest of the time God will give me. I want you to help me do just that. Can each of you promise me that you will help me?"

Stella said softly, "You can rest assured that each of us will be by your side the entire time. We will help you in any way that you ask."

Each one nodded.

"I am so glad that you all feel like that because when the time comes, I want you to help me die," Gracie said firmly.

"What do you mean, Gracie, by helping you die?" Tilly said sharply.

Sadie shot Tilly a warning look, but Tilly did not care.

Her voice cracked with fear, "Gracie, there is no way that I could help you die. I will be right there holding your hand but do not ask us to help you die. That is just plain wrong."

Gracie became silent. The only sound heard was the crackling of the fire.

Tilly could not remain silent, "Gracie, you are talking foolishly."

"I am just asking for help. If I am suffering, and there is no more that can be done, just help me go. I am ready. I am not afraid. Just place a pillow over my head and push down. Pretend I am Lindsey Grace, and you are holding me as I held her. I want to die just as she died surrounded by the ones I love. I don't want to suffer and be crying out to die or plugged into all kinds of machines, keeping my shell of a body alive with no hope."

She took a short breath and then continued, "Soon, everything that I have said tonight and everything I am asking will be just a wrinkle in time."

"How can you say it will just be a wrinkle in time? You cannot imagine how I feel right now about the possibility of losing you, and then you ask us to help you die. You're asking for mercy killing." Tilly argued.

The rest shook their heads as if in disbelief. There was no use in arguing with her. Sadie looked at the rest of the girls letting them know not to make any more comments.

Sadie grabbed Gracie's hand and said, "Honey, it's getting late. You need your rest. We will all sit down and talk about this later."

"I am tired, but I need to finish. I want to thank each of you for tonight. I love you all so much. After all, you have been my family, my only family, for many years."

"Let's get you back to the beach house and in bed," Tilly said and then remembered Gracie wanted to be treated normally.

Tilly continued, "We are just as tired and sleepy as you are. It has been a long day spying on Trace, and you never did tell us what you did when you went into the motel."

"I sure didn't. If you don't mind, can I tell you in the morning, Stella?" Gracie said as she struggled to stand and then slowly turned toward the beach house.

"In the morning, it will be a perfect time to tell me. I am just too sleepy to think about Trace now," Stella lied.

Sadie kicked sand over the fire and then poured water on it to make sure the flame was out. She watched as the others helped Gracie back to the beach house. She finally felt as if a tremendous burden had been lifted from her shoulders. Everyone knew the truth. Sadie now had another burden to bear. She didn't know exactly how she felt about mercy killing. She had witnessed people suffer many times before their death when she was a registered nurse. She had never questioned God on how and when he decided it was time for the person to go. It had always hurt her to watch one of her patients lay and suffer. How would she be able to watch one of her best friends suffer and not do something? Especially now since Gracie had asked for help.

She looked toward the moon that was still as bright and full as when they first walked out on the beach earlier in the night.

Warm tears streamed down her face, and she could not make them stop, no matter how hard she tried. No one could see her, and she needed the time to let all the emotions that she had been bottling up for all these days be released.

She felt a light touch on her shoulder. She turned around to find Hannah at her side.

"Sweet pea, don't do this to yourself. You were strong for Gracie when she needed you. Now let us be strong for you. Remember, she has asked all of us to do something we do not believe in doing. Don't try to carry this on your shoulders. We will figure out what to do, but we will do it together. Don't put this on yourself the way you do everything else. We will do what needs to be done at the right time. Now, come back to the beach house. I will fix you a cup of coffee and bring it to your bedroom. It's time you get some rest. We have already made sure Gracie is in bed."

Sadie did not argue. They walked swiftly back to the beach house. She took a quick bath washing the sand from her body and then crawled in bed. Hannah brought her in a hot cup of coffee, gave her a quick kiss on the top of her head, and then left the room.

Sadie sipped her coffee but had to wipe tears from her cheek to keep them from running into the cup. How was she ever going to make the decision on this one?

The next morning everyone seemed to want to stay in their bedrooms and not enter the main part of the beach house. It was as if they were trying to hide away from what the new day may bring.

Sadie decided to crawl out of bed, get dressed, and face what the day held.

She walked into the kitchen and made a large pot of coffee. Then she opened the refrigerator door to find things to cook for breakfast. Cooking always made her feel better. She hoped it would be a form of medicine for her today.

The aroma of breakfast soon pulled everyone from their beds.

"Miss Paula Dean is at it again," JoBeth said, walking into the kitchen while stretching her arms as wide as she could.

"Good morning, JoBeth. Were you able to get any sleep last night?"

"Very little sleep, Sadie. Gracie gave us a lot to try to swallow at one time. My heart goes out to her, and I don't know how to help."

"Just being here for her is all we can do until she gets back to the doctor, and they do some more tests," Sadie said, once again talking like a nurse. "Then, I'm afraid she is going to need us more than ever."

JoBeth didn't question what Sadie had just said. She just did not want to handle it right now.

JoBeth reached for a cup, poured herself some coffee, and walked out on the balcony.

Sadie looked around the kitchen at all the food she had prepared. She shook her head and headed to join JoBeth.

"JoBeth, I thought maybe cooking would make me feel better or clear my head, but it didn't work."

"What are we going to do, Sadie? Why in the world did Gracie ask us to help her die?"

"She's scared. She has always been able to provide for herself and do things in her own way. If her life is not productive, she doesn't want to linger any longer. I truly feel the way she described it to us last night on the beach is the way she wants her life to end."

"What if she keeps on about it?"

Sadie sighed and said, "I don't know, JoBeth. I just don't know."

JoBeth put her arm around Sadie and said, "We will all figure this thing out together. It will be all of us helping make the decision. Remember that, Sadie, and let some of the worries leave you. I am worried about you."

Sadie smiled at JoBeth's remark. It had only been a few weeks earlier that Sadie had told JoBeth that she was worried about her.

They leaned against the rail, looking out toward the beach.

"Isn't it funny how time seems just to stand still when you stare out across the ocean?" Sadie remarked.

"Yes, it does," Stella said as she joined them.

Sadie could not help to notice that Stella had a glow on her face, and her blue eyes seem to twinkle once again. Maybe she was facing facts about Trace and was going to take her life in another direction without him.

"I need us to spend the entire day together. I want us to do whatever Gracie feels like doing. It might be walking on the beach or just sitting out here in a lounge chair."

"Don't you want to try to take more pictures of Trace and his young friend?" JoBeth asked.

Stella calmly said, "Somehow, all that is not important to me anymore. I cannot continue to fight for a man that does not care whether I win or not. I am tired. I am too old to continue pretending that he is off on a business trip and cannot wait to come home to me. I don't deserve that, and I am not going to take it anymore. I am finished. He can have his young friends, but he will not be crawling back in my bed again."

Tilly and Hannah were standing at the open balcony door.

Hannah walked to Stella's side, hugged her, and said, "I am so proud of you. I wish I had been that strong the first, second, and even third time I knew that Gordon was having an affair. I wished I had been the one to say get lost instead of him walking out the way he did. I think I would have felt better about myself."

"Well, I know I have got a lot of planning to do, but I don't want him knowing I know about this affair right now. He is not leaving me penniless. I helped him be what he is today, and half of everything is going to be mine whether he likes it or not."

"That's the way to think, girl. Take him to the cleaners." Tilly said, smiling.

"You got to have proof of his infidelity, Stella. You have that with the pictures we have made this weekend, but you are still going to have to be careful," Gracie said as she quietly came out on the balcony to join them.

Surprised that she was out of bed, they all turned to face her. Tilly grabbed a chair for her to sit in, and Hannah reached for a pillow to place at her back. Sadie watched but kept her distance. She knew that Gracie had never liked a lot of attention. She wondered how she was going to react to this.

"Ladies, thank you, but I am not an invalid yet. Please let me do for myself as long as I can. There will be plenty of time to treat me like an old woman when I reach ninety."

"Well, excuse me for breathing," Tilly said.

Gracie smiled, "There you go. That is exactly what I want. I want things to be as normal as they can. I hope that I don't sound mean, and you all understand."

"We understand, and we will try not to be a mother hen to you," JoBeth said, smiling, remembering how they had given her special attention during the crisis in her life.

"It looks as though Sadie has plans to feed an army this morning. Shall we eat and then get started spying on Trace again today, Stella?" Gracie asked, trying to sound strong.

"No, as I was telling the others, I want this day to be our day. I want to spend it doing the things that you feel up to doing. Last night was the first time I had walked barefoot on the beach in years. I want to do that again. I want to go out on the fishing pier and watch men catch fish until their bucket is full. I want to eat ice cream while walking on the beach and let the sun slowly melt it while I fight to get it licked off the cone. I want to act like a child with the friends I love. There is only one thing I would like to know, and then I ask that no one brings up the name of Trace again today."

"What do you want to know, Stella?" Tilly asked.

"Gracie, yesterday you went into the hotel, and we waited and waited. When you got back, you were too exhausted to tell us what happened. I would love to know what you did if you feel like talking about it now."

"Oh yes, I feel like talking about it. I was almost caught by Trace. When I got out of the van, I was unsure of what to do first. Therefore, I went into the motel hallway. There was a house cleaner getting ready to go inside a room to do her morning cleaning. I told her I was supposed to meet your dear husband for a business meeting, and I was running late. I told her I had left the number of the room inside the car, and I didn't have enough time to run back to get it. I made it sound like your husband was very strict about being on time, and I was concerned about losing my job. She immediately got her chart and looked up the room number. I thanked her and got on the elevator. When I got off and stepped into the hallway, I could tell they had been eating all their meals inside the room and wasn't planning on coming out."

"How did you know that?" Tilly questioned.

"There were two trays from breakfast beside the door, and a do not disturb sign hanging from the doorknob. A menu list tagged on the door for what they wanted for dinner was waiting to be picked up. That was a dead giveaway. They intend to stay in that room until it is time to head back to Monroe. Trace does not want anyone to see them together, and he is taking all the precautions he can."

"How in the world did you get a picture of the two of them?" Sadie asked.

Gracie smiled the conquering smile and continued, "I got back into the elevator, went to the ground floor, and found the pool. I knew all the rooms were oceanfront and would face the pool area. I walked around, acting as though I was a paid guest at this fine hotel. So, I counted the floors and carefully looked at the balconies. There they were, leaning on the rails looking out across the ocean. He had his arm around her shoulder, and she had hers around his waist. I pulled out the camera and acted as if I were taking pictures of the pool. I slowly guided the camera right up toward the building and then started my upward motion to their balcony. I clicked several pictures of them. Then she noticed what I was doing, and she started posing and waving as if she were in a Christmas parade."

Gracie chuckled and then continued, "I could barely hold the camera for shaking so hard. Then, when Trace realized I was taking pictures of them, he jumped back into the room. I could hear her ask him where he was going. That sent a warning signal to me that he was heading my way. I waved back at her as if I was just a tourist that wanted memory pictures, and then I took off. I ran to the side where they place the big trash dumpsters, opened the wooden fence, and went inside. I knew he would not be able to see me there. I watched through a crack as he raced by, heading straight to the pool. He stretched his head from side to side, frantically looking for me. Then when he realized I was nowhere in sight, he went huffing back inside the hotel. You should have seen the look on his face. He had that look of a deer caught in the headlights of a car. I was so scared I thought I was going to pass out right then and there."

The girls, including Stella, laughed.

"I waited a few more minutes, and then I hurried back to the safety of the van and my friends."

Suddenly, Tilly started clapping. This encouraged the others to clap as well.

"You are certainly the woman of the day, Gracie. I would have never thought of doing that, and I certainly would have never had the courage," Hannah admitted.

"You have the courage, Hannah. You just don't give yourself credit. You are the only one of us that talked to a man from a dating service and then dared to meet him," Tilly said.

"I think Tilly has had too much sun. She is paying me a compliment," Hannah said, laughing.

"Ladies, I think it is time for us to get this day started. Let's go inside, eat, and then we will decide what we will do first. This is going to be our day to spend doing whatever we want to do," Sadie said, trying to sound happy.

"That's right. It is going to be a day we will always remember," Gracie added.

The morning meal was a struggle to finish. Each made sure Gracie's illness was not mentioned during breakfast, even though it remained in each one's mind.

After changing into beach clothes, they slowly began the day they wanted to make special for Gracie. They walked from the balcony and then paused briefly at the bottom step.

Tilly asked, "Gracie, are you sure you are up to this walk? We can always sit on the balcony sipping sweet ice tea. That would make for a fun day for me."

"I'll walk slowly, and if I get to feeling fatigue, we can turn back around," Gracie assured her.

They each slid off their shoes, dropped them on the bottom step, and began their journey.

JoBeth wiggled her toes in the sand and said, "The warm sand between your toes feels so good. It brings back memories of my childhood. Mama would bring me to the beach, and we would play all day. Daddy never seemed to find time to come with us. That was all right, though. Mama always bought us cotton candy at the pier. She could have never done that if Dad had been with us. He would have said it had too much sugar, and I might gain more weight."

No one commented but continued their walk side by side, each one in deep thought of their memories of childhood summers.

Gracie calmly said, "The problem with the past, whether good or bad, is that it always stays with you. You can keep it squeezed tightly inside for years, and then suddenly it comes creeping back into your life, taking control of your very being."

"You sure are getting deep in your thoughts, Gracie," Tilly said, trying to smile.

"I guess I am. I need to stop that."

Gracie pointed and said, "Look, JoBeth, there is the pier, and we can get all the cotton candy we can stuff in our mouths."

"We can also check and see if anyone is catching fish," Stella said.

Soon, they were on the pier resting under the shelter, eating cotton candy, and watching the fishermen bring in their catch for the day.

"Wouldn't it be nice if we could bottle this moment in time so we could remember it forever?" Hannah remarked.

"Well, I brought Gracie's camera. I just know that nice man over there that keeps staring at us would be willing to take our picture," Tilly said.

"Well, maybe he likes our looks," Hannah remarked while smiling at the man.

Sadie reached for the camera and walked toward him. Soon, they were both headed back toward the group with the camera in his hand.

"I would be pleased to take you lovely ladies' picture," he said, grinning.

They gathered around one another, with Gracie in the center. They each smiled, but their hearts were filled with sadness. Each one determined not to let it show on the picture that would forever remain a memory.

The man patiently took his time making several pictures. It was apparent he was more interested in spending time with them than participating in a photoshoot.

When he finally snapped the last one, he said, "I certainly would like to have one of these pictures so I could remember you, beautiful ladies."

"That is so sweet of you to say. Write your name and address on a piece of paper, and we will see that you get one," Gracie said in a southern flirting way.

He quickly wrote all the information down and handed the paper to Gracie. After a few minutes of small talk, he excused himself and continued his walk on the pier.

"Gracie, should you have done that?" JoBeth questioned.

"What do I have to lose?" Gracie said, laughing.

No one laughed at her remark.

"That was supposed to be funny," Gracie said, giving them all a stern look.

"Gracie, you can't expect us to laugh at a remark like that," Sadie said.

"Lighten up, girls," Gracie sternly said and then started walking back down the pier.

It was apparent she was ready to go back to the beach house. The others followed, quickly catching up with her.

It didn't take long before Sadie could see the beach house insight. She glanced toward Gracie. It was clear that the walk had been too much for her.

Sadie acting as if she was out of breath, said, "Can we just sit down on the sand and rest for a bit?"

"That sounds good to me," Hannah said, taking a deep breath. "I can tell I am out of shape."

Gracie smiled and sat down with the others in the warm sand. She knew they were taking this rest for her benefit.

Tilly stuck her feet in the sand, covering them completely up. The others did the same.

"My, we must be a pretty sight. Here we are six aging gracefully women sitting in a row with our feet covered with sand," Stella said, laughing.

"Well, I know one man on the pier that certainly liked our looks." Tilly bragged.

"I have his name and address to prove it. Is it all right with everyone if I send him one of the pictures in a thank you card from all of us?" Gracie asked.

They all nodded in agreement.

Tilly said, "I think that would be great. That way, you won't forever be a mystery woman that he met on the pier."

Sadie gave Tilly a stern look. A look that made Tilly quickly realize she should not have used the words *mystery woman*.

"All right, I said it, Gracie. I didn't intend for it to sound mean, but you have always been a mystery to us."

"I guess I have, but it wasn't on purpose. You can ask me anything. Now, I am not saying I will give you the complete answer. Remember, I never enjoyed playing the truth or dare game."

Tilly ignored the look of the others and said, "Well, Gracie, I would like to know how we ended up staying in a beautifully furnished beach house. It was even stocked with food that was a favorite of each of ours. How did you plan all this?"

Gracie stood up, faced them, and said, "All these years, I knew I was called the mystery woman of the group. I rather grew to like that label, and I think you all enjoyed me remaining mysterious. Therefore, if we are playing the game, I guess I will take the dare instead of telling the truth. So, I will dare myself to try to walk back to the beach house."

She gave them all that sly smile of hers, turned, and started slowly walking.

Tilly threw her arms into the air, letting herself fall completely backward in the sand. She lay there laughing.

She shouted toward Gracie, "I give up, Gracie. Do you hear me? I give up."

Hannah stood up, extended her hand toward Tilly, and said, "Take my hand, and I'll help you up, you silly thing."

Tilly reached for her hand, stood up, and wiped the sand from her clothes.

"Hannah, please carry the camera. I am going to catch up with Gracie," Tilly said.

She rushed and wrapped her arm in Gracie's and then calmly said, "It's nice to have a mystery woman in our lives."

Gracie smiled but remained silent.

The others stayed several feet behind, allowing Gracie and Tilly to share this time together.

Stella whispered, "I wonder how many more walks on the beach we can share with Gracie?"

Sadie whispered back, "Enjoy this one. I'm afraid it will be her last one."

"Don't say that, Sadie," JoBeth cried.

Hannah quickly said, "Girls, dry your tears. We are almost at the beach house. Gracie wanted this day to be one she could remember, and I don't want her to remember the tears we shed for her. We can do that behind closed doors when she can't hear us."

"You're right, Hannah," JoBeth said while drying her tears with the sleeve of her blouse.

"Come on, girls, let's run up ahead of them as if we are racing. We need to make this a day we can all remember with Gracie," said Stella.

They ran, caught up with Tilly and Gracie, and then ran as fast as they could ahead of them.

Sadie stopped, turned to them, and said, "The last one to the beach house has to pour the others a glass of tea."

Then she started running once again to catch up with the others.

Tilly winked at Gracie and said, "We might as well take our time. They don't realize I drank the last of the tea this morning. The joke is on them. Tea will have to be made if they intend to get any."

Gracie smiled and continued to walk slowly, letting Tilly help hold her up. Neither said a word. Tilly fought back the tears, and so did Gracie.

Finally reaching the beach house, Sadie turned to see how much longer it would take Gracie and Tilly to get there.

"They are almost here, but Gracie really looks out of it," Hannah said.

"Tilly needs help getting her up the steps. You girls stay here and act as if you are getting us all some tea. I will go and help," Sadie suggested.

Sadie quickly went to Gracie's side and placed her arms around her waist. She pulled Gracie toward her. With Tilly on one side and Sadie on the other, they were able to help her up the balcony steps.

Gracie pointed to one of the chairs and said, "That's a nice place to place this old body."

"Sounds good to me," Tilly said as she flopped down in a chair beside her. "I am tuckered out. Oh, by the way, Sadie, you may have beaten us back to the house, but I drank all the tea this morning."

"We noticed, and the others are making it as we speak," she said as she sat down beside Gracie.

"I'll go in and help. Anyone interested in a light lunch of chicken salad sandwiches?" Tilly asked, trying to sound upbeat.

"Tilly, that sounds great. I love your chicken salad. That is just what I want to eat." Gracie said, smiling.

Tilly walked inside, shouting, "I am making chicken salad, so the rest of you get busy making tea and a dessert."

Sadie shook her head and said, "God bless her. She is one bossy little woman."

Gracie weakly smiled.

"Let's be honest, Gracie. I know you are getting worse, and it is much faster than I was led to believe. When is your next doctor's appointment?"

"Tuesday," Gracie said, without further comment.

"Is it chemo, or do you see the doctor?"

"I'm seeing the doctor. I don't intend to take chemo anymore."

"Do what?" Sadie said loudly.

Everyone in the kitchen became silent but didn't come out on the balcony. They, instead, came closer to the door, trying to hear what was being discussed.

"I know your listening in there, girls. No need to eavesdrop! I'm telling you all. No more chemo for me."

JoBeth was the first to come out from behind the door, followed by the others.

She softly said, "You told me not to give up on solving my eating disorder. Why are you giving up?"

"This is quite different, JoBeth," Gracie said as she ran her fingers through her hair, bringing out large amounts between her fingertips. "I noticed it this morning when I brushed my hair. I guess it is getting worse."

"Stop, Gracie," Tilly said while pulling Gracie's hand from her hair.

"I figured in less than two weeks, I will have to wear a wig or a cute little baseball cap. If this chemo is not helping, why should I continue to take it? It is making me weaker than a newborn kitten. I stay tired, and I fight nausea all the time, and now, my hair is coming out. I'm not giving up, but if it's not helping, why am I putting myself through more pain and stress?"

"We can't force you to do something you are against, but we just don't want you to give up," Hannah said.

"Let us go to the doctor with you Tuesday. I know you are a private person, but please let us be there for you," Sadie said, pleading.

"It's settled, we are going with you, or I'm not making you your favorite chicken salad tonight," Tilly said, trying to sound tuff.

"All right, you win. You will get to meet my doctors. One is new and is coming from Duke University to meet me in the Charlotte office. I talked to him this weekend, and he plans to see me."

Sadie remembered walking out on the balcony during one of Gracie's phone calls. She wondered if this was the conversation she had overheard.

"You have doctors from Duke? You must have some great connections, girlfriend," Tilly remarked.

"Doesn't help to have all the connections in the world if there is nothing left they can do," Gracie said calmly.

"Sounds like you have already given up," Tilly said sternly.

"Tilly, I'm getting hungry for those sandwiches you have promised Gracie," Sadie said, trying to change the subject.

"All right, I get the drift. It's time for me to shut up and leave Gracie alone to make her own mind up."

Gracie smiled and said, "Thank you, Tilly, for continuing to treat me like you do the others."

Tilly reached down, hugged Gracie, turned, and went back inside to start making lunch.

The others followed, leaving Sadie and Gracie alone once again.

"Sadie, I can't keep fighting if there is nothing to fight for," Gracie whispered.

"Just keep the faith and stay focused on living."

"I know you're talking like a nurse again, Sadie."

"No, honey, I'm talking like a friend that has known and loved you for many years. Now, let's go inside. I want you to rest until we bring you a tray to your room."

"I will do just that," Gracie said as she slowly raised herself from the chair with Sadie's help.

Sadie walked Gracie directly to the bedroom and straight to the bed.

She opened the window wide so the cool beach breeze could blow in. It softly blew the curtains from side to side. Sadie watched as Gracie quickly fell asleep. Then she tiptoed from the bedroom, shutting the door behind her.

She glanced toward the kitchen, where the girls were busy making one of Gracie's favorite meals.

Sadie walked toward them and said, "We need to have everything packed and ready to go back to Monroe early in the morning. If we start early, we can beat the traffic."

She paused and then continued, "Can we all go out on the balcony? We need to talk. Gracie is asleep right now, but I don't want the chance of her hearing us if she would wake up."

"We have everything under control in the kitchen. We can eat anytime Gracie feels like it. If she is asleep, we might let lunch turn into supper. She looked like she needed all the rest she could get," Hannah said while placing the tea pitcher inside the refrigerator.

"You're right. We will let her sleep as long as she can," Tilly said as she and the others followed Sadie out to the balcony.

"I don't think I will be able to enjoy the beach again," Tilly said as she looked out across the ocean.

"Don't say that, Tilly. Gracie would not want us to feel like that about something we have always enjoyed and loved," JoBeth said.

"Why do I feel this is going to be our last weekend together?" Stella asked.

"It's not going to be our last weekend with Gracie. We are just scared for her, and we don't know what the future is going to hold."

Sadie paused, took a deep breath, and continued, "We will go with her Tuesday. It's not going to be good, and I want to prepare you for that."

"I know this is going to sound strange, but I'm sitting here knowing that Trace is about fifteen miles from here in a hotel room with another woman, and I don't even care. My only thought is that Gracie will not be in our lives much longer. That doesn't say much for my marriage," Stella said, without hesitating.

"Have you decided what you are going to do when you get home and have to face him?" Tilly asked.

"I know that I am going to be as brave as Gracie is right now. If she can face death with the attitude she has, I can surely face an unfaithful husband without blinking an eye."

"I would love to be a fly on the wall when you confront him about everything," Tilly said, smiling.

"The good Lord knows I have tried to be a good wife all these years. It has been hard knowing what he did and trying to keep it to myself."

"Stella, I wish you had felt like you could come to us before now. We could have at least been a shoulder you could lean on," Hannah said.

"I was ashamed. I somehow felt it was my fault he was having one affair after the other. I kept hoping that things would change, and our marriage would be the way I had always dreamed it would be. I guess when you have been married as long as we have, you just let things go and look the other way. Well, I am tired of looking the other way. It is time for me to do something but enough about me. What are we going to do about Gracie's request?"

Sadie seemed nervous by the question. "I still say when the time comes, we will know what to do."

Tilly just rolled her eyes, got up from her chair, and walked toward the rail of the balcony.

Sadie knew that Tilly was upset. "Truth be told, Tilly, none of us knows what we will do. It's not our nature to help someone die, and now the first time in our life, we have been asked to do just that. I am hoping Gracie will see the effect it is having on us and won't bring the subject up again."

"You all know how much I love Gracie, but I have never been able to deal with death very well," Hannah said, in almost a whisper.

"Why do you say that?" Tilly questioned, with a puzzled look on her face.

"I really don't want to say because it might sound silly."

"Why, Hannah, when have you ever said anything that came out silly?" Tilly said sarcastically.

"Stop it, Tilly," Sadie said. "Hannah, honey, tell us why you feel like that."

"When I was about four years old, my great-grandmother died. In those years, they would bring the body back to the home and place the casket in the living room. Well, I was scared to go into that room, so I hid in one of the closets in a bedroom. Mama found me and thought it would be best if she held me and let me see my great-grandmother in the coffin. I guess she thought she was doing what was right, which would help me overcome my fear of death. I can remember her holding me tightly in her arms while I struggled to get down. She walked right up to the coffin, bent down, kissed my great-grandmother on the cheek, and then told me to do the same. I remember closing my eyes as she brought me closer to the casket. I squeezed my eyes even tighter and didn't move my head. Then I felt her cold cheek against my lips. I screamed to the top of my lungs, bringing the entire family rushing into the room."

"Oh my goodness, what happened then?" Stella asked.

"Father rushed in, grabbed me out of my mama's arms, and took me outside. I felt safe once I was in his arms and in the fresh air."

"Hannah, are you making this up?" JoBeth asked.

"Why would she make anything up like that?" Tilly said, taking up for Hannah.

"Hannah, people a long time ago felt that was a sign of showing their respect for their departed loved one. I've seen people do that even now. It was just not very smart of your mother to do it to you at such an early age and against your will," Sadie said.

"Now, do you understand why I might not be strong enough to stand by Gracie when the time comes?"

"Hannah, you will find the strength," Sadie said while placing her hand on Hannah's shoulder.

"Hannah, it sounds like your mother was right out of the twilight zone," Tilly said, without giving her remark a second thought.

Hannah looked at Sadie and laughed, "I see the look you are trying to give Tilly. Don't worry about it, because in this case, I completely agree with her. Mother meant well by what she did, but I had nightmares for years."

Hannah jumped from her chair, went to Tilly, kissed her on the cheek, and said, "I'm a big girl now, no more nightmares."

Tilly pretended to wipe the kiss from her cheek.

Suddenly, everyone started to laugh and then stopped as if they were ashamed of having this reaction.

Sadie quickly said, "Don't feel guilty because you laughed for a moment. We are grieving over Gracie, and she is still with us. We have to stop it and stop it now. We need to cherish every moment we have with her and laugh when something is funny. She asked us today to treat her as if she wasn't sick. That is the very reason she kept it away from all of us as long as she did. Starting now, things are going to be different. Do you all agree?"

There was only the sound of splashing waves against the shore until finally, Tilly spoke up. "You are right, Sadie. I think I can speak for the rest of us, that it is time we straighten up. We are a strong group of women, and it is time to show our strength. We will treat Gracie the way she wants to be treated."

"Do you think that Gracie would like to hear what Mother did to me?" Hannah asked.

Tilly shook her head and said, "No, Hannah, you don't need to tell anyone else that story. We will keep that to ourselves."

Giggling, JoBeth said, "Yes, we will keep that to ourselves. Now, let's get back inside and make sure we got everything cooked for supper."

Everyone followed JoBeth's lead as she walked back into the beach house. Sadie stayed behind, looking out at the water. She could see people walking along the beach. Some people were stretched out on beach towels enjoying the sun, and others were swimming in the water's edge. How happy everyone looked. Only months ago, her little group of friends didn't seem to have a care in the world.

How quickly life can change!

Chapter 14

The pain of losing a friend can remain
with you for the rest of your life.
Hold on to the memory of their smile,
*   their laugh and the unique way they made*
you feel.
*   In the winter of your life, you can reflect on*
that friendship turning
*   your winter into spring, once again.*

Sadie sat on her front porch, rocking back and forth in her chair, sipping on her third cup of coffee. She smiled to herself as she wondered if she was trying to drown her sorrow with this decaffeinated brew.

She tried to erase the drive back from the beach from her mind. The long drive home was nightmarish. Sadie had to stop the van and pull it over to the side of the road several times to allow Gracie to throw up. The only way they could help her was to dampen tissues with water from their water bottles and wipe the sweat from her face. Sadness engulfed everyone leaving total silence after each stop. Tilly tried several times to start a silly argument with Hannah to lighten the mood, but that did not even work.

Sadie had begged Gracie to spend the night with her. Gracie made it clear to everyone that she was going home and needed to be alone. She insisted there were several things she had to take care of. Her statement had left a big question mark in everyone's mind, but no one questioned her.

Sadie's thoughts of the day quickly ended when she looked up, seeing JoBeth pulling into her driveway.

She jumped from her chair to greet her. As she got closer to the car, she could see that JoBeth had a look on her face that Sadie had not seen in several weeks. She knew JoBeth was in trouble.

She slowly got out of the car and stood motionless, looking at Sadie.

"You don't have to say a word, JoBeth. I know what is going on. I saw you were struggling several times this weekend to make yourself eat."

JoBeth walked to the back of her car and opened her truck. She pulled out two suitcases and said, "Can I stay with you for a while? I cannot stay by myself. I don't go back to therapy until Wednesday. I'm fighting hard, but

I know I'm not strong enough to fight this alone."

Sadie grabbed for a suitcase and did not say a word. She reached for JoBeth's hand and led her toward the house.

"Have you eaten this afternoon?" Sadie questioned.

"Yes," JoBeth answered and then put her head down.

"Did you throw it back up?"

The silence was JoBeth's answer.

"At least you're not telling me a lie. That is a good sign."

Sadie reached for the suitcase that JoBeth was still holding. She carried them into her guest bedroom, leaving her standing like a statue in the hallway.

"Please don't be mad or disappointed in me, Sadie."

"Honey, I'm not. Actually, I was half expecting this very thing. It takes a lot to heal one's self from an eating disorder. You cannot do it in just a few weeks. It takes a long time. I figured the stress all of us are under with Gracie would affect you in this way. You are fighting your own little battle. No, it's not cancer, but it is eating away at you."

"Please don't tell the others, especially Gracie. She has been so proud of me. She is fighting for her life, and I am doing the opposite. Why am I doing this to myself?"

"You came here tonight, and you are admitting you need help again. JoBeth, you are going to be all right. Stress just got the best of you, and you don't know how to handle it. You are a fighter, and I am going to help you."

"I have always thought of you as being our compass, Sadie. You direct us in the right way to go. You always have an answer for everything. I shouldn't ask you to keep this a secret from the others, but I just don't want them to know how weak I am. Also, Gracie is going to need all our strength. They don't need to worry about me.

She paused and once again put her head down as if she was ashamed, "Sadie, this is not fair to you. I shouldn't ask you for your silence."

Again, Sadie felt like she had a ton of bricks placed upon her shoulders, but she would honor JoBeth's wishes just as she had for Gracie.

"I want you to promise me that you will start going to therapy two times a week. If the others ask, you can simply say you have therapy now two times a week instead of one. That wouldn't be telling them a lie or holding anything back."

"I promise, and I will be honest with Dr. Roberts. I will see what he has in mind. I just hope he doesn't feel I need to be admitted back into rehab."

"I honestly don't see that happening if you stay honest with everyone and yourself."

"I will, Sadie. I promise."

"Well, let's start by going into the kitchen and fixing us something very light. I won't push a big meal on you now, but be prepared to eat exactly what I tell you to eat tomorrow. Don't even consider getting out of my sight."

JoBeth smiled and followed Sadie into the kitchen.

She opened the refrigerator looking for ingredients for a salad, while JoBeth gathered everything for grilled cheese sandwiches.

"Where is everyone at?" Tilly called from the hallway.

Sadie gave JoBeth a reassuring smile, letting her know that it was all right.

"Looks like we need to make more sandwiches," Sadie said.

Tilly strolled into the kitchen with Hannah right behind her. She walked directly toward the stove, grabbed the coffee pot, and poured herself a cup of coffee.

"Hannah and I were talking on the phone and just felt the need to come over. I called Stella to see if she wanted to come, but Trace had not gotten home yet. I guess she is going to confront him with everything she knows tonight. I hope she stays strong and stands up to him."

"She will do what she thinks is best when she feels the time is right. I think we all saw a side of her during the weekend that lets us know she won't be on the losing end of whatever might happen." Sadie said, smiling.

Hannah quickly remarked, "Well, she best have all her ducks in a row before she talks to Trace about the weekend. He is one smooth talker, and I feel he will have an answer for everything."

"She needs to wait until the pictures are developed, make several copies and then sock it to him," Tilly giggled.

JoBeth nervously said, "Gracie has the camera. Do you think she is going to feel like having the film developed? We should have thought of that when we let her out at her house. Sadie, we need to call her and tell her that we will take care of having the film developed. She doesn't need to worry about anything."

"You're right. I was going to call her anyway to check on her. I'll tell her that we will pick the film up when we pick her up tomorrow to go to her doctor's visit."

"I am so nervous about tomorrow," Hannah said.

"How do you think Gracie feels? She's the one that is living this nightmare," Tilly said bluntly.

JoBeth went to Hannah's defense, "She didn't mean anything by that, Tilly. We are all nervous and would rather be anywhere but there."

Tilly acted as if the statement wasn't directed to her. She proceeded to go to the cabinet to remove plates for the sandwiches.

Sadie gave a quick wink to the others, letting them know ignoring Tilly would be in the best interest of everyone at this time.

Hannah smiled and said, "Oh, I have news. I would love to wait and share it with Stella and Gracie, but I just can't hold it in."

"Tell us, Hannah, and I sure hope it is good news. We need some for a change," JoBeth said.

"It is great news. Cole has been dating a nice girl for several months now, and he is going to ask her to marry him."

"Does that mean he will bring her with him when he moves back home?" Tilly asked.

"Tilly, I have little patience for your pettiness, and that was petty for you to say that," Hannah said bravely.

Tilly rolled her eyes and crossed her arms. It was a clear sign that she disagreed with Hannah, but she did not seem to have a fight in this. Hannah had won.

"Mark one up for Hannah," laughed Sadie.

"I am sorry once again, Hannah. Forgive me, I am in an agitated state this afternoon, and I am taking it out on my friends," Tilly confessed.

"There. That was short, to the point, and easy to say. I am proud of you, Tilly," JoBeth said, teasing her friend.

"Does anyone else have any good news they could share?" Sadie asked.

"Well, I have talked to Bruce several times on the phone since we have gotten back home. He told me he missed me so much. He is so sweet," Hannah said, smiling.

"Tell us some things about him. You haven't let us in on much about his life," Tilly said.

"Well, he has never been married. He came close at one time, but he said it just didn't work out. His father died about ten years ago, and he has been taking care of his mother ever since. He's been a complete gentleman so far."

"Meaning?" Tilly asked.

"Meaning, I often wish he wouldn't be," Hannah said, blushing.

Tilly quickly said, "Hannah, be ashamed."

"Why should she be ashamed? She is almost sixty years old. She needs some excitement in her life," JoBeth laughed.

Tilly shook her head and said, "We need to change the subject. Therefore, I vote we take our sandwiches and salad and have a picnic on the deck. We need to soak up as much of this afternoon's summer sun as we can. It won't be long before it starts getting chilly."

"I agree. While you girls get everything ready, I will call Gracie," Sadie said.

"By the way, Sadie, how did you get the van back to the rental service? You would have needed one of us to drive you back," Hannah questioned.

"In less than ten minutes after getting home, the rental service came and picked it up. The young man said someone called and said it was ready to be returned. I didn't question who it was. I'm sure Gracie called them. She has a way of taking care of things without letting us know."

"It has been taken care of, so we don't need to question her about it. We probably wouldn't get a clear answer anyway, but it doesn't matter," Hannah said.

The others nodded while gathering plates and glasses for their meal. Sadie watched them as they walked out on the deck. She reached for the phone and slowly started to make her call to Gracie.

Suddenly, Sadie felt a light touch on her shoulder. She jumped and turned to face Stella. She placed the phone back on the receiver.

"Stella, you startled me. Tilly said that you were at home waiting for Trace."

"Where are the others?" Stella asked.

Sadie pointed toward the deck.

"Well, it looks like I am just in time to eat."

"Yes, grab you a plate. It looks like they have already started. We fixed enough for an army."

"You always do," Stella said, reaching for a plate and walked out to the deck.

They greeted Stella and continued to eat. Stella lowered her head, said her silent blessing, and reached for a sandwich.

Hannah, between bites, said, "Did you call Gracie?"

"No," Sadie replied. "I started to, and Stella came in. I will call her when we finish."

"I talked to her before I came over here. She is feeling much better but said she was going to call it an early night. She wants us to pick her up at eight in the morning. She said that way we would have plenty of time before her nine o'clock appointment."

"Stella, when I called you earlier, you said that you were waiting on Trace. Do you want to tell us what happened?" Tilly questioned.

"When I was talking to Gracie, she said that she had already taken care of having the pictures developed. We talked a little more, and we feel like I need that proof in my hands before I talk to him. So, when he came in, I gave him a *BIG* welcome home kiss and told him I had to leave immediately because Gracie needed me."

She giggled but continued. "I reached for his BMW keys that he was still holding in his hands. I rushed out, telling him I was taking his car, and shut the door quickly behind me. I didn't give him time to ask me why I was taking his car. I rather think I surprised him with the welcoming kiss and the quick exit out the door."

"I would have loved to have seen his reaction," Tilly said, smiling.

"I'm afraid I didn't stick around to see much of a reaction from him myself. I was close to tears and had to get out of the house. All I could see when I looked in his eyes was the love he has for the new young one on his list."

"You don't call that love, Stella. You call it lust." Tilly was quick to say.

"Well, whatever it is called, it still hurts. We at one time had a great marriage, or at least I thought we did. That was years ago, but it was a good marriage. I can at least have those memories."

Hannah softly said, "Well, my marriage was just the opposite. I loved him right from the start, but I'm not sure why Gordon married me. I guess I am just a romantic at heart. There was something I always needed from him. I never got it, but now I know it was because he didn't have it in him to give to me. It is just that simple."

"Well, after the remark you said in the kitchen, you sound like you are hoping Bruce will have that something for you," Tilly said, once again speaking before she thinks.

JoBeth said in a sharp voice, "Well, Miss Tilly, we will hope that Bruce is the man for Hannah."

Tilly quickly said, "I wasn't suggesting that he jumps right down on his knees and ask for her hand in marriage. I was simply trying to state that I hope he is the one that makes Hannah happy."

Tilly reached for the tea pitcher, grabbed Hannah's glass, and poured her more tea.

Hannah smiled.

Stella suddenly started laughing, "I can remember Mama telling me after Trace and I got married that we should never go to bed angry at one another. If we had followed her advice, we would have never gone to bed."

Everyone around the table started laughing.

"I wish Gracie could be here with us," Tilly said, almost in a whisper.

Sadie took a deep breath and said, "I know, Tilly. We all wish she were here."

The waiting room in the doctor's office wasn't crowded yet. Gracie had made sure she was early and would be the first patient for the doctor to see. Everyone but Gracie looked around nervously. She seemed to have accepted her verdict from the doctors without hearing it yet.

"I wish that you all would smile. I am not going to my grave this minute," Gracie said.

"There, she goes again. Sadie, tell her not to talk like that," Hannah whispered in Sadie's ear.

"Gracie, Hannah said there you go again and not to talk like that," Sadie said loudly so the rest could hear it.

Gracie laughed and then said, "All right, Hannah, I will be a good girl and not make any more remarks like that."

Sadie could not get over the attitude that Gracie had. She admired her strength and hoped it could continue.

Tilly quickly stood, walked toward the table with all the magazines, and picked one up. Her face had suddenly turned blood red. She sat back down and quickly fanned herself with the magazine.

Stella elbowed Sadie and said, "What in the world is going on with Tilly?"

"Tilly, are you all right?" Sadie questioned.

"Hot flash, that's all. Work of the devil is what I call them!" Tilly said, fanning as fast as she could.

"Work of the devil? Tilly, you are always saying that I say some stupid things, but I think you have topped anything that I have ever said." Hannah said, laughing.

"Don't laugh at me. It is not funny. These are real feelings. They start from the top of my head and go to the bottom of my feet. It feels like I am on fire. That is why I said it is the work of the devil because it lights me up like a flame."

"I have never heard hot flashes described in that way, Tilly. That should be written down in a medical book." Hannah teased once again.

Sadie leaned toward Gracie and said, "This is a change. Usually, Tilly is always getting the best of Hannah. Now the table seems to be turning."

Gracie smiled, "Maybe hot flashes are Tilly's punishment for all the years she has been so critical of Hannah."

"You think so?" Sadie said, giggling.

Suddenly, a slim young nurse appeared in the waiting room.

She walked toward Gracie and said, "The doctor will see you now."

"Can my friends come with me?" Gracie asked.

"I'm sure there wouldn't be a problem with that." She said and turned away.

"Follow me, girls," Gracie said, attempting to make her voice sound strong.

They followed, but they certainly were not smiling. Tilly was still wiping her face with a wet tissue Hannah had finally handed her. Hannah was so nervous she could barely put one foot in front of the other. Stella and JoBeth were so scared you could see it written all over their face. Sadie was the only one besides

Gracie that was holding their fear inside and not letting it show.

Sadie turned to the others and whispered, "It's written all over your face that this is frightening you. Don't let it show for Gracie's sake."

They nodded, continued to follow behind Sadie and Gracie, and tried to act brave. However, they knew this would not be good news for Gracie, and they felt they were walking the last mile with her.

A man that was obviously the doctor stood in the hallway and greeted Gracie with a hug.

"Good morning, Gracie. I see you brought your friends. It is nice to meet all of you. Everyone come on in and find a seat," he said as he pointed toward his office door.

He walked in behind them and took his place at his desk.

"I have heard so much about each of you that I feel as if you are also friends of mine."

Sadie looked at the wooden nameplate that sat on the doctor's desk and said, "We have heard very nice things about you as well, Doctor Duncan." Sadie lied but thought it was the right thing to say at the moment. Actually, Gracie had never discussed who her doctor was. She had always been private about her life, so they did not feel the need to know her doctor's name. They were just concerned that he was the best doctor for her to have.

He continued, "Gracie, I am glad that you agreed to see the doctor that I was telling you about on the phone the other day. After we talked, I called Doctor David Young from Duke. He is running a little late this morning, but he should be here any minute. I sent all your records, including your recent MRI's, CT scans, and blood work, to him. He has read over them, but he still wants to do some of his own tests. We will discuss your case and tell you what we think needs to be done next."

"I don't think the chemo has helped me, and I really don't want to take anymore," Gracie said without hesitation.

"It might be too early for us to determine that, Gracie. Please, let's discuss that after he gets here. I hope you have prepared to stay all day because I have cleared my calendar. This is your day, Gracie, and we intend to devote it all to you," he said, forcing a smile.

"Now, ladies, I must ask you to wait in the waiting room. It will be a long day, so talk to my secretary at the front desk, and she can direct you to the lounge. If you need anything, just ask her, and she will see that you get it."

Sadie stood and walked toward Gracie. She hugged her and said, "We will be in the waiting room. If you need us, I am sure your kind doctor will come and get us."

"You can rest assure I will," he said, getting up from his chair, standing and showing the manners of a gentleman that he was.

The others hugged Gracie and then followed Sadie out of the room, down the hall, and into the waiting room.

They each found a chair and sat down. Tilly was the first to speak, "All I can say is that Gracie really must know some high up people. Look around at this office. We are the only ones in here, and Gracie seems to be the only patient for the entire day."

She walked to the front desk and said, "When is Dr. Duncan's next patient due?"

The nurse calmly looked up and said, "He cleared his patient appointments completely today for Miss Gracie."

Tilly smiled and walked from the desk and straight to Sadie.

"See what I mean. He actually did schedule only her for the entire day. What doctor does that for a patient?"

"I don't know, but I am glad that he did," Sadie said, trying not to sound that she was once again questioning Gracie and her life.

A young man quickly walked into the room, made a quick hello gesture to the nurse, and walked directly down the hall.

"Well, that must have been the doctor from Duke University Hospital," remarked Stella.

"Good, they can start the exam for Gracie," Hannah said, reaching for a magazine from the table.

The nurse slowly walked past the girls, straight to the door, and locked it. She turned to them and said, "Ladies, I have hot coffee made and fresh pastries. Just make yourself welcome to them any time today. Also, there will be lunch brought in for each of you."

Saying this, she turned and went back to her desk as if she didn't need to explain.

Tilly quickly rushed to Sadie's side and said, "What do you make of that?"

"I say the coffee sure smells good, and I think I could eat one of those pastries right now."

She looked toward JoBeth and said, "Join me, JoBeth. I am hungry, and I am sure you are also."

They each decided to get a cup of coffee, pulled their chairs close together, and began their friendship chatting.

"We need to make ourselves comfortable and try not to speculate what this day is going to bring. I don't know what Gracie is facing right now, but I don't feel it is good. She is going to need us when the doctors are finished more than ever before," Sadie explained.

Hannah put her head down, cleared her throat as if she needed to say something but stopped.

"Hannah, did you say something?" Tilly asked.

"Well, I want to, but I don't know if this is the right time."

"Oh yes, this is definitely the right time. Honey, what's wrong? Is it about Gracie?" Sadie questioned.

"Of course, I am worried sick about her, but I got a bizarre phone call last night. I still can't get over it."

"Hannah, tell us. Was it something about your father?" Stella asked.

"No, it was Gordon."

"Gordon! What in the world did he want?" Tilly roared.

Hannah slowly began, "Well, he started by asking me to forgive him. Do you know how many years it has been since he left me?"

She didn't give them time to answer. "He asked me if he could see me."

"I sure hope you told him exactly where to go, and I certainly don't mean on a trip," Tilly said as if she was mad enough to spit nails.

"He continued to tell me how he had made such a mistake in his life by leaving me the way he did. Of course, he never brought up the fact he had a woman in every port, and he wasn't even a sailor."

"Old joke, Hannah, but it still works," JoBeth said, laughing.

"He kept on and on telling me he still had feelings for me. He is like an emotional vampire that sucks the life out of me even after all these years," Hannah said sadly.

Tilly took her hand and said, "Hannah, God doesn't want you to be stupid."

"You're right. There was just so much mental abuse I could take."

"That's right, Hannah, and you took your fair share and then some," Tilly said.

"Why did he finally come to his senses and realize what a fine woman you are after all these years?" Sadie asked.

"Is everyone ready for this?" Hannah paused and then continued. "He has diabetes and is slowly losing his eyesight. That is why he is acting as if I am the love of his life. He is losing his sight, and I guarantee the woman he is living with now doesn't want to have anything to do with him."

"Oh, that man, what nerve he has trying to get you back when he has nowhere to turn," Stella said.

"You're not going to allow him to come crawling back, are you?" Tilly asked

Hannah looked Tilly right in the eyes and said, "The old Hannah would have taken him back without any questions. I am not the old Hannah. I told him that I was truly sorry that he was sick, and I wished the best for him. You know he almost had my sympathy until he told me to remember that it takes two for a marriage to work."

Tilly laughed and then said, "What did you tell him then?"

"Frankly, I'm not interested in hearing anymore that you have got to say. I loved you more than life itself at one time, but the love has been dead for a long time."

"You said all that?" Stella questioned.

"Then I said goodbye and hung the phone up."

"Hannah, I am so proud of you," JoBeth said, hugging her.

"I kept thinking about Gracie and how we were going to be there for her no matter what is ahead. I sort of felt guilty, but then I remembered how he had treated me and how I felt like his doormat for so many years. After giving it some thought, I truly was able to sleep last night without feeling guilty about how I talked to him."

"Good for you, honey. Good for you," Sadie said, smiling.

Sadie realized that she wouldn't have to worry about Hannah anymore. She was finally a freethinking woman that wasn't going to be told what to do and when to do it. She had finally completely gotten over Gordon. Even after all the years that Gordon had been gone, there was still something that seemed to hold Hannah back. They each had seen it but never told her how they felt. Sadie knew now that Hannah was ready to embrace Bruce as more than just a friend.

"Ladies, I hate to interrupt, but lunch has been delivered. I have it all set up for you in the back. It is ready anytime that you are," the nurse said, smiling.

They hesitated as if they didn't want to move from the spot.

The nurse once again spoke, "I know what you are thinking, but she is nowhere near ready to come out. They are taking more CT scans, and after that, they plan to do another test. She is in good hands. Come on and follow me. I will show you where everything is."

Sadie stood up and followed the nurse with the rest as always following Sadie's lead.

They walked into a small room, and right in the middle was a table filled with sandwiches, potato salad, slaw, several jars of pickles, and chips. There were several different kinds of desserts.

The nurse pointed to an ice cooler and said, "I ordered sweet tea. I hope that was all right. You will find it in the cooler."

Sadie smiled and said, "Thank you so much. You have been so nice to us."

"Miss Gracie is a lovely lady and has always been one of my favorite people. We want only the best for her and her friends," she said and then left the room to go back to her desk.

"She seems like she has known Gracie for a very long time. I wonder if it is because Gracie has been coming to this doctor for many years." Stella questioned.

Sadie shrugged, "Could be, but I'm not sure."

They each sat down and then grabbed each other's hands quickly. As always, the blessing was going to be asked no matter where they were.

"God, please be with Gracie and give her the strength she is going to need now and later. Thank You for this food, and bless the person that got it for us. Amen." Tilly said softly.

Each one went through the motions of eating. Their hearts and minds were with Gracie and what she was going through now. Sadie kept looking at JoBeth, trying to encourage her to eat just a little more. She let her eyes do the talking without saying a word. JoBeth smiled, placed another chip in her mouth, only to please Sadie.

"Why don't we clean up our mess and then take our dessert and a cup of coffee back into the waiting room. I know the nurse said it would be a long time before Gracie can come out, but I think we would all feel better waiting in there," Sadie said.

They all agreed and quickly cleaned the table, making sure everything was put away in the refrigerator that sat in the corner of the room. Then they gathered what they wanted for their dessert and walked back into the waiting room.

"Is it all right if we eat our dessert in the waiting room?" Sadie asked the nurse.

"Of course, it is. By the way, I went back to check on the progress with Miss Gracie. The doctor said it should be about two more hours and he will come and get you. They are waiting on the results of some tests right now."

She continued, "They said it was all right for her to eat. I am going right now to fix her a plate and take it to her."

Tilly said, with her lips quivering, "She will love the chicken salad, so please fix her two sandwiches."

The nurse nodded, smiled, and walked back toward the little room to fix the sandwiches.

"How in the world am I going to stay strong for Gracie? I can't even tell someone to fix her a chicken salad sandwich without almost breaking down."

"When you need strength, it will come. I promise," Sadie assured her.

"You keep reassuring us, but Sadie, I agree with Tilly. It's going to be hard," Stella said.

"We all keep looking for Sadie to give us the courage, and she keeps giving us everything she can. We have to quit laying all our problems with her. So, with that being said, I have a confession," said JoBeth.

"We already know, JoBeth. You are having trouble with that darn eating disorder of yours, and you have done some backsliding. I guess that is what it is called," Tilly said bluntly.

"How did you know?" JoBeth questioned, looking puzzled.

"Well, we aren't fools. When we came over to Sadie's last night, there you were. It also helped that we could see your suitcases in the guest bedroom. That was a dead giveaway," said Stella.

"How bad is it?" Hannah asked.

"Bad enough that I didn't trust myself to be alone. I had asked Sadie not to tell you, but I see now that wasn't fair to her. I do ask you, though, not to tell Gracie. She has been so proud of me, and she certainly does not need to worry. I will promise the rest of you, as I did, Sadie, that I will fight this even harder. I will win."

Hannah handed JoBeth a chocolate chip cookie and said, "We know you will, and we are here to help you in any way that we can."

JoBeth smiled and accepted the cookie.

"Ladies, is there anything else anybody needs to get off their chest or finally come clean about?" Sadie asked, teasing.

"Give me some time to think, and I can probably come up with something in my life that I need to confess," Tilly said.

"No confessing, but I wish that you all could have seen the look on Trace's face this morning," Stella said, with a slightly smug look.

"Spill the beans, Stella. Tell us what happened," Tilly said excitedly.

"I got up early this morning and was waiting for him downstairs with a cup of coffee in my hands. I put on a fake smile, said good morning, and handed him the coffee. He reached for it, and when he did, I planted a great big kiss on those lips of his. Then I calmly told him to have a great day at work and that I would call him later. Then I turned, and out the door, I went."

Hannah asked, "What did he do?"

"I don't know. I didn't give him a chance to do or say anything. I went out the door in a flash, got in my car, and pulled off."

"That is classic, Stella. You are acting differently just enough to make him wonder if something is going on in your life," Sadie said.

"I am going to stay away from him as much as I can, but not enough that he will ask any questions. The fact is I am still hurting from finally seeing the truth right in front of me that I have known for months. I have got to decide how to handle everything, and staying away is the best for me right now."

"I think you are handling it the correct way. I am proud of you," Tilly said.

Sadie looked down the hall nervously as Gracie slowly walked toward them. They jumped to their feet and hurriedly walked toward her.

"Is it over? Are they through with you for the day? Can you leave now?" Tilly asked, without taking a breath.

"They are discussing my case, or that is what they told me. Then they want to discuss the next step in my treatment. Right now, I just want to sit down. I have been poked and stuck with needles so many times that I am sore all over."

"Oh, honey, here sit down," Hannah said as she pulled a chair close to Gracie.

"Would you like to have something to drink or eat?" Stella asked.

"I don't want anything right now." She looked toward the nurse and smiled. "Tina brought me a sandwich and a glass of tea earlier."

"Were you able to eat it?" Sadie asked.

"I ate a little bit. Now, everyone quit looking at me as if you don't know what to say or do. Nothing they did today is going to affect what is already going on inside me. I really don't know why I agreed to see Doctor Young from Duke. I know my body, and I don't need to hear the verdict from another doctor."

Sadie looked at the others. No one said a word.

"Well, tell me what has been going on out here all day. I am sorry, girls, you must have been bored to death waiting for me," Gracie said as she took a deep breath and tried to relax in the soft chair.

"We have talked about everything. We will fill you in later when we get you home. I want you to stay with me tonight," Sadie said.

"I won't give you an argument on that. I can almost hear your bed calling my name right now."

Tilly laughed and said, "Do you think you can make room for the rest of us, Sadie?"

Sadie smiled, "It's never been a problem before."

The nurse walked toward Gracie, touched her softly on the arm, and said, "Doctor Duncan said he would like to see you now. He would like your friends to come as well."

"Well, ladies, are you ready?" Gracie questioned as she slowly rose from the chair.

Tilly reached for Gracie's arm, but Sadie slowly shook her head, letting Tilly realize this was not a good idea at this time.

Gracie looked around and said, "Have you girls ever seen the movie Dead Man Walking?"

"There she goes again, Sadie. Tell her to stop," Tilly said.

"Gracie, Tilly told me to tell you to stop. So I guess you need to stop," Sadie said, trying her best to sound upbeat.

They walked down the hall right beside Gracie. They could see Doctor Duncan standing at his door.

"Come on in, ladies," he said.

He reached for Gracie's arm and helped her to the chair closest to his desk. The others found a seat.

Doctor Young walked into the room and introduced himself.

He sat on the edge of Doctor Duncan's desk and said, "Miss Gracie, I am sorry that we have put you through so much today. You must be exhausted."

"To be honest, I am," Gracie said.

Doctor Duncan cleared his throat and then began, "Gracie, you and I have been friends for many years. There is no way that I am going to sit here and lie to you. Knowing you the way I do, I know you would not want me to do that. I wanted to bring in David because I wanted a second opinion."

He paused to see Gracie's reaction, and then he began again. "The chemo has not helped. We have compared all your MRI's and CT scans. Your cancer is getting progressively worse."

Doctor Young spoke, getting right to the point, "We have several options. We can operate and then go aggressive with chemo and radiation."

"Will that take away the cancer or just prolong my life for a few months with the pain getting worse and worse each day?" Gracie said as if this was just a normal conversation.

"It will assure you of a few more months," he said.

The girls looked at Gracie as if they wanted to say something but didn't know what to say. Therefore, they continued to stay quiet as they listened to the doctor explaining the situation to Gracie.

Tilly bit the bottom of her lip, almost to the point of it bleeding. She was determined not to cry. Gracie was so brave that she was determined to do so as well.

Doctor Young continued talking, sounding very impersonal, "If you decide to have the operation, we will schedule it as soon as possible. I suggest after that you call a home health care nurse to help take care of you, or you might want to go into a Hospice Care House."

"I can see that I will jump at either one of these options. Do I need to tell you right now, or do I have at least five minutes to decide?" Gracie said, looking the young doctor straight in the eyes.

He stood, turned to Doctor Duncan, and said, "I see that I have not used the bedside manner once again that you have suggested so many times."

He turned to Gracie, "I see that I have presented a lot to you at one time. I am sorry that I could not have given you good news. You are a very strong-willed lady, and I wish the best for you."

He took Gracie's hand, held it briefly, turned, and left the room.

Doctor Duncan started to speak immediately, "I am so sorry he stated everything that way. He is young, best in his field, but no compassion at all."

Gracie cleared her throat and said, "I knew it was bad, and I have known it for several weeks. I also knew I wasn't getting any better."

She continued, "Your optimism anchored me through this entire cancer journey, but I'm tired. I am ready for this journey to be over."

He pulled away from his desk and went to Gracie's side. He bent down beside her chair and said, "Please don't give a final answer now. Consider an operation and then maybe chemo and radiation. It's not like you to give up."

Sadie felt a heavy emotion sit in her chest and throat, blocking her breath and leaving her anxious. She could not hold back any longer.

"Honey, you don't have to make a decision this very minute. Just listen to Doctor Duncan and give it a few days for everything to sink in. You can make a decision then."

"If I don't do anything except just live this nightmare day by day, how long do I have left?" Gracie asked.

You could hear the anguish in his voice, "Gracie, I can't give you a time limit. Only God knows that."

"You can give me an educated guess. Just give me that much."

He hesitated to what seemed to be minutes. He then said, "Six to eight weeks without the operation and possibly six months with the operation. I don't like to play God, Gracie, you know that."

It was apparent this was causing him great pain.

Gracie reached for his hand, placed it in hers, and said, "We have been good friends for as long as I can remember. I have always trusted you. Now, look me straight in the eyes, George. What would you do if you were deciding for yourself?"

He softly said, almost in a whisper, "I would leave this office and live life to its fullest as much as I could, just as you are now. I would not have the operation."

She smiled and said, "Thank you. Don't ever think that you have decided for me. I don't want that hanging over your head. I have the presence of mind to think clearly, and I have made my own decision."

He stood and placed a kiss on her forehead and went back to his desk. He wrote on his prescription pad and then handed the paper to Sadie.

"See that this gets filled as soon as possible. Make sure she takes them as often as I have put them down. She doesn't need to wait until she feels the pain. She can be stubborn about things like this. I am sure you all know that, though."

He continued, "Gracie, when it gets to the point you can't take the pain at home any longer, that is when we will make some more decisions. Again, don't think about that now. I just want you to know there is an option."

"We will be taking care of her," Tilly said nervously.

The others nodded.

He looked down, took his pen, wrote something, and handed it to Sadie.

"This is a number you can reach me at any time. Don't hesitate to use it."

Sadie folded the paper and held it tightly in her hand. This somehow gave her a feeling of security.

Gracie stood and said, "Well, George, we are going to go now. I have a nice comfortable bed at Sadie's waiting for me, and I sure am tired."

He stood once again and walked everyone into the hallway. He stopped Sadie and whispered as the others walked away.

"It's going to get worse very fast. Please call me every day and let me know her progress. Gracie and I go back a long way, and I know she will probably not darken this door again as a patient if she can help it. When she said no more chemo, I knew she meant it. If you see that pain medicine is not helping, call me, and I will do something else."

Sadie nodded, unable to say anything, not even thank you. She rushed to catch up with the others.

She walked toward the nurse's desk and said, "Thank you for the kindness you have shown us today."

The nurse smiling sympathetically, said, "No need to thank me. I hope Miss Gracie has a good night tonight."

Sadie nodded and then turned to the others.

"Tilly, I could use that hand that you were going to help me with earlier when Sadie gave you that look. I can surely use the help now. I am all tuckered out."

Tilly carefully placed her arm under Gracie's and helped her toward the door.

"Only if you tell us later just how you know this Doctor George Duncan," Tilly said, trying to tease.

"That's my Tilly," Gracie said slowly. "Yep, that's my Tilly."

As Sadie pulled into the driveway, there on her front porch sat two suitcases. She pulled the car to a stop and stared at them.

"I don't have to ask who those belong to, but I would love to know how they got there. Gracie, could you help us out by telling us who brought your suitcases over here for you?" Sadie said calmly.

Gracie slowly opened the car door and said, "Let's just say the mystery woman is still working her web of mystery."

The others looked at one another with that familiar puzzled look. They were not about to question Gracie at this point.

Tilly raced around to the side of the car and asked, "Gracie, do you need my help?"

"Yes, I do. Thank you."

Tilly helped her out of the car, up the steps, and into the house. Hannah grabbed for the suitcases and carried them into the guest room that was soon to become home to Gracie.

"I'm tired. I'm going to rest for a bit." Gracie said, sounding weaker than she had before.

Hannah followed her into the bedroom, turned the covers back, and then questioned, "Is there anything I can do before I leave? I need to run home and pack myself a small overnight case. I am also going to pick us up something from a take-out. Is there anything that you might feel like eating?"

"I think maybe Chinese food sounds good. That is if everyone else wants that," Gracie said as she lay across the bed.

Hannah reached for a light quilt that was lying across a chair, walked toward the bed, and placed it across Gracie.

"Rest well, honey. I will be back later."

Gracie smiled but stayed silent.

Hannah gave Gracie one more quick look and then walked out of the room, closing the door behind her.

The others were sitting in the kitchen, waiting for the coffee to perk.

Hannah said, "Tilly, ride with me. I need to go home to pick some things up, and I will dart by your house for you to do the same."

"That sounds good to me. Sadie, is there anything we can do before we go?"

Sadie shook her head.

"Oh, by the way, I will bring us something to eat back. I asked Gracie what she thought she would be able to eat, and she said Chinese food," Hannah said.

"Whatever Gracie wants is what we will eat," remarked Sadie.

Stella grabbed for her pocketbook and said, "JoBeth, will you come with me? This way, I will not have to be one on one with Trace. I will tell him that I am spending the night with the girls, and you can talk to him while I pack. Will you please do that for me?"

JoBeth smiled and said, "Sure, and I promise to be a good girl and not hit him square in the nose. Do you get the idea I don't like your husband?"

Sadie was surprised that this remark had come from JoBeth and not Tilly.

Tilly said, "I don't think there is a person in this room that likes him, except for you, Stella. I sure hope that will soon change."

Stella walked toward the door with JoBeth right behind her.

"All right, everybody, we will return shortly." She did not want to make any type of comment about Trace. Her love for him was still there, but she did not dare admit it, not even to herself.

Everyone left at the same time, leaving Sadie staring at the coffee pot that had finally decided to perk. Even after all these years, she still used the first coffee pot that she and Mitchell had received as a wedding gift. She watched as the coffee came right up to the little clear top of the percolator and jump up and down, letting her know it was ready. Funny how she could still remember opening this gift at her bridal shower and thinking about how she didn't know the first thing about making coffee. That seemed a million years ago and at least ten thousand cups of coffee later.

"They don't make coffee pots like they once did," she whispered to herself and smiled.

"Sadie Sue, can you come in here when you get a chance?" Gracie called from the bedroom.

Sadie hurriedly went to the bedroom and, leaning against the doorjamb, asked, "Are you all right, Gracie? Do you need anything?"

"I would like to talk for a bit if you have time."

Sadie pulled a chair close to the bed and said, "I always have time to talk to my friend, especially when she calls me Sadie Sue."

"Have you ever wondered why I only call you that at times?"

"Yes, but I figured that when you wanted me to know the reason that you would tell me."

"I always felt that if I called you Sadie Sue, you would take me more seriously and know that what I was going to say was very important. I guess calling you Sadie Sue made me feel I was getting your full attention."

"You always have my full attention. You know that, Gracie."

"I know it, but it just felt right calling you that. For some reason, it also gave me the courage to talk to you about whatever was bothering me."

"Well, Sadie Sue is right here, ready to listen."

Gracie paused and then slowly began, "I can feel myself getting worse. It feels like it is happening minute by minute. I can't get over how I had the strength last week to walk on the beach, chase after Trace, and even drive the van, and I don't feel like even raising my head from this pillow right now. This cancer is draining me in ways I never dreamed. I was sure that when George diagnosed me months ago that I would have at least a year. I know now I don't, Sadie."

"I wish there were something I could do to help you," Sadie said. "I was a nurse for so many years, and I feel so helpless now."

"You are helping me in more ways than you will ever know. I don't want you to be sad because I'm not. I am ready to go. I know God is waiting for me. I can close my eyes and see Him holding Lindsey Grace in His arms. When I get there, He will place her in mine. I can take her and hold her tightly against my heart, knowing I didn't kill her. I can hold her without guilt and shame. You made me realize that, and I will never be able to repay you for giving that to me."

She took a deep breath, and Sadie saw she needed to rest.

"Gracie, do you need some of the pain medicine we picked up before coming home?"

Gracie nodded.

Sadie swiftly left the room, went straight to her pocketbook, and got the medication. She filled a glass with water and returned to the bedroom.

She handed it to Gracie and said, "You are going to take it every two hours, and then the pain won't get ahead of you. When it gets worse, we will do something else."

Gracie looked straight into Sadie's eyes and then said, almost pleading, "I can depend on you, can't I?"

Sadie turned away from Gracie's stare. She knew what she was asking once again without saying the actual words.

"I'll rest," Gracie assured her. "Then, when the others get back, we'll visit some more."

Sadie nodded and left the room.

She went straight to her bedroom. Once inside, with the doors safely closed behind her, she kicked off her shoes and lay across the bed. She closed her eyes, but visions of what the future held for Gracie kept entering her mind. The feeling of helplessness engulfed her once again. She reached inside her pocket and pulled out the number for Doctor Duncan. She didn't feel entirely alone now.

Sadie could hear the sound of footsteps walking in the hallway. She jumped quickly from the bed. She had gone hard and fast to sleep. Her body had needed this rest. She felt as though, once again, she had the mental and physical strength to help Gracie better.

She walked toward the kitchen, and suddenly the aroma of shrimp-fried rice filled her nostrils. She looked at the kitchen table and realized immediately that Hannah must have bought a little bit of everything on the menu.

Tilly and Hannah smiled as they continued to take the food from the brown bags.

Stella walked into the kitchen, carrying a large box, which held a chocolate cake.

"We decided to go by the bakery and pick a few things up. This way, Sadie, you don't have to worry about baking. We know how you love to bake, but we are going to be taking some of the chores from you."

"Is Gracie still resting?" Hannah asked.

"Yes, I gave her a dose of pain medicine. It will help, but I know that later on, it's going to take a different medication to help her."

Tilly reached for a cup and went in the direction of the coffee pot.

"It's probably going to be very strong. It has been heating every since you girls left. I'm afraid I fell asleep and forgot to unplug it."

"The stronger, the better for me right now," Stella said.

"Stella had a slight run-in with Trace," remarked JoBeth.

"What do you mean? I thought you were going to be there with her, JoBeth, so nothing would happen." Tilly said bluntly.

"Don't blame her, Tilly. We walked in, and Trace wanted to know where I had been for so long. Then he followed me upstairs while I packed. He asked me if I was leaving him. When I told him I was staying with Sadie for a few days due to Gracie's illness, he acted as if he was disappointed. It's clear to me now that he wants me to make the first move."

"See, Gracie is right. You have got to wait until you have enough evidence that you can get your fair share. Then you can walk away from your marriage, not having to struggle for money the rest of your life," Tilly said.

"That is exactly what I have been trying to do, but this afternoon it was hard. I held my tongue, finished packing, turned to him, and kissed him on the cheek. I told him that if he needed me to please call. Again, that strange look came over his face as if he didn't know what to do. So, that is good. I am still ahead of the game."

She continued, "Then he followed me downstairs as if he was going to tell me something. JoBeth walked toward him and said something about his tie bringing out the blue in his eyes, and he seemed to melt into the floor."

JoBeth laughed and said, "I didn't know what to say, and that was the first thing that popped in my mind. I want to know what you whispered in his ear."

Stella calmly said, "He had already asked me if I was leaving him when we had our discussion upstairs. I didn't feel like I should leave that hanging. So, I whispered and said, darling, I don't know why you thought I was leaving you. My friends mean everything to me, but you are my life."

"So, that is why that look came over his face, and he became speechless?"

Stella nodded, "That's it. As I said, I am playing his game, and right now, my score is much higher than his. I plan to keep it that way as long as I can."

"Sadie," Gracie called.

"I'm coming, Gracie," Sadie said and went immediately toward the bedroom. The others followed.

Sadie turned toward them and whispered, "Be as cheerful as you can without overdoing it." Then she opened the bedroom door.

"Do you need anything, honey?" Sadie questioned as she walked toward the bed.

Gracie looked at them and said, "I could hear you all talking, and I guess I wanted to be included."

"Would you like to eat a little supper now?" Tilly asked.

"I'm really not hungry."

Sadie spoke up, "Gracie, you are going to have to try. The medication that you are on will make you very sick on your stomach if you don't have a little food in it."

Gracie laughed, "Well, I wouldn't want to make my stomach hurt."

She paused and then continued, "Sorry, ladies, I know you don't know how to handle it when I make one of my sick jokes."

"Well, to be completely honest, we don't know how to take it," Tilly remarked.

"Just take it as a joke and go on. It makes me feel better when I can joke about my condition."

"Then you make all the jokes you want to, and we will do our best to laugh with you. Don't count on us laughing every time, though," JoBeth said.

Gracie smiled and said, "I'll try a little food now since we have that settled."

She leaned up in bed as if she was going to try to get up. She slowly went back into her pillow.

Sadie saw that Gracie didn't have the strength to leave her bed.

"I think tonight we will bring the meal to you. Do you mind if we all join you while we eat?"

Gracie shook her head.

As they were leaving the room, Tilly turned back to Gracie and said, "Don't think we are going to make this a habit, but for tonight you are going to get your meal in bed and special attention from your friends."

She winked at Gracie and continued, "We will be right back."

As they reached the kitchen, they each started gathering the things they needed. Sadie got a bed tray while Tilly fixed Gracie a small plate of food.

Tilly said, "I am not a bit hungry."

"I don't think any of us are. Just put a little bit on your plate to make it appear we are eating with her," Sadie instructed.

"Well, we will certainly be eating Chinese food for the next few days. Why Hannah and I got this much is beyond me," Tilly said.

Within minutes, everything was ready, and they headed back to Gracie's bedroom.

Sadie placed another pillow under Gracie's head and then laid the bed tray on her lap.

"Girls, let's join hands. I think it might be my time to ask the blessing," Gracie said while reaching for their hands.

"God, we thank you for the ones that prepared this food."

She stopped. No one said a word. Sadie opened one eye to see if she was all right.

Finally, Gracie calmly began again but with a stronger voice, "God, this isn't really a prayer to bless this food. I pray that You will give my friends the courage to let me go without being so sad. Give them strength, dear God, to know it is all right. Amen"

Silence took over the room.

Finally, while holding an egg roll in the air and turning it around and around, Tilly said, "I love Chinese food, but I have never been able to figure out why they call an egg roll an egg roll. There are no eggs in it, and it doesn't roll."

Tilly's words broke the silence, and everyone, including Gracie, attempted to laugh.

"I don't know why either, Tilly, but they sure are delicious, "JoBeth said as she took a big bite of her egg roll.

Tilly laid her plate down on the bedside table and said, "I will be right back."

All eyes watched her as she left the room.

Hannah said, "She is probably going to go and get an encyclopedia to see if she can find information about an egg roll."

Tilly entered the room, carrying a large bag. She reached her hand in and pulled out a Braves baseball cap. She went straight to Gracie and placed it on her head. Then she reached in once again, pulling out several and tossing them to the others. They immediately put them on their heads.

"Now, we all have baseball caps just like you, Gracie. The store where I bought the caps makes real cute scarfs, but I thought that right now, a baseball cap will do the trick."

"This will work perfectly while my hair is growing back," Gracie said while adjusting her cap. "Friends, I haven't changed my mind about anything. I won't be taking any more chemo, and I'm not going to have the operation. So please respect my decision and don't question me or pressure me into doing something I know is needless."

Sadie spoke immediately, "We respect your decision. We will not ask you to try other things. It's your life, Gracie, and you live the rest of it the way you desire."

Gracie smiled and said, "I have several things I would like to talk to you about tonight. I will say them tonight, and then we don't have to bring them up again."

"Our mystery woman is going to tell us something without us asking. I can't believe it," Tilly said.

Gracie began, "Stella, tomorrow, go to my house. You all know where I keep the front door key. When you get inside, you will find on the top of my desk a large envelope. Inside are the pictures we took of Trace and his newest friend. I ask you not to do anything at this time with the pictures. Don't ask me any questions, but please just take my advice and wait a while longer. You will know when the time is right and exactly what you need to do."

Stella nodded.

She continued, "The picture of us that was taken by the man on the pier has been mailed. He will receive it in a few days. The picture was placed in a thank you card with all our names on it. I hope that was all right with each of you. I felt he would like to know our names."

Once again, she turned her attention to Stella, "Laying beside the envelope, you will find six picture frames with the picture he made for us inside. Please bring them back with you for each of us."

Once again, Stella nodded.

"Two more things, and then I turn it over to whoever wants to ask me questions, but I don't promise I will answer them."

Sadie had noticed Gracie pushing her food around on her plate the entire time. She had absolutely no appetite. She had not taken a single bite of food.

Sadie walked toward the bed and removed the tray without saying a word.

Gracie took a deep breath and continued, "I want you all to know that my final arrangements have been made. I mean everything right down to the clothes I will be wearing, to the flowers that will be placed on top of my casket."

"You're just a wealth of information tonight, Gracie. Wouldn't you like to save some to share with us in the morning?" Tilly asked.

"No, I want it all out and in the open tonight. Then you won't have to keep wondering what to dress me in or where to have my funeral. You know all those little things that have to be done once someone has died. I don't have any family left. You have been the only family I have had since my husband died. So there is no need to try to go looking for a family that doesn't exist."

She reached under her pillow, pulled out a small sealed envelope, and handed it to Sadie.

"Sadie Sue, I ask you in front of the others not to open the envelope until I die. The minute I die, open the envelope and call the number on the piece of paper. Tell the one on the other end it is over, and then just hang up. There is no need to say anything else. Remember, all you need to say is *it is over*."

"I hear and obey, Gracie," Sadie said, knowing this must be very important because she had called her Sadie Sue.

The girls looked as puzzled about this envelope as Sadie did. Tilly was just about to ask a question about it, but Gracie said, "No questions about this envelope, and then there will be no lies."

Tilly shrugged her shoulders, pulled her chair closer to the bed, and said, "Then I will ask you another question. Gracie, we have all been wondering about something and hope you will give us an answer. Today it seemed you were much closer to Doctor Duncan than just patient and doctor. What is the connection between you two?"

Gracie smiled and said, "I knew that question was coming, and it is one I gladly will answer. He was Reece's doctor. He was very young and just starting his practice. I remember being very scared that he didn't know what he was doing. I soon realized I didn't have to worry. After the death of Reece, George became a close friend of mine. He wanted it to turn into more, but my heart still belonged to Reece, and I knew there would never be another man that could walk in his shoes. He realized this and moved on with his life. We have continued to stay friends throughout the years."

"Why did you never mention him all this time?" Hannah questioned.

Tilly spoke immediately, "Hannah, has Gracie ever completely let us in on her life?"

"I can answer that. No, I admit I haven't," Gracie said. "But it isn't that I didn't trust you or didn't love you. You have been the closest thing to a family anyone could have. As I said earlier, you all have been my family, and I deeply thank you for sharing your lives and your love with me."

Once again, Tilly was the only one asking the questions, "Gracie, you said you had two things that you wanted to tell us. What is the second thing?"

"That's right, and when I talk to you about this, I ask that no one comment."

She reached for her stomach and moaned.

"No more talk tonight, Gracie. It is time for your medication." Sadie pointed to the door and said, "Let's go."

"No, please. Just listen to what I need to say tonight," Gracie said, pleading.

Stella said, "All right, but this is it."

"I want you as my friends to help me die. I asked you at the beach, but I did not get an answer. So, I ask this of you again. I don't want to linger. Sadie, you were a nurse, and in your heart, I know you still are. You will know when it is time, and I ask that you honor my request. Now, I see that each of you wants to say something. I again ask that you do not. I have made my request, and I hope it will be honored. I will not ask again, no matter how much pain I am in."

She grabbed for her stomach and said, "Sadie, I sure could use that medication now."

They watched as Gracie grabbed for the side of the bed and held tightly as her knuckles turned white. Sadie raced out of the bedroom and quickly came back with two pills instead of one with a glass of water.

"Take this, Gracie. It will ease the pain faster than just one."

Gracie eagerly took the pills and then said, "Everything happens for a reason, and that is the way I am accepting this cancer. I am no better than anyone else is, so I don't say why me. I only say, why not me. Now, let me rest, and I expect you all to get a good night's sleep so we can talk only about happy things tomorrow."

They each gave Gracie a soft hug and left the room carrying their plates that hadn't been touched either. Sadie left the door slightly open to hear her if she needed anything during the night.

They placed their paper plates inside the trash can and went into the den, so Gracie would not hear their conversation.

Sadie was the first to speak, "We need to think this over."

Tilly bluntly said, "No, kidding!"

Sadie held the envelope, waving it back and forth in the air.

"You promised not to open it, and we will make sure you don't. Even though it sure is tempting," Hannah admitted.

"All these years, we have teased that Gracie was a mystery woman. We would have never dreamed just how much of one she really is," Tilly stated.

"Ladies, I can't take anymore. I have to get up early in the morning to let Dr. Roberts know I need more therapy sessions. No mystery about me, I have been a weak person, and now there are more days of therapy in my life. Thank you all for helping me get through these last couple of days. I wish I were as strong as Gracie."

JoBeth made a motion of throwing them a kiss, headed to the bedroom, and continued, "Good night, dear friends. I will leave my door open, so I can also hear Gracie if she needs something."

Tilly sat down beside Sadie and asked, "God bless Gracie for trying, but if she isn't scared, why is she asking us to help her die?"

Sadie shook her head and said, "I don't know. At one time, I thought it was because she was scared of death and wanted us to help so she would go fast, but now I don't have an answer."

Stella reached for Sadie's hand and said, "Honey, we all need to go to bed and just think this thing over silently. We need to search our own hearts. You told us several days ago that we would know what to do when the time comes, and we will."

She hugged Sadie and said, "Now, if I am sharing the bedroom with JoBeth, I need to get on in there so I won't mess up her beauty sleep. Good night, all."

Tilly stood up, reached for Hannah's hand, and said, "Come on, girl, I guess that means you and I are sharing a room. I sure hope you keep your snoring down tonight."

Hannah turned to Sadie and asked, "Sadie, do I snore?"

Sadie nodded, "Yes, Tilly is right. She is not teasing you."

As Hannah and Tilly left the room, Sadie could hear Hannah commenting that she was not a snorer.

She smiled, knowing that nothing would ever change between those two.

She quietly walked to Gracie's bedroom door and stood listening to see if she was asleep. She could hear her softly breathing. The medication had taken effect, giving Gracie some relief. Sadie took a deep breath, realizing that at least it had done the job tonight.

She walked back toward the couch, grabbed a pillow, and placed it under her head. She reached into her pocket and pulled out the envelope once again. The temptation of opening it popped into her mind. She once again reached inside her pocket and brought out the piece of paper that had the number for Doctor Duncan.

The thought of calling him raced through her mind, but she felt it was too soon to let him know how Gracie was doing. She placed them both safely inside her pocket and closed her eyes. She hoped that sleep would come quickly.

Chapter 15

The bond of sisterhood
is felt through one's heart,
seen through one's eyes,
moreover, it lingers forever in one's mind.
    Therefore, a true friend is a special gift
from God.

Sadie sat at the kitchen table with her hands wrapped tightly around her coffee cup. The warmth of the cup felt good on her fingers. The aroma of coffee had always given her a happy feeling, but it wasn't working this morning. Happy moments had been very few and far between since she had learned her friend was dying. Each of the women had accepted the verdict and, in their own way, was dealing with it.

JoBeth came rushing into the room. She looked tired. It was apparent she had only gotten a few hours of sleep.

"Sadie, is it all right if I ask Tilly to go with me to therapy this morning? I know that Stella will be going to Gracie's house to pick up the pictures, and that will leave only Hannah here with you to take care of Gracie."

"We will be fine. I haven't checked in on Gracie yet this morning. I felt it was all right for her to miss her medicine this morning as long as she was getting some sleep. She sure didn't get much after midnight last night."

"I know. I can't get over how this has taken over her body so fast."

Sadie nodded and said, "I'm calling Doctor Duncan later this morning and see what he might suggest."

Tilly came into the room, stretching and rubbing her eyes. It didn't take her long to grab for her first cup of coffee for the morning.

"I couldn't help but hear that you wanted me to go with you today, JoBeth. What time do we need to leave?"

"We need to leave as soon as we can both get ready. I really don't have an appointment with Doctor Roberts. I am going to try to catch him before he starts his day with other appointments."

"Sadie, can you come in here?" Stella called from Gracie's bedroom.

Sadie didn't bother to answer. She hurried from her chair and straight to the bedroom. It didn't take long for her to see that Gracie needed her medication.

Sadie raced back into the kitchen, grabbed a glass of water and the medicine. She had a sick feeling hit the pit of her stomach.

"Why didn't I check on her earlier," she whispered to herself.

While entering the room, she could see Stella wiping Gracie's forehead with a cold cloth.

"Don't look so scared, ladies," Gracie said. "I have been lying here for a long time, and I let the pain jump on me without realizing it. Sadie, I see that look on your face as if you feel you should be doing more."

"Hush and take your medicine. We can talk about this later," Sadie said while putting the pills directly into Gracie's mouth.

Making sure Gracie had swallowed the pills, Sadie said, "Now, I'm going to fix you some oatmeal, but if you don't feel like you can keep it down, don't eat it."

Gracie gave her a thumb's up.

Sadie left the room with Tilly right behind her. The others stayed to keep watch over Gracie.

Sadie stayed silent while she gathered the ingredients for breakfast.

"What's going on in that brain of yours, Sadie?" Tilly questioned.

"That everything is going too fast. I am still a nurse at heart even though I am retired, and I can sense something is not right. Gracie has seemed to go downhill since we have come back from the beach. It is much too fast, and I can't understand it. I feel there should be something that could be done to slow the cancer down."

Tilly grabbed Sadie's shoulders and directed her to a chair.

"Now, you're going to sit down and listen to what I have come up with. Sadie, I have tossed and turned all night thinking about Gracie. I have wondered the same thing. As private as she has always been, this could have been going on for months and months. Looking back, I am sure it has. Do you remember all the times she was late for our meetings? She never would say why, and we finally quit asking."

Tilly continued, "All we can do now is make her as comfortable as we can and not start second-guessing our actions."

"I know you're right, but it is still frustrating."

Sadie eased from the chair and continued her task of fixing the oatmeal.

Tilly continued to talk, "Sadie, the problem with you is that you have always been a fixer, and this can't be fixed."

"So, I am a fixer?" Sadie said, sounding agitated.

"Yes, but in a good way, Sadie. Don't take it as criticism. You are a good fixer."

Sadie could not help but laugh, "I know you were complimenting me, Tilly. Honestly, I do."

She finished fixing Gracie's breakfast and placed it on a tray.

Tilly reached for it and said, "I will take it to her. Let us take care of Gracie until we have to leave. You rest some. Honestly, Sadie, you look like you have aged over the last few weeks."

"Thank you for sharing that with me."

Tilly stopped in her tracks, turned around, and said, "There I go again, putting my size eight foot in my mouth."

Sadie shook her head and grinned. She knew she looked tired, but she did not realize she had aged. Keeping other people's secrets was beginning to affect her, but at least there were no more secrets. The others could help now, knowing exactly what was going on. She took a deep breath, and then a thought raced in her head. What if more secrets were floating around?

She listened as her friends whispered in the other room. She smiled to herself as she thought of all the years they had shared together. Now, she knew exactly what she had to do. She could not hold back any longer. She reached into her pocket and pulled out Doctor Duncan's personal phone number. She made sure she kept this number with her at all times.

There just had to be something else that could give Gracie more time.

He answered on the third ring. For some reason, hearing his voice made her heart beat faster. She had not had this reaction for many years.

She actually blushed when she heard his voice. She finally uttered a soft hello.

"Good morning, Sadie."

"Good morning, Doctor Duncan, I am sorry to be calling you so early, but I am concerned about Gracie."

"Please, to start with, I am not Doctor Duncan to a friend of Gracie's. Please call me George. I hope it was all right that I have been calling you, Sadie?"

She decided to ignore the question and continued her conversation keeping it entirely on Gracie.

"George," she said, finding it hard to call him that. "I am worried about Gracie. I know that her being my close friend would lead you to believe I am overreacting. I am trying to look at her condition through a nurse's eye. She is getting worse, and it is happening much faster than I feel it should."

"I was concerned this was going to happen. I will come over and just pop in for a few minutes before I go to the office. I will change her medicine and see if that might help her a little more. What do you think her pain level is at this time?"

"Knowing Gracie, it is a lot worse than she is letting on, but I feel it is very close to a ten," Sadie said, once again talking like a woman that was confident in her past occupation.

"I'll see you in about thirty minutes, Sadie."

He then said goodbye, with Sadie still holding the phone to her ear. He had not asked for her address. Maybe it was written on Gracie's medical record. She had probably put her down as an emergency contact. She decided to wipe this from her mind.

She could not get over the emotion she was having. When he had called her by her first name, it made her feel strange, but in a good way. This was something she could not wipe from her mind.

She darted into her bedroom, changing her clothes. She took an extra-long look in the mirror. She hoped that Tilly was not right about her aging. Once again, she felt herself blushing at the thought that she had let enter her mind. She shook her head as if trying to shake off this unwanted reaction.

She went straight to the kitchen, making a fresh pot of coffee. Tilly entered the room with Gracie's tray.

"She ate a few bites. We could tell she was trying. It seemed to be making her sick before it reached her lips. We remembered what you had told her about not eating if she felt it would make her sick, so we didn't insist," Tilly said while placing the tray on the table.

While pointing to her watch, JoBeth said, "Tilly, we need to go."

"Give me five minutes, and I will be right out," she said, racing to the bedroom.

"Sadie, we will be back as soon as we can. I don't know how long therapy is going to be today. It is usually an hour, but after I talk to Doctor Roberts, I don't know what will happen."

Sadie put her arms around JoBeth and hugged her. "You are talking like you are going to the principal's office. It is going to be fine. You feel as if you have backslid on your recovery, but I can honestly tell you that Doctor Roberts is going to look at this as if you have taken two steps forward."

"You are always right about everything, so I hope you are right this time."

Tilly walked back into the room and grabbed for JoBeth's hand.

"Let's go, kid. Do you think I could sit in on the therapy session?"

"Oh, Sadie, what am I going to do?" JoBeth said in a nervous tone.

Sadie laughed and said, "No, Tilly, you can't sit in on the therapy session. The others would not allow that."

In that self-satisfied tone that only those who are used to being positive of themselves can achieve, Tilly said, "I am sure that I could put some input in how they could help themselves in any situation."

After seeing the smile on Sadie's face, JoBeth said, "I am sure you could, Tilly. We will talk about it on the ride over."

As they were walking out of the room, Sadie heard Tilly proudly say, "Finally, I am appreciated."

Sadie smiled to herself, knowing that Tilly would never change.

She started walking toward Gracie's door when Stella quietly came out of the room.

"No need to check on her. She is asleep. Hannah and I stayed with her until the pain medicine got in her system. She should sleep until I get back. I would like for Hannah to go with me to Gracie's if you can handle things here until we get back."

"That will be fine. I called George, and he is coming over to check on Gracie. I know we will all feel better knowing he is going to keep a close watch on her."

"You called who?" Stella questioned.

Sadie quickly corrected herself, "I called Doctor Duncan, but he asked me to call him George. I guess I forgot that you didn't know his first name. Sorry about that. Anyway, he is coming by shortly."

Hannah walked in during the conversation, "So, it is George now?"

Sadie ignored the question and started to tidy the kitchen. She turned her back from them and then smiled. Now, she was the one showing some mystery in her life. She felt anxious to talk to Gracie about this.

"Don't you turn away without letting us in on what is going on," Hannah said.

Turning back once again to face them, she said, "Honey, I promise nothing is going on. He simply asked me to call him George instead of Doctor Duncan."

Stella put her finger to her mouth and said, "Hush, Hannah, don't talk so loud. Gracie needs to sleep, and we need to get going." She winked at Sadie and continued, "We will be back as soon as we can. You and George have a good morning."

Sadie reached for a dishtowel, threw it at Stella, and said, "Get out of here, you two, before I get angry."

Hannah laughed and said, "Going, going, gone." They both raced out the door.

Sadie turned back to the sink and continued with the dishes. Her mind kept going back to Gracie. She placed the last plate in the sink, took the dishtowel, wiped her hands, and walked softly toward her bedroom door. She opened it carefully so it would not awaken her. Gracie was still asleep. Sadie looked long and hard at her friend that lay so lifeless in her bed. She shut the door and went back into the kitchen.

Within minutes, she heard a knock at the front door. She didn't waste any time getting there.

George stood smiling as Sadie opened the screen door wide, allowing him to walk inside the hallway.

"I hope I haven't overreacted and got you over here out of fear, but you did say you wanted to know how she was doing each day."

"I am glad that you called," he said as he followed her into the kitchen.

She pointed to a chair for him to sit down.

"It seems this is the main part of my house. Everyone always ends up in here with a coffee cup in their hand," she teased while handing him a cup.

"That is just what I need this morning," he said, lifting his cup while Sadie poured the coffee for him.

He slowly sipped a taste of the coffee, making sure it wasn't too hot.

"That's good, and it hit the spot. Now tell me what you have been noticing about Gracie before I go in to see her."

She lowered her voice and said, "Last week, she was walking around, and now it is as if she can't get out of bed. I know she was in pain while we were at the beach over the weekend, but at least she was trying. Now, it is either that she has given up or cannot be the Gracie we know. As strong a person that I have always known her to be leads me to believe she is much worse."

George continued to drink his coffee as he attentively listened to Sadie. It was apparent he respected her knowledge of medicine.

"Sadie, I don't know how much Gracie has let you and the others know about her condition, but I have been treating her for over a year now."

Sadie lowered her head and said, "That just answered my question. She is in the last stages of this cancer. Am I correct?"

"I am afraid you are. I wanted to try to operate months ago and then try chemo and radiation. She refused and only consented to chemo. After hearing the percentages of recovery, she decided that an operation was not to happen. I thought maybe bringing in another doctor the other day would convince her to reconsider. Then after the exam, we put her through. I knew it would be in vain. When she directly asked me, there was no way I was going to sit behind that desk and lie to her. She has been too good of a friend for me to do something that I know would be in vain."

He took another sip of his coffee and then questioned, "How long have you known Gracie?"

"Oh my, it has been so many years that I am really unsure of the exact amount. We met her the day her husband died."

"That indeed has been many years. He was a good man, and they were very much in love. I was his doctor. That is how Gracie and I became friends. I don't mind saying that I was somewhat sweet on her or thought I was. She never paid me a bit of attention except as a friend. Our friendship grew as the years went by but continued to remain just friends."

He said this as if Sadie needed to know they were "just" friends and had never been a romantic couple.

Silence filled the room as if neither knew what to say at this point.

Finally, Sadie stood up and said, "Let's see if she is awake."

George reached for his bag and followed Sadie toward the room.

As she opened the door, Gracie turned to see who was entering the room.

"Good morning, my dear friend. Did you come over to see if I had made it through another day?" Gracie asked.

"Well, I can see that you are in your usual funny mood," George said while bending down and placing a kiss on her forehead.

He pulled a chair close to her bed and continued, "Now, can we get serious for a minute? I want to know how you are feeling."

"I have had better days. I know I don't have much longer, but I don't want to spend all my last days in the hospital."

Sadie sat down softly at the foot of her bed and said, "You don't have to worry about that. You can stay right here until you decide it is time to go to the hospital. George, how do you feel about that?"

He looked at Sadie and said, "With you being her caregiver, I will send over certain things that you will need. I am going to change the pain medicine to something much stronger. Sadie, you will be able to do everything a nurse would do at the hospital, so for right now, it is all right for her to remain here."

Gracie said, "So I take it I don't have the amount of time you told me in your office."

"You told me to be straight with you," he said, with his voice becoming much softer. "Gracie, do you have all your affairs in order?"

"Yes, I do. I had everything in order months ago. Don't look so sad, George. I'm not asking you to speak at my funeral."

"Yes, she told us that she has everything planned right down to the flowers on the casket," said Sadie.

"Why does that not surprise me?" George said while taking his stethoscope and placing it on Gracie's chest.

"I see my two favorite friends are on first-name terms now."

"Hush, Gracie, while I listen to your heart. Can you set up for me?"

Sadie walked over to the bed and helped Gracie sit up.

George placed the stethoscope on her upper back and said, "Take a deep breath for me."

Gracie took a deep breath and then immediately started coughing. Sadie looked at George, and he slowly shook his head.

Sadie carefully lowered Gracie back onto the pillow and reached for the water pitcher.

She poured a glass of water and said, "Take small sips, honey. It will help the cough."

She did as Sadie asked.

Gracie finally stopped coughing and slowly said, "Well, I know not to take deep breaths anymore."

George touched her softly on her hand and said, "You beat all I've ever seen, Gracie."

She grabbed her stomach. She did not say a word, but her pain was written all over her face.

"What's your pain level? Gracie, be honest about this," George pleaded.

"I'm not going to lie about it. I am close to a ten on the pain scale."

George nodded and looked toward his bag. He swiftly opened it and reached inside. He brought out a needle and then reached in again for a vial.

Gracie turned her head toward Sadie as George inserted the needle into her arm.

"This will give you faster relief than the pills by mouth. I will see to it that this is what you will get from now on," he said.

"George, you are a dear friend," Gracie said while closing her eyes.

George touched her on the shoulder and said, "You should be able to rest now. Do not let the pain get ahead of you. If you feel you need it before the scheduled time, let Sadie know."

Gracie's lips quivered as she said, "I will. Now both of you get out of here and let this dying woman rest."

Sadie shook her head and softly said, "There she goes again."

"Oh, calm down, Sadie. I was trying to lighten the mood. Everyone is dying a little bit every day. I just have the privilege of knowing that my days are definitely numbered. Now, let me get some sleep. I feel the medicine working on me right now. I am in much less pain, and I can barely keep my eyes open."

Sadie turned and started to walk out of the room with George right behind her.

Gracie suddenly said, "George, did I tell you that Sadie is an exceptional woman?"

"No, you didn't tell me, but I realize that. I think you both are very remarkable women."

Gracie, in a frail voice, said, "That's right."

Sadie and George returned to the kitchen once again. He placed his bag on the kitchen table, opened it, removed needles and more medicine.

He handed them to Sadie and said, "This will do until I get more supplies sent over. I will take care of everything as soon as I get to the office. You will be getting everything you will need within two hours."

Sadie looked at the vial George had given her. She knew that this medicine would help with the pain much better than the pills. Maybe now Gracie could get the rest she needed. She also knew this was the medicine used when the patients were closer to death.

George realized this and said, "I know what you are thinking, Sadie. I don't see Gracie making it even a month now. I wouldn't be a bit surprised if she has only two weeks or less left. Cancer has spread, and I fear it is in her lungs now. The chemo that I was finally able to get her to take was of limited benefit. Looking back, I guess I shouldn't have taken that route, but I was trying so hard to help her in any way that was medically possible."

He paused as if he was giving the situation much thought and then said, "I could have you bring her to the hospital for a CT scan of her lungs to confirm my suspicions, but there is no use. I am going to treat her aggressively with pain medicine. We will keep her as calm and pain-free as possible."

"She is the strongest woman I have ever known to face death the way she is doing," Sadie said while walking him toward the door.

"You are a strong woman, as well. You are acting bravely, knowing that you are losing your friend. I think you and her are both made from the same mold. I know she is friends with the others, but it appears you and her have some kind of special bond."

Sadie thought for a moment and admitted, "I guess you are right. We do have a special bond of friendship."

George reached for Sadie's hand and gently held it firmly in his.

He softly spoke, "It is going to be very hard the next few days. Please don't hesitate to call me at any time, night or day."

Without pulling her hand away, Sadie said, "Thank you, George. That makes me feel better."

He smiled, turned, and walked out the door. Sadie followed behind him and watched as he got into his car.

He looked toward her, smiled, and gave her a quick wave goodbye. She turned and walked slowly back inside. She suddenly felt exhausted and alone.

Walking toward Gracie's bedroom door, she took a glance inside. Gracie was asleep and appeared to be pain-free at this time.

She went to her bedroom and lay across her bed. She closed her eyes, and sleep came quickly to her exhausted body.

Sadie woke to voices speaking softly from another part of the house. She jumped swiftly from the bed and raced to Gracie's room, making sure she didn't need anything. She opened the door slightly and looked inside. Gracie was still asleep.

She once again heard the whispers and realized they were coming from the living room. The closer she walked toward the room, she realized it was Tilly and the others talking.

"Am I the only voice of wisdom in this room?" Tilly raged, raising her voice.

"Hush, Tilly. Lower your tone, or you are going to wake Gracie. What is going on?" Sadie questioned.

"The same thing we have been discussing behind your back for days, Sadie. We were talking about Gracie's request that we help her die. Tilly just got a little out of sorts," Stella said.

Tilly started to say something, but Sadie interrupted, "Please don't bring this up again. Now, since everyone is here, I need to tell you something."

All eyes went to Sadie, and the girls became silent.

"I am sure that I won't be telling you something right now that hasn't entered your minds, but Gracie probably hasn't but a few days left. After George checked her this morning, he suspects the cancer has entered her lungs. She wants to stay here as long as possible. I assured her that it was all right. We, as a group, can handle this together. It will be hard to watch a friend slowly die. Now, if one of you doesn't feel like you can do this, then I ask you to be honest and admit it. I can completely understand it."

Hannah walked toward Sadie, looked around the room at the others, and said, "I want to speak for everyone. We are all in this together. We will each make Gracie's last days as peaceful and happy as we can."

Stella spoke up, "That's right. You just tell us what to do, and we will do it."

JoBeth and Tilly both nodded their heads in agreement.

"I knew you all would feel this way, but I had to make sure." Sadie continued, "Someone should be coming over with things we will need for Gracie. I will explain as time goes on what we will need to do."

Sadie walked toward the couch and sat down. She couldn't help but notice Stella holding on to a large envelope.

Stella held it in the air and said, "Yes, here it is. All the proof I will need to take Trace to the cleaners. I'm taking Gracie's advice and not approaching him about it right now. Gracie took some interesting pictures. The one she took with them on the balcony is a winner. You can almost see the guilt on his face."

Stella took the package, tossed it on the coffee table, and stated, "If anyone wants to look at them, they will be right here."

"Look what else we have," Tilly said as she handed each a picture placed in a silver frame.

"Oh my goodness, just look at us," Hannah said, beaming. "This is precious to me. What a special thing Gracie has done."

Sadie held the frame carefully. There they were, the six of them sitting side by side on the fishing pier. It had seemed so long ago, and it had only been days.

"When did Gracie have time to do all this?" Tilly questioned.

"We will never find out because we aren't going to question her about anything that we don't understand," JoBeth said, looking directly at Tilly.

"I'm not even thinking about asking her, thank you," Tilly blurted, sternly directing her statement right back to JoBeth.

"Hush, girls. We don't need to argue about these. Somehow she got them developed and ready to give to us, and that is a very special accomplishment," Sadie said tenderly.

Stella turned to the window, looked out, and said, "I thought I heard someone pull up. It's a van. Sadie, it must be someone with the things we will need for Gracie."

Tilly went to the door and opened it wide as two men quickly gathered everything and brought it inside.

Sadie was glad to see that George had sent over a portable oxygen tank, a wheelchair, and a small brown package. She knew this held the medication that would help relieve some of Gracie's pain.

Sadie signed for the equipment, and the men were gone as fast as they had arrived.

Looking at the wheelchair, Tilly said, "I sure hope she is going to be able to use this. She looked so frail this morning that I truly have my doubts."

Sadie didn't comment, but she felt the same way.

They each shared the responsibility of putting everything where it belonged. Sadie reached for the brown package and tucked it under her arm. She then went into the living room and got the picture she knew Gracie had made for herself.

She tiptoed into Gracie's bedroom and placed the picture frame on the bedside table.

"No need to tiptoe around, Sadie. I wasn't asleep," Gracie whispered.

Sadie reached for the frame, held it close to Gracie, and said, "Just look at the six of us. We are six extremely fine-looking women, aren't we?"

Gracie nodded.

"That was so sweet of you to do this for all of us, Gracie."

Sadie turned to place it back on the nightstand when she saw a blood-stained tissue in the trashcan.

She bent over, looked carefully inside, and calmly asked, "Gracie, how long have you been coughing up blood?"

Without hesitation, Gracie admitted, "Actually, it started while we were at the beach, but I don't want to talk about it. I want to know what you think about George."

Sadie reached for clean tissues and placed them in the trashcan covering the blood-stained ones. There wasn't any need for the others to know about this right now.

She pulled a chair as close as she could to the bed and sat down. Gracie looked her straight in the eyes and once again asked the same question.

"Oh, dear," Sadie sighed. "I see you aren't going to let this go until I give you some kind of answer."

Gracie smiled, "You know me much too well."

Sadie giggled and said, "Oh, do I? I wonder sometimes. Anyway, I will answer your question about George. I think he is a charming man that is very fond of you."

Gracie placed her hand firmly on her stomach and said, "Only as a friend, sweetie. He would make a very nice companion for you. You do know that, don't you? You are so busy taking care of everyone that you leave yourself out. You need someone. It wouldn't be betraying Mitchell. He would want you to be happy."

"Gracie, don't try to play matchmaker, and don't pretend you aren't in pain."

Sadie calmly rose from the chair and went to the package that she had placed on the dresser. She opened it, removing several needles and the pain medicine that George had promised he would send. She placed everything in the top drawer and walked toward Gracie with a prepared needle.

Gracie reached for Sadie's hand and said, "Can you ask the others to come here? I would love to hear about their day as I am falling asleep. I know what this shot will do to me within minutes of it entering my system. It does help Sadie, and I am thankful for that, but I would like to hear my friend's voices, their laughter, and all the silliness we have enjoyed all these years."

Sadie went to the door and, as cheerfully as she could, announced, "Girls, get yourself in here. Gracie wants to know what you crazy women have been doing today."

They each came rushing in, grabbed a chair, and pulled them as close to the bed as they could.

Tilly was the first to speak, "Gracie, I went to therapy with JoBeth today. I wanted to attend the session, but everyone agreed that I was not allowed inside. I can't understand why. I don't have the slightest clue why they wouldn't let me have therapy with them."

JoBeth laughed and said, "It's because you need to be in a type of therapy of another kind."

"What do you mean by that? Gracie, tell her not to talk to me like that," Tilly stated, acting as if she was upset.

Gracie smiled, turned to Sadie, and said, "You can give me the medication now. This is what I have waited for all day. I needed a good laugh with my friends."

She paused and then softly whispered, "Stella, tell me about your day."

Sadie carefully wiped Gracie's arm with the alcohol swab and then gave her the shot. She had given thousands in her career, but somehow this was different. This was her lifetime friend.

Stella took a deep breath and began, "Well, Gracie, I got the pictures you had waiting for me at your house. Those pictures are everything I need to make Trace look like the true dog he is. Oh, by the way, I called him around lunchtime and told him I would be here for a few days. I was charming. You would have been very proud of me, Gracie. I acted as if everything was just fine between us."

Gracie smiled and closed her eyes. The girls kept talking as if she could hear everything. They knew the pain medicine was working, but they continued as if Gracie heard every word they said.

JoBeth bit her bottom lip to keep from crying and said, "Doctor Roberts looked very nice today in his black suit and red pinstriped tie. Stella would have really had a fit over him today. He wants me to come to therapy twice a week. Maybe she can go with me the next time and flirt with him like she did the first time she saw him."

For the next twenty minutes or so, the girls continued to talk in their Southern lady charm. It was all they could do to keep from crying. However, they were determined to make it feel like they were still around the breakfast table, sipping their coffee, making small talk, and enjoying one another's company as they had done for many years. This was what Gracie wanted from them tonight, and they were determined to do just what she requested.

The room went silent, and everyone looked at Sadie. She motioned for them to leave the room. She gave Gracie one more quick look and then followed the others.

They each walked directly to the kitchen and sat around the table. They were mentally exhausted.

Tilly finally spoke, "For a few minutes, it was like old times with us all chatting together. I hope Gracie felt that as well."

"I think she did, Tilly. I truly think she did," Sadie said, sounding exhausted.

"Ladies, it's getting late. I think you all could use some rest. Sadie, I'm going to sit with Gracie tonight. I will come and get you if she wakes to need something for pain. I will put some pillows and quilts on the floor close to her bed. I promise I will wake if she even turns over. We can't give shots, Sadie, but we can give you some rest by taking turns sitting with her," Hannah said, sounding in control of the situation.

"Thank you, Hannah. That is sweet of you," Sadie said, smiling.

"We can't make her better, but we can show her just how much we love her every single day she has left," Tilly said, fighting hard not to cry.

"That's right," Stella added.

JoBeth touched Sadie on the hand and said, "Get to bed. We will do whatever needs to be done in this kitchen. We will also make sure that Tilly keeps her talking down to a whisper."

Sadie slowly rose from the chair and said, "I am tired, ladies. I think I will go on to bed."

She walked from the room but suddenly stuck her head back around the corner of the door and said, "Oh, have I told you silly group of women lately that I love you all very much?"

They smiled but couldn't say anything. Their sadness was much more than they could handle right now. They tidied the kitchen without saying a word, hugged each other, and followed Sadie's lead of going to bed.

Hannah was the only one that remained in the kitchen. She reached for the coffee pot and gave it a good shake making sure there was enough coffee for her if she needed it during the night. She was nervous, but she would not let the others know.

She walked toward the hall closet, opened the door, grabbing for pillows and quilts. She quietly entered Gracie's room and placed them on the floor close to her bed. She lay down and faced Gracie, watching her breathe slowly. Each time Gracie's chest would rise, Hannah would feel a sigh of relief, knowing she was still alive. She was still holding on to life.

Hannah silently prayed, "God, thank you for giving me this dear friend all these years."

A sense of relief came over Hannah. She closed her eyes and knew everything was going to be all right tonight. She could sleep, knowing God was watching over them all.

The next few weeks were very hard on the women. They were upbeat while in the presence of Gracie but were engulfed entirely in an emotional fog when they left her bedside. Each passing day it was evident that Gracie was getting much worse. She had to depend on the oxygen tank the majority of the day, and pain medicine was needed much more now.

George would make daily visits, but there wasn't any more he could do. He continued to encourage her to go to the hospital, but she refused. Sadie would smile, letting him know it was all right, and they would continue to take care of her at home. There would come a time when she would have to give in and go, but that would be Gracie's decision.

The day had started out in the usual way. Tilly had given Gracie a sponge bath and then encouraged her to eat.

"Gracie, are you sure you can't eat just a bite of this oatmeal? You are beginning to look like a stick woman." Tilly said in her usual manner.

Gracie smiled and stated, "No, Tilly, but I will try later on."

She paused, attempted to talk, and finally said, "Tilly, you still treat me like the others. If you feel sorry for me, you sure do hide it well."

"You told me at the beach that you wanted to be treated without pity. So, I guess I can be as rude to you as I do them. I really don't mean some of the things I say. Do you know that?"

Gracie nodded.

"I sure hope the others know that, also. Sometimes the words pop out of my mouth before they run through my brain. I guess I don't have the gift of sorting through them before it is too late."

Gracie reached for Tilly's hand and pleaded, "Don't change, Tilly. That is what makes you so unique. I have always known not to ask you anything unless I wanted the complete truth. Whether it hurts or not, you are going to be honest and tell it like it is."

"Well, I don't mean to change the subject, but do you think you feel like sitting in the wheelchair for a while? I could roll you out into the living room or maybe sit on the deck for a while. It is such a pretty day, and we won't be seeing many more of them."

"No, I guess you are right about that," Gracie said.

"I didn't mean it like that, Gracie. I meant...."

"Tilly, I knew exactly what you meant. Summer will soon be over, and the days are going to turn chilly. We need to enjoy every bit of the warm sun we have left."

"Yes, that is exactly what I meant. Gosh, for a minute, I thought I had put my foot in my mouth once again."

"I would like to try the wheelchair for a while, Tilly."

Tilly took one arm and placed it softly under Gracie's legs and the other around her back. It didn't take any effort to lift her from the bed and into the wheelchair.

"I am certainly not a muscle woman. Gracie, you are skin and bones. I've given this remark some thought before I say it. You are going to blow away if you don't try to start eating."

Gracie took her finger and made a motion for Tilly to come closer. Tilly bent down and placed her ear right at Gracie's mouth.

Gracie giggled slightly and teased, "I'm watching my figure."

Tilly jumped back and laughed. "I give up, Gracie. I won't push you to eat anymore."

Tilly placed the portable oxygen tank on the back of the wheelchair and said, "Gracie, your oxygen is right here anytime you need it."

Gracie gave her a thumb's up in her usual manner when she wasn't quite able to answer.

She rolled Gracie into the living room and then hollered, "Everyone come here. Look who is paying us a visit."

JoBeth came from the kitchen, followed by Stella.

"It is great seeing you in another room besides that bedroom," Stella remarked while giving Gracie a kiss on the forehead.

"Hannah and Sadie will be surprised when they come back in. They went to get the mail from the mailbox."

Tilly quickly blurted, "Well, Sadie went to the mailbox, but Hannah goes outside to call her friend, Bruce. Bruce this, and Bruce that, is all I hear from her lately."

"Sounds like you might be a little jealous," Sadie said, walking into the room. "Gracie, I am so glad you are feeling well enough that we can all gather in here instead of that bedroom. It's getting a little dreary in there. What do you think about us painting it a brighter color?"

Gracie tried to reach for her oxygen tank and slowly said, "No need to repaint right now, Sadie. I am getting rather used to the room."

Tilly raced to help Gracie with her oxygen.

Hannah entered the room, placing her cell phone in her pocket. She glanced at Gracie and said, "Good for you, honey. Does this mean you feel stronger today?"

Gracie nodded. The others knew she wasn't telling the truth. They knew she was doing this for them.

Sadie waved an envelope in the air and announced, "Well, since we have all gathered in our little group, it is time for me to show you what came in the mail."

Everyone looked at Sadie with a questioning look on their face, including Gracie.

Sadie turned the envelope around so everyone could see it and said, "Look, it is from the man from the pier."

"Open it," Tilly urged excitedly.

Sadie opened the letter and then read the note inside.

Dear ladies,

It was my pleasure to take a picture of the most

beautiful six women I have ever met in my life. I wish we could

have shared more time together, enjoying the warm beach

weather while sitting on the pier. Thank you for sending me a

picture. It has a special place on the top of my

fireplace mantel.

I hope our paths will once again cross in the future.

Sincerely,
Russell

"He sounds like one smooth talker," Tilly blurted out.

"Actually, Tilly, he sounds like a very nice Southern gentleman just letting us know how pleased he was to receive the picture," Hannah said in an attempt to take up for the man.

Stella added her thoughts, "Well, it might be that you both are just a little bit correct about this. He does sound a bit of a player, but he is calling us the most beautiful women he has ever met. I put it this way, he must be a brilliant man."

"Well, speaking of players. What did your husband say when you went home last night for the first time in a couple of weeks?" Tilly asked, expecting an answer.

Stella pulled her chair closer to Gracie and said, "I walked in, and he was sitting in his big leather chair reading his newspaper. I went right over to him, grabbed the paper from his hands, and gave it a sling. Then I popped my butt right on his lap."

She giggled but continued, "Gracie, you should have seen the look on his face. I didn't give him time to remark before I planted a great big kiss on his two-timing lips. Again, he didn't say a word. Then I told him that I was home for the night, but I was going to take a quick bath and jump in bed. I had an awful headache and intended to go right to sleep. Then I jumped from his lap and went upstairs. He came to bed about twenty minutes later, but I pretended I was asleep."

Hannah questioned, "What did he say to you this morning?"

"Not a thing because I didn't give him a chance. I was up and gone before he even thought about getting ready for work. I left him a note beside his briefcase, telling him I was spending a night with Sadie again. I also told him if he needs me to call. Now, has anyone heard the phone ringing off the hook?"

Gracie reached her hand toward Stella's, gave it a soft pat, and said, "I am so proud of you. This, for right now, is the way you should handle it. Give it time. Trust me. You will know when to bring it all out. Just trust me."

Stella leaned toward Gracie and whispered, "I trust you, and I will do exactly what you have told me to do."

Almost breathless, Gracie said, "It would be so much fun to roast wieners again the way we did at the beach."

"Do you think you are up to making a trip back to the beach?' Tilly said, once again, not thinking about what she was asking.

Gracie knew this and smiled, "Sometimes, Tilly, we have to wait and put our dreams on hold for a while."

"That doesn't mean we can't roast wieners over the outside grill. If that is what you want, that is exactly what we are going to do for lunch. We will just all pretend we are at the beach. We might even throw a beach ball around in the backyard," Sadie said, trying to sound cheerful.

"Yes, and we could take off our shoes and pretend we are walking in the sand," Hannah chimed in.

"Just please, no truth or dare games permitted at this picnic," Tilly said.

"That's right, Tilly. No games of truth or dare at our parties anymore," Gracie said, placing her head against the handle of the wheelchair.

Sadie saw the reaction on Gracie's face and knew it was time to get her back in bed with more pain medicine. She made a motion for the girls, and they flew into action.

"Well, Gracie, you need to rest some before we get this party started. So, here we go," Tilly said as she rolled Gracie back to her room.

Hannah followed right behind her, and together they carefully placed her back to bed. Gracie smiled weakly but didn't say a word. Sadie immediately came in and gave her a shot.

Gracie made the motion of saying thank you with her lips, but not a sound came out. Instead, she closed her eyes and fell asleep instantly.

They left the room and went straight to the kitchen.

Tilly was the first to ask, "Sadie, are we going through the act of a party? She is not going to be able to do it. I don't understand what is going on."

Sadie sighed, "Oh, Tilly, I'm not sure I understand either. But trust me, if Gracie wants another party at the beach, we are going to give her as close to one as we can."

Again, Tilly asked, "What is your point, exactly?"

"Exactly, what she said," Hannah spoke up. "We are going to roll Gracie out on the deck, pretend that grill is a big blazing campfire, and then we are going to roast wieners."

"Yes," Stella spoke up. "We might have alligator tears running down our cheeks when we do this, but we won't let Gracie see them."

"That is right," JoBeth said as she grabbed for a paper towel to wipe her eyes. "I'm leaving now to go to the store to buy stupid beach balls and a bag of sand. This is Gracie's way of telling us goodbye, and I, for one, am going to help her do it."

JoBeth turned and rushed out the door.

Tilly spoke up, "Well, I take it she didn't want anyone of us going with her."

Sadie shook her head and said, "Hush, Tilly, and get the wieners out of the freezer. JoBeth needs this time to cry. That is what each one of us has been doing behind closed doors. I know it, and you know it as well."

Tilly turned and went straight for the freezer. Yes, she had cried into her pillow many nights. The thoughts of losing Gracie had not gotten any better with all the tears she had shed. Sometimes acting the ruff and tuff one of the group just didn't work no matter how hard she tried.

JoBeth returned from the store with several beach balls and a large bag of sand. With the help of the others, the balls were soon inflated and placed around the deck. Stella put some of the sand in a large bowl, and the rest she spread across the yard, making it resemble as close to sand dunes as she could.

Then everyone but Sadie got busy in the kitchen preparing food that was supposed to be for a beach party.

Sadie tiptoed into Gracie's room and stood by her bed.

"I'm still here, Sadie, but barely. You told me several weeks ago to be honest with you, and that is what I am doing now."

"Gracie, we are going to have our little party in here. I don't want you using any more of your energy than what is needed right now."

"No, I can do this," Gracie whispered, almost breathless. "It's important that I do this."

Sadie shook her head but went directly to the corner where they kept the wheelchair and pulled it close to the bed. She wrapped her arms around Gracie and lifted her into the chair.

Without warning, Gracie coughed, and blood covered her gown.

Sadie reached for a tissue and wiped Gracie's mouth. Then, she went to the top drawer, pulled out another gown, carefully removed the soiled one, and redressed Gracie.

"I know, Gracie, you want this to be my and your secret for right now."

"Yes, honey, but soon, very soon, there will be no more secrets left in me. You and the others will know everything. I promise this is the last secret I ask you to keep from them. They aren't as strong as you and I, my dear Sadie Sue."

Sadie reached for the box of tissues and placed them on Gracie's lap. Then, she pushed the wheelchair out of the room, bites down on her lip to keep from crying, and agreed, "That's right. They aren't as strong as me, and you are."

The others were already on the deck. They were putting all their efforts into making this a party Gracie would enjoy. Tilly placed a tape of beach music in the CD player and started dancing around in an attempt to make Gracie smile.

Stella brought the bowl of sand and kneeled beside Gracie. She gently removed her bedroom shoes and lifted Gracie's feet into the bowl.

"Wiggly your toes and close your eyes, and you will be able to pretend we are all sitting in the sand as we did weeks ago," Stella said, without crying.

Gracie closed her eyes and made every effort she could to wiggle her toes in the bowl of sand.

"It's working, honey. I am at the beach with my dear friends. I can see the waves beating against the pier."

"Pretend you can smell the ocean breeze and maybe even taste that cotton candy we bought from the pier," Stella said, continuing to paint a picture in Gracie's mind.

Gracie smiled through her tears as she talked to the girls, "I think this might be the best party we have ever had. I am so proud to say that our little Southern Belle Breakfast Club will live on and on."

"We haven't even brought out the food yet, and she is still treating this like a party," Tilly whispered to Sadie.

"There is no need to bring the food out. Just let her sit silently for as long as she wants. This is her party, and we will play by her rules," Sadie said firmly.

Gracie opened her eyes and stared straight at her friends and said, "Ladies, you know what I am about to say, and I promised I wouldn't ask again, but please start listening with your hearts. I'm tired. I am so very tired."

Tilly edged herself to the wheelchair, bent down, and began to speak to Gracie. She couldn't say a word. Blood was running from Gracie's mouth and down her chin. Tilly grabbed the tissues and began to wipe the blood away. The others rushed to her side.

Sadie reached for Gracie's hand, held it firmly, and said, "Are you ready to go to the hospital now, honey?"

With every ounce of her remaining strength Gracie said, "Yes, I am ready to go now."

Sadie calmly turned to the others and said, "Tilly, call 911 and tell them to hurry."

She pulled the piece of paper she had kept in her pocket all these weeks, handed it to Stella, and said, "Go to your cell phone and call George. Tell him we will be at the hospital as soon as the ambulance gets us there. The rest of you help me get Gracie cleaned up. She is not going to the hospital looking like this."

Nervously, they each did as Sadie had told them.

She carefully wheeled Gracie back into the house and said, "Gracie, it is going to be all right. We will take care of everything."

Sadie was unsure if Gracie understood her at this point.

In less than two hours, the girls were in Gracie's hospital room, pacing the floor.

Gracie seemed restless, slowly moving around in the bed. Sadie knew that this meant she was in deep pain.

George walked into the room and said, "I have ordered her the strongest pain medicine there is. The nurse should be here any minute with it."

He pulled Sadie aside and whispered, "How are you holding up?"

"Well, I will put it like this. I know my best friend is dying, and she is in more pain than we can ever imagine, and there is nothing I can do for her. That is ripping my heart out. I could scream to the top of my lungs, but nothing will change. I am trying to be strong for the others, but I am almost at my limit of bravery. You asked me, and so you got it. So, I guess you might say I'm not holding up very well, but I will be all right," Sadie said, with tears running down her cheek.

He pulled out a handkerchief and dabbed her tears. Then he placed the handkerchief in her hand.

He wrapped his hands around hers and said, "I wouldn't consider you as being her best friend if you felt any other way. I have got to go now and check on the patient down the hall, but I will be back as often as I can."

As he opened the door to go out, the nurse immediately walked in. She carried a needle with what Sadie hoped would stop the pain completely for Gracie.

As the nurse inserted the needle into Gracie's arm, she moaned.

Sadie rushed to her bedside, reached for her hand, and said, "We're right here, honey. We aren't going anywhere."

Sadie looked sharply at the nurse and said, "Why didn't you put that in her I V line? Then you wouldn't have to stick her again."

The nurse tried to make an excuse, but Tilly spoke up.

"Don't try to fool an old fool," Tilly said and pointed to Sadie. "She is a nurse, and she knows exactly what she is talking about. So, don't try pulling anything over her eyes."

The young nurse shrugged her shoulders and stomped out of the room.

"Tilly, I wish you had worded that another way. I don't feel like an old fool," Sadie said, with a slight smirk on her face.

"Sorry, poor choice of words."

Tilly walked over to Gracie's bed, leaned down, and whispered something in her ear.

Walking back to Sadie, she said, "All right, I know she didn't hear me, but I told her I had put my foot in my mouth again. A little something between Gracie and me."

The door opened once again. An orderly came in, carrying a large number of blankets and pillows. Behind him, another man came pushing in a large recliner.

"I will be bringing in each of you ladies one just as soon as I find enough. That is orders from Doctor Duncan," he said.

Within ten minutes, each one had a recliner of their own.

"I guess it pays to know people at the top," Hannah remarked while placing her pillow and blanket in the recliner.

Gracie turned to one side and opened her eyes. She looked directly at her friends and smiled but said nothing.

Tilly whispered to the others, "She still knows us."

Sadie walked toward Gracie's bedside, touched her softly on her foot, and said, "Yes, she still knows us."

She walked back toward the others and said, "You need to get some rest. You will need it."

"Is she, is she dying now, Sadie?" JoBeth whispered.

Sadie nodded and talked low, "Dying for some comes in stages. I was hoping that death would come quickly for Gracie, but it doesn't appear it is. Don't get scared when you see her breathing change. That is a part of dying, girls.

Keep remembering, when she finally takes the last breath here, she will take another one in Heaven. She will no longer be in pain that she has had to endure all these months."

"Is she going to be in any more pain now," Tilly questioned.

"I hope not, Tilly," Sadie answered.

Hannah said, "Ladies, Sadie said to try to get some rest. So, find a recliner and lay down."

Sadie smiled at the others and pulled a chair close to Gracie's bed.

Several hours passed, and Sadie was still wide awake, watching Gracie breathe. It had seemed that she had stopped breathing several times, but then she would take a long breath and start her regular breathing once again.

Sadie rocked back and forth in her chair with a blanket pulled around her shoulders, fighting sleep.

Suddenly, Gracie cried out in pain. They jumped from their recliners and rushed to her bedside.

"What is going on, Sadie?" Tilly questioned.

"She's in pain, a great deal of pain. I have pressed the call button, so a nurse should be here any minute.'

The door opened and in walked the nurse.

"What seems to be the problem?" She asked casually.

Tilly wasn't about to hold back, "What do you mean by that remark? She is dying and in a lot of pain. She needs her pain medicine, and she needs it now."

"Well, I looked on her chart before I came in, and she isn't due for any right now."

"What difference does it matter now how much you give her and when you give it. She is dying and in pain," Tilly screamed out.

Gracie moaned louder.

Tilly continued, and the others weren't about to stop her, "We aren't asking for a kidney here."

The nurse turned around and headed out the door with Tilly right behind her.

Screaming at the top of her lungs, Tilly said, "Give her more morphine. Do you hear me? Right now! Just make her comfortable, for goodness sake; just make her stop crying out in pain."

Tilly stomped her foot, infuriated that the nurse didn't act as if she cared. She came back into the room with tears running down her cheek.

Sadie looked down at Gracie. Her breathing once again appeared to stop for what seemed to be minutes. Then she took a deep breath and once again moaned in deep pain.

She opened her eyes and stared straight at Sadie.

"Does she know us now, Sadie?" Stella asked.

"No, honey. She is past knowing us at this point." Sadie said, hoping that would give them some comfort.

Stella took a wet cloth and wiped the sweat forming in big drops on Gracie's forehead.

Tilly said while pacing back and forth in the room, "When is she going to bring the morphine?"

Sadie calmly said, "Tilly, shut the door and stand against it."

Tilly does what Sadie says without questioning her. The others walk slowly toward Gracie's bed. Hannah reaches for Gracie's thin hand and places it in hers. JoBeth goes to the footboard and lays her hands on Gracie's feet. Stella reached for a pillow and handed it to Sadie. Sadie slowly bends near Gracie with the pillow in her hand.

Gracie was pronounced dead at 2:45 a.m.

The girls stood in the hospital waiting room as if they were waiting for Gracie to walk out the door to meet them.

Sadie suddenly remembered the envelope that Gracie had given her that held the mysterious telephone number. She grabbed for her pocketbook and reached inside. Her fingers curled around the envelope. She gave it a tight squeeze as if hesitating to pull it out. She finally closed her eyes tightly and removed the envelope. Sadie had held it several times since placing it there, but she had honored Gracie's wishes. She had not looked inside its contents. She realized it was only a telephone number, but removing it now meant she would have to repeat those final three words she didn't want to say aloud.

"Stella, can I use your cell phone for a minute. There is something we almost forgot to do." Sadie said while reaching for the phone and opening the envelope at the same time.

She pulled out a small piece of paper with a single telephone number scribbled on it. She slowly pressed the numbers on the cell phone.

She held the phone to her ear and finally heard a strange voice say, "Hello."

Sadie paused for a few seconds. Then with tears running down, her cheek said, "It is over."

She listened as the stranger spoke, "I will call you when the arrangements have been made. Thank you." Then he was gone without saying another word.

Sadie slowly turned to the others and said, "We go home now."

Chapter 16

Gracie's Goodbye

Dear friends, don't shed tears since I have gone away
For I'm with you in your heart and thoughts every day
Think of me when you walk on the beach barefoot in the sand
Think of me and the long walks we took hand in hand
Think of me when you see the blooming of a flower
Think of me during a spring shower
Think of me when you walk through the morning dew
Think of me when the day is through
So cherish my memory now that I am gone
Let my life through you live on
and on
and on

They were finally back at Sadie's, sitting around the table with coffee cups in hand. It felt funny to glance toward the empty chair that Gracie always occupied.

The grandfather clock that stood in the corner of the hallway chimed six times.

"We need to try to get at least a couple of hours of sleep. I don't know when the mystery man will call us to let us know what the arrangements are going to be. Still, we need to have some rest behind us so we can be prepared for that," Sadie said slowly.

"This all seems like a nightmare," said Stella.

"I have the strangest feeling that it's not going to get any better for a while," Hannah remarked.

"Why do you say that?" Tilly asked.

Hannah thought for a moment and said, "I don't know. I just have a strange feeling that something is going to happen."

JoBeth quickly spoke up, "Hannah, it's just that you are tired. We all are. We need to listen to Sadie and get some shut-eye."

They stood and started to walk to their bedroom when suddenly the phone rang.

"Who in the world could that be at this time of the morning?" Tilly questioned.

"I don't know, but I am sure Sadie will find out," Hannah said as if she was once again teasing Tilly.

Sadie reached for the phone and said, "Hello."

They stood in silence to hear her conservation, but Sadie just stood there without saying a word. It was evident that the party on the other end was doing all the talking.

Finally, she looked puzzled and said, "All right. Thank you." She placed the receiver back on the hook and turned toward them.

Shaking her head, she said, "You will never guess what that was about in a million years."

"It had to be about Gracie," Stella announced.

"Well, you are right about that part. That was the mystery man on the other end. He once again did not announce his name. The only reason he called is to tell us the arrangements are complete. He said that he was given strict instructions to call us first."

She took a deep breath, shook her head, and said, "He didn't say who told him that."

"Well, what time is the funeral tomorrow?" Tilly asked.

"What do you mean tomorrow? Graveside service is today at two o'clock at Lakeland Memorial Park. There is no visitation, no meeting at someone's home, just a quick graveside service." Sadie said, still in disbelief.

Stella, fighting back exhaustion, yawned and said, "Really, none of this should surprise us. Gracie said she didn't have any family. We were her family. We appeared to be her only friends except for George. He never was in the picture, or at least not when we were around. Face it, girls, we spent time together almost every day of the week. She didn't have anyone else."

"Oh yes, and by the way, girls, there is something else I need to tell you," Sadie said.

"What else is left to surprise us with, Sadie?" Tilly questioned.

"Only the fact that a driver will pick us up today at one o'clock right here and take us to the graveside and where ever we would like to go afterward."

Hannah nervously asked, "Where in the world would we want to go after Gracie's service? Sadie, what is going on? Should we get into a strange car with someone we don't know and then let him take us who knows where? This is making me nervous."

"I'm not nervous. It's depressing me," Tilly ranted.

"Look at it as another adventure that we are on. Except for this time, Gracie isn't with us. We will figure it all out in time. Now, isn't that what Gracie always said, Sadie?" Stella said with tears in her eyes.

Sadie nodded, "That's exactly what she said, and somehow I feel like Gracie is still with us in all this."

"Is she sort of still playing the truth or dare game with us?" Tilly questioned.

"Hush, Tilly, that makes cold chills go up and down my spine," Hannah said, once again sounding very nervous.

"Both of you hush and listen to me. We need to get our act together. Before you know, the time will be for us to wait for that driver to pick us up. Now, I, for one, intend on wearing a black dress and maybe even a pillbox hat with a black net veil to the service. I am fixing up fancy for Gracie," Sadie said, smiling.

"Well, I want to fix up fancy, too, but I don't have a black dress," Tilly said sadly.

JoBeth said, "I think we all agree that we want to look good for Gracie. So, I need to run home to see what is in my closet."

Stella reached toward her pocketbook, opened it, and brought out a bright, shiny charge card.

Sounding excited, she said, "Well, you all are getting your wish today. This little card is going to make your wish come true."

"What will Trace say?" JoBeth asked.

"I don't care what he will say. The card is in his name, and he gave it to me years ago. I guess during one of his *feel guilty* times. So we will use it and not feel guilty." Stella said with a wicked laugh.

"I can assure you that Gracie would like your style right now," Sadie said, remembering back on things Gracie would say.

She took a deep breath and continued, "We can't get into the stores until they open. That means we need to be at the mall by nine o'clock and get busy buying. Then it is back here to get ready and wait for our chariot. Why don't we try to get at least a little rest before we start this day? Gracie wouldn't want us to have puffy eyes and drooping eyelids at her service."

They all nodded and headed in different directions to take a short nap.

Sadie yelled out to them, "I don't want to hear any crying when you get by yourselves. Remember, Gracie requested there would be no tears shed for her after her death."

She went to her bedroom and lay across the bed.

Whispering to herself, she said, "Gracie, that was another hard request to ask of us!"

Then slowly but surely, tears formed in her eyes, rolled down her cheek and fell on the pillow as they had done so many times before.

Once again, Sadie whispered to herself, "Some promises just aren't meant to keep."

Three hours at a mall and a charge card can make an evil woman out of a usually average, money-saving person.

Tilly walked into Sadie's living room and plopped down in the chair, letting her shopping bags fall to the floor.

"Now, I know what the old saying means to shop till you drop," Tilly said in a loud voice so the others could hear her.

"I didn't even take time to go to the restroom while we were there," Hannah said as she placed her packages on the chair and raced from the room.

Sadie carefully carried a round-shaped box along with her other packages. Then, she sat down on the couch, opened the lid, and pulled out a hat, "When I made a comment about the pillbox hat, I never dreamed they were still made. It is beautiful."

"The trick is to go to the right store. Not just any retail store has things like that," Stella commented.

"Yes, and the price you paid for it shows just that," Hannah said, coming back from the bathroom.

"I didn't pay for all our goodies; dear Trace did. He was so happy to be able to brighten our day. He even made plans at the florist that two dozen long stem red roses will be placed on Gracie's grave every month for the next year. Don't you think that was sweet of him?" Stella said with a devilish look on her face.

Hannah whispered to Tilly, "Did he really do that? He must be changing."

Tilly looked at Hannah and said, "Silly, he didn't do that. Stella called the florist and had it arranged in his name."

"That's right, and I don't know what I am going to come up with next for that nice husband of mine to do."

"Well, while you are giving that some thought, we have got to get dressed. We don't have but an hour before our driver comes, and we need to be waiting on my front porch when he does. We are not going to be late for Gracie's service."

Tilly nervously laughed and said, "Gracie was late for everything. Do you think she will be late for her own funeral?"

"Tilly, she would have expected that comment from you and loved every word of it," teased JoBeth

"I know. That is why I said it," Tilly said while leaving the room in a rush. She was determined for the others not to see her tears.

Each one grabbed their packages of dresses and hats and left the room determined to be ready and waiting in less than an hour.

Tilly stood on the front porch and looked straight toward the highway.

"Well, here we are, but where is our ride?" She impatiently asked.

"Your guess is as good as mine. We're just going to make sure we follow the instructions that were given," Sadie said, sounding impatient as well.

Hannah took a few steps off the porch, stretched her arm out, with palm up, and said, "Oh no, it's starting to rain."

Stella walked out on the porch with a large bag in her hand, "I couldn't sleep this morning, so I turned the television on and heard the weather forecast. We might get heavy rain, and Trace thought we might need these black umbrellas at the service."

Reaching in the bag for an umbrella, Tilly remarked, "There he goes again, being super nice. What a man! What a man!"

"I know he just never quits surprising me," Stella said smugly.

"Well, bless that mystery person's heart. Look pulling in your driveway, Sadie," Tilly announced excitedly.

Sadie couldn't believe her eyes. A long, black limousine had pulled into her driveway. A man dressed in black politely got out, walked toward the front porch, took off his hat, placed it at his waist, and said, "My name is Cooper, and I am your driver for the day. Are you ladies ready?"

JoBeth opened the door, walked out to stand with the others, and whispered to Sadie, "What do we do?"

Tilly was the first to respond. She took the porch steps two at a time, turned around to the others, and said, "We let this nice gentleman take us for a ride."

He calmly went around to the side of the limousine and opened the door while each one slowly and gracefully took their seat.

"Our first destination, ladies, is to Miss Gracie's service at Lakeland Memorial Park. If you need anything, please do not hesitate to ask." He shut the door, walked around the other side of the limousine, and got in the driver's seat.

He slowly pulled out of the driveway, with each one looking wide-eyed at the other.

Tilly pointed toward her window and said, "Look at your neighbor, staring. We can see him, but he can't see us with these tinted windows."

Then Tilly stuck her tongue out as far as she could at the staring neighbor.

"Gosh, that felt good. I haven't done anything like that since I was a child."

Stella shook her head and whispered to Sadie, "Our nutty friend is a child."

Tilly quickly said, "I heard that, but I don't care. Gracie said she liked me just the way I am, so there!"

Suddenly, it seemed like the rain clouds opened up and dropped all the water that was inside of them right on top of the limousine. The driver immediately switched on his windshield wipers.

His voice came over the speaker, "I am sorry that it will be raining on Miss Gracie's service. I will drive you as close to the gravesite as possible."

Sadie politely said, "Thank you, Cooper."

"How did he do that?" Tilly questioned.

Stella pointed to a little box, "Tilly, that is a speaker. He has the controls right in front of him to speak to us. It's similar to a baby monitor. That is the simplest way I can explain it."

"Oh yes, I've seen it in movies," Tilly quickly said.

"I think it was sweet of him to say he is sorry that it is raining, but this is the way the day should be," JoBeth said.

"Why do you say that?" Tilly questioned.

JoBeth looked at each one and said, "I remember the first day we met Gracie. She walked into the restaurant like a wet little puppy. She was soaked and had such sad-looking puppy dog eyes. I certainly remember those eyes. It had been pouring down rain, and I couldn't help but think at the time that she must have just stood right in it and let herself get soaked."

"She didn't realize what coming into that restaurant on that day did to make our lives better," Sadie said, remembering back to those long away years.

"That's right. We were blessed with a friendship we will always cherish," said Hannah.

Again Cooper spoke, "Ladies, we have reached our destination. I am attempting to find a place that will be close so you won't get wet."

"Bless his heart. He is just the sweetest little thing," Tilly said and then continued, "Do you think we could ask him in for a cup of coffee when he drives us back to your house?"

"That would be fine with me, but Tilly, I honestly don't know what we are doing from one minute to the next. We have got to just play this by ear," Sadie said, trying to sound as confident about things as she could.

Cooper held the door with an umbrella placed as close to them as he could get.

They each stepped out and gathered in their little group. They looked very distinguished in their black dresses and hats while holding tightly to their black umbrellas.

They each looked at Sadie to see what she was going to do.

"Well, ladies, it doesn't appear to be many people here, so I guess we could walk toward the tent. That will help keep the rain off of us," she said as she headed in that direction.

As they drew closer, they could see the casket covered with dozens of long-stemmed red roses.

"Don't look at me. The order that I put in Trace's name doesn't start until next month," Stella said, surprised as the others.

"Remember, Gracie said she had everything taken care of right down to the flowers on her casket," Hannah remarked.

Tilly giggled and said, "Well, our girl did herself right. I bet that big spread of roses set her back close to a thousand dollars."

Within minutes, several more limousines appeared and parked close to the gravesite. Each limousine held at least six men in black suits. They walked directly toward the gravesite without saying a word to one another.

Tilly whispered as low as she could in Sadie's ear, "Sadie, I am getting nervous again. It looks like the FBI is invading us."

Hannah walked toward Tilly, pinched her on the arm, and said, "Hush, they might hear you. I heard you from where I was standing. Just don't stare at them. Just act normal."

The men made a circle around the tent. They each opened their umbrellas to shield the rain from their faces.

Sadie jumped as she felt someone touch her shoulder. She turned to face George.

"Sorry I am late. I had an emergency operation that I had to take care of before I came."

Sadie smiled and said, "I am glad you were able to be here."

He slowly took his hand and cuffed her elbow. She liked the feel of his touch. She didn't attempt to move.

A man from the group walked close to the casket and started to speak. Sadie found it strange that he didn't introduce himself.

"Miss Gracie wanted her service to be very private and simple. We honor her wishes, as we always have. She wanted the Lord's Prayer spoken by everyone and then the service to be immediately over."

He paused and then began, "Our Father which art in heaven, Hallowed be Thy name. Thy kingdom come. Thy will be done on earth, as it is in heaven ...."

Everyone followed his lead and repeated the words. Sadie said them in her mind, but the words just couldn't form on her lips. All she could think about was losing her best friend and never being able to hear her voice again. Yes, she loved the other girls deeply, but Gracie and she shared a bond that she would never be able to share with the others.

George placed his arm around her waist, gave her a slight squeeze, and whispered, "It's all right to be sad. I know Gracie told you to be strong, but sometimes it's best to let your emotions show."

Sadie laid her head against his shoulder for a brief moment and then moved away quickly. She hadn't meant for this to happen.

George reached into his pocket, pulled out his pager, and whispered, "Sadie, I am so sorry. I am needed back at the hospital. Things aren't going well with my patient, who just went through the operation. I told my nurse to page me immediately if there was a problem."

"It's all right, George. Gracie would have understood."

"Sadie, would it be forward of me to ask you out for a cup of coffee later this week?"

Sadie smiled and whispered back, "Give me a call. I will look forward to hearing from you."

He smiled, turned, and rushed toward his car.

Tilly leaned toward Sadie and said, "That was rude of him to take off running like that."

"The hospital paged him. One of his patients took a turn for the worse," Sadie said, feeling as if she had to explain.

"Oh, well, in that case, it is all right," Tilly remarked as if she had approved his actions.

The man finished the prayer, turned, and headed back to his waiting limousine. The other men followed his lead except for one man, which was heading straight in the direction of the girls.

"What now, Sadie?" Tilly said, once again sounding scared.

"We play it by ear, honey. That is all I know to do," Sadie said, directing her statement to not only Tilly but the others as well.

He walked directly to them, stood for a moment, and said, "Good afternoon. I have been instructed to ask you to do as I say. May I continue, Sadie Sue?"

Sadie knew immediately that Gracie had given this man his orders. She nodded her head, letting him know he could continue.

Suddenly, Cooper appeared and stood right beside the man in black.

"Cooper will take you to your next destination. I can see a look of fear or mistrust on some of your faces. Please know that you are in safe hands."

He paused for a second and then continued, "I give you my condolences. Miss Gracie was a fine woman that will truly be missed."

He turned to Cooper and said, "Cooper will now take you to Parker and Son Law Office. You will have all your questions answered at this time. I wish you, ladies, well."

He turned and walked away, leaving the girls still in a fog of confusion.

Cooper softly said, "Will you please follow me?"

Sadie looked toward the casket and said, "Cooper, can we please have a minute to say our final goodbyes to Gracie?"

He nodded and then stepped aside.

Sadie walked toward the casket with the others right at her heels.

She bent down as if she was talking directly to Gracie and said, "We don't know what in the world is going on, Gracie, but you have got to be at the bottom of all this. I guess this is your famous truth or dare game, and we seem to be taking the dares. We're going to miss you, dear friend. You always kept us guessing just what was behind those beautiful, sad eyes of yours."

"I always liked the mystery part of you, Gracie. You had a style all your own, and you will truly be missed," JoBeth added.

"That is the same way I feel about you, Gracie. You helped me keep my head straight about Trace. I am still following your advice. I will try hard, but I sure wish you were still around telling me what is best for me to do," Stella said, fighting back her tears.

Hannah placed her hand on the casket and said, "Thank you for believing in me the way you did. Bruce always said you were one classy lady. I think so, too."

Tilly stepped up to the casket, looked around at the others, and then finally said, "I know I am only talking to a casket, but the others seem to be doing it. I guess I need to also. Here goes! You made me feel special. Gracie, no matter what dumb things came out of my mouth, you never seem to get upset. Actually, you seem to like the things I would say."

She paused, looked around at the others, and then continued, "Well, I guess that is all I have to say. The others seem to be getting a little impatient with me. You know how they are at times. I love you, Gracie, and remember to kiss Lindsey Grace for me. I know you are holding her right now, just the way you said you would."

Stella touched her on the shoulder and said, "Tilly, you beat all I have ever seen. Here I am getting upset with what you are saying, and then you come back and say something sweet like that. You are truly always surprising us."

They grabbed for one another's hands and walked hand in hand toward Cooper.

He smiled and walked toward the limousine with the girls following close behind him.

As he opened the door for each to get in, he said, "I'm glad it quit raining. It has turned out to be a nice day."

"Cooper," Tilly said in a flirting tone. "Does anyone ever ride upfront with you?"

"On occasion, there have been times I have had the pleasure of people joining me."

"Can I ride in the front then? I think that would be fun."

"It would be a pleasure for you to accompany me," he said, directing her to the front of the limousine.

The others watched as he opened her door for her, and she slides in.

"Look at that silly little thing making a monkey out of herself," exclaimed JoBeth.

"I know. I wish I had thought of it first," Stella said, sounding jealous.

Cooper pulled slowly onto the highway and headed toward their next destination.

"I am changing the subject here," Hannah said. "Gracie's body isn't even cold in the grave, and we are headed to a lawyer's office. Doesn't that sound a little strange to everyone?"

JoBeth quickly announced, "Technically, Hannah, the body starts getting cold just seconds after death and ...."

Hannah stopped her in mid-sentence, "JoBeth, I was just using that as an example. I know all that medical stuff. I'm trying to tell you I don't feel right about this. It is making me extremely nervous."

"Between you getting nervous and Tilly getting depressed, we have got to come up with some type of medication for the both of you," Sadie said, teasing.

She continued, "We will find out what we need to know in a few minutes. We are only ten minutes away from the lawyer's office. If we don't get the answers we need, then I will get nervous right along with you."

This seemed to satisfy Hannah, but not for long.

She pointed to the front and said, "Look at that, Tilly. She keeps talking, and Cooper is taking his eyes off the road to look in her direction. What if we have a wreck?"

Sadie shook her head and said, "Trust me, Hannah, if we wreck, this thing is so long that it will take forever for us to feel any type of impact. Now, sit back and enjoy this ride. It will be the last time we ever get to ride in anything like this again. Sit back, close your eyes, and make yourself feel like someone rich and important. That is what I am trying to achieve."

Hannah sat back, closed her eyes, and said, "I'll try, but if we wreck, I can say I told you so."

Sadie looked toward JoBeth and winked. She knew there was no reasoning with Hannah at this point. She smiled to herself and, once again, wished Gracie could see what was going on with her group of friends.

Within ten minutes, Cooper was pulling in front of Parker and Son Law Office.

Stella questioned, "Sadie, do you know anything about this group?"

"Only that they are a very old and trusted firm. They have been in this town for as long as I can remember. It seems the entire family from generation to generation has continued to practice law."

JoBeth whispered in Sadie's ear, "I know how Hannah has been feeling. I am feeling extremely nervous about this myself."

"I know what you mean. But, try not to let it show, or Hannah is going to flip out on us," Sadie whispered back.

JoBeth nodded.

Cooper came quickly to open the door, with Tilly following close behind.

As they stepped out, Sadie looked around to see if there were any more men in black suits coming around the corner.

Cooper closed the door behind them and then said, "Follow me, please."

"Isn't he just the sweetest thing you have ever laid your eyes on, girls?" Tilly asked.

"Get over it, Tilly," Stella said. "Don't you have any concerns about what might happen to us when we walk through those doors?"

"Gosh, I didn't think about that. Sadie, do you think they know....."

Sadie put her finger to her mouth and said, "Hush Tilly, just go in and keep silent. Everything will be all right."

Cooper opened the door for them and said, "I will be waiting for you when the meeting is over. You can tell me your destination then."

"Well, Sadie, it appears we are going to get to ride in that long black thing at least one more time," Hannah said, acting pleased.

Sadie thought to herself that her little group of friends had finally gone over the edge and was taking her with them. She quickly shook her head, trying to shake this feeling from her mind.

They continued to walk into the building and entered an enormous foyer. Antique furniture filled almost every inch of the room, but it did not appear to make the room look cluttered. The look of the walls combined with the furniture made you have a warm feeling when entering. Sadie admired the plasterwork on the high ceiling and the enormous chandeliers. She wished she could enjoy the beauty of it all, but her mind kept racing back to what was going to happen to them.

A side door opened and out walked a tall, distinguished, looking man. Sadie remembered seeing him at the funeral. He had been one of those strange men in a black suit.

He walked toward them, smiling.

Sadie whispered to Stella, "He is smiling. Maybe that is a good sign for us."

He extended his hand first to Sadie and said, "Nice to finally meet each of you ladies. I am Ray Parker. I was and am Miss Gracie's lawyer. If you follow me, I am sure I can answer all your questions." He then turned and walked toward the door of his office.

Sadie turned to the others and motioned for them to follow.

They entered his large office. There around his desk sat five chairs, just waiting for each of them.

He waited as they took their seats, and then he sat. The thought of him being a true Southern gentleman entered Sadie's mind.

"Is there anything that I could get you, ladies? Maybe a cup of coffee, water, or sweet ice tea would ease your nerves."

"Is it that obvious?" Sadie questioned.

"Yes, actually it is, but that is understandable. Now, would you care for something to drink?" He once again questioned.

They shook their heads.

"Well, then I guess I need to get down to business. First, I need to tell you a few things that will better help you understand the situation you are in right now."

Sadie glanced at the others to see their reaction. They looked back at Sadie but didn't say a word.

"Frankly, Mr. Parker, we are grateful that you are getting straight to the point," Sadie said sternly.

"Yes, I understand that each of you has been under a lot of stress while taking care of Miss Gracie."

Sadie realized she had heard the Miss Gracie comment from several people today. They seemed to have been all very secretive men. She didn't know what to expect.

She took a deep breath and once again said, "Yes, actually, we are exhausted and would like to return home so we can reflect on the memories we all hold for Gracie. We need to be together to share our own private time."

"I will be as quick as possible with this meeting. I understand the need for your privacy. I will start by reading a letter from Miss Gracie. Feel free to stop me at any time."

Tilly raised her hand and said, "Stop."

Sadie gave her a stern look that made Tilly realize to let the man do the talking in this case.

"I will be glad to answer any question you might have," he said politely.

"Well, actually, I don't have one. I was just testing you," Tilly said quickly.

Stella looked at Sadie and giggled right out loud.

Sadie felt like she needed to make some kind of explanation for what just happened.

She slowly said, "Mr. Parker, you will have to forgive us. We have all been under a lot of stress. I guess our nerves are getting the best of us, and it is affecting each of us differently, especially Tilly. Now, if you don't mind, please continue."

He reached for a group of papers on his desk, cleared his throat, and said, "Now, as I was saying. I will begin with a letter that Miss Gracie wrote for all of you."

He began,

My dear girlfriends,

Since you are here listening to this long letter and I am sure sitting impatiently, that only means that I am no longer with you. Sadie Sue, you were right. God does answer prayers in His own way. I had asked you all not to shed tears, but I will take that back. Cry if you want, but not much. Remember, I am right where I have wanted to be for a very long time.

Now, we will get down to business so you all can get on with your lives. I am dragging my feet on this because I don't know where to start. I know you have always felt I was a big mystery in your lives. I know I gave that impression, but I did not know any other way to be. I remember the first time I walked into that restaurant on that cold rainy morning. My baby had died months earlier, and now I had lost my husband as well. I had no family and no desire to live. I sat there, realizing that I had nothing else to live for, so I was planning my suicide. Then you ask me over to join the table for a simple cup of coffee. That changed my entire life. I couldn't believe total strangers could take a person that looked as bad as I did that morning and show love toward them. Well, as you realize, I changed my plans for that day. I went through with the funeral of my husband and then continued to join your little coffee club.

There wasn't a day that went by that I came so close telling you my secret, but as each day grew into weeks and then into months, I realized you loved me for just being me. I feared that if I told you I was rich, it would somehow change our relationship. I was foolish, and I realize now that nothing could change the bond we have had over all these years. Now, I know you are each wondering just how rich this old woman was. Well, they tell me that probably at this point, I am worth well over twenty million. See, I know you all so well right now. You are wondering how in the world I got so rich. You know the old saying born with a silver spoon in one's mouth. Well, that was me. Father was rich. I married into money, and I always had brilliant lawyers that I could trust to put my money in whatever could make it continue to grow. After losing my baby and my husband, money just wasn't important to me. Besides, I had met my Southern Belle Breakfast Club group, and I didn't need money in my life. After my husband and I were married, we soon learned that people looked at you and treated you differently if they knew you had money. I just pretended there was no money in my life. Except for charities and a few people, I helped without them knowing it. I just pretended it no longer existed.

The beach house we all enjoyed a few weeks ago is mine, but now it is the five of yours to share equally. You also own a much bigger home in the North Carolina mountains and one in Key West, Florida. So including the house I have lived in all these years makes you four houses I give to you. Do as you please with them, but I hoped that you all could take extended vacations together in them.

I have instructed Ray to divide all my monies into six equal parts. Now, you are wondering why six since there are only five of you. Someday, someone will enter your life just the way I did that morning, and she or he will be that sixth person to give that share. I know between the five of you, the right decision will be made. It will be your decision on whether to let that person know where the money came from. I was the mystery woman, but I am there no more. So again, that is your decision whether or not you want to become a mystery.

Hannah, here is the answer to a question you had about your father. I had a private detective find out all the information I gave to *you about him. He searched all his records and his life. You had a wonderful father, and I am glad that you got to meet him. Your half-brothers are wonderful as well. They have all the kind qualities your father did. I hope you will consider letting them into your life. Hannah, trust me on this that they would welcome you into their life with open arms. Ray will give you a folder of all the information my private detective collected on them.*

Now, Stella, it is your time. You came to us and opened your heart to the way Trace was doing you, and it tore me apart. I immediately had a private detective follow his every move. He took pictures of things that you do not know about. He went into records that only a detective knew how to do. Ray has an envelope that will be given to you at the end of this meeting. I want you to use it wisely. You will find that he has money hidden in banks overseas and several banks spread across the United States. It is money that you would not be able to get your hands on unless you knew exactly how. Ray will help you with this if you feel the need for his help. Also, don't worry about the money you are receiving from me. Ray has already arranged that there is no way Trace can get his hands on it. Trust him, girls, the way I have all these years. He will not let you down. Also, if you decide to use him as a lawyer, there is no need to pay him. I have taken care of that little problem as well.

I know all this is a lot to absorb at one time. While sitting around that table, sipping on that hot cup of coffee, I know everything will slowly come together, and this will all make sense. I genuinely hope that I have not left out anything that you needed to know about me.

I want to thank each of you for sharing your lives and family with me. I felt a part of your lives during the years, and I wouldn't have traded that for anything in the world. Now, enough about me, for I am sure the last few months, it has been all about me. It was take care of Gracie, is Gracie all right, what can we do to make Gracie feel better. Now, it is your turn to let it be about each of you. Enjoy every bit of life you have left. Don't be scared to take chances. I don't know how to close this letter, or maybe I fear I may have left some unanswered questions. If that is the possibility, then just make up the answers. I am sure that would work just fine. Oh yes, one more thing, always keep people guessing. We will keep that mystery only between the six of us. Remember that, my lifelong friends, always keep people guessing,

All my love to each of you over and over,
Gracie

Stella was the first to speak, "I think I am ready for something to drink now, but I'm afraid it needs to be stronger than what you suggested earlier. You wouldn't happen to have a shot of whiskey or bourbon in your desk drawer, do you?"

Mr. Parker laughed and said, "No, but I am sure that I could arrange to have some brought in."

"I am afraid this is just so overwhelming that I can't even think straight. We never had a clue that she was rich. It wouldn't have made any difference, but we never dreamed of this," said Sadie.

Mr. Parker reached inside his desk drawer and pulled out several envelopes. He handed them each one.

"Inside, you will see what your share of the money is and answers to many of the questions you may have."

Then he reached in the other drawer, pulled out two more, and said, "Hannah, this one is yours, and Stella, this is an essential one. As you see on the top, Gracie has written use with care. This can destroy your husband, and Gracie wanted to make sure he didn't take you down with him. There are tapes, documents, and pictures inside the envelope. I suggest you read over everything carefully and then get out of the marriage. I also suggest you don't let him know anything in this envelope. Then after you are divorced, take it to whomever you want to handle it. After seeing and going over everything with the detective, I know he will be headed to prison. That is why Gracie wanted me to fix your share of the money where your husband could not touch it."

He paused briefly and said, "All these years, I have handled Gracie's affairs. I hope you will have confidence in me as she has and will consider me your lawyer."

They each looked at the other but didn't say a word.

He stood and reached his hand out to Sadie and said, "I was told anytime I wanted to get serious and let you know I was telling you something significant, that I was to call you Sadie Sue. Well, Sadie Sue, all of you talk this over. Let it take several days to really sink in what has happened and then come back to see me. You can then let me know if you trust me enough to be your lawyer. I do want each of you to know that Miss Gracie was more than a client to all of us. The men in the black suits today could each tell you a story about her. They were lawyers appointed to different charities that she has given money to over a long period of years. They were sworn to stay silent as well. Now, before you go, are there any more questions?"

Sadie raised her hand and teasingly said, "Stop, I have a question."

Tilly laughed, "You are acting just like I did about an hour ago."

Mr. Parker smiled and said, "Remember, you never have to raise your hand to ask a question in this office."

"I know, I was teasing, but I truly do have a question. Gracie gave me a telephone number before she got to her worse point in her illness. I was to call it when she died and only say the words it is over. Who was on the other end of the telephone?"

He looked sad and said, "Your words were spoken to me. I knew that I would eventually get that phone call, and I dreaded even thinking about when that time would come. This was Gracie's wish that everything be ready for her death, and none of you would have to pick out a casket or make any type of arrangements. She didn't want her best friends to have to handle that part of her death. Therefore, she instructed me to handle everything, and I did what she wanted. I told her to have you call me and simply say it is over. I didn't want to hear the word death, or Gracie has died. All I needed was those three simple words. I am sure you are also wondering why the service was done so quickly after her death. That was another wish she requested. She wanted her burial to be as quick as possible. The way she stated it to me was when I die, take me directly, and throw me in a grave."

Sadie smiled and said, "Yes, that sounds like a comment Gracie would make."

"I don't know if you truly realize what a brave woman she was," Mr. Parker stated.

"We had the privilege of being friends with her for over thirty years. So, I think we know her better than anyone," Tilly blurted out.

Hannah touched Tilly on the shoulder and said, "Tilly, think about it. Did we ever really know the true Gracie?"

"I can answer that," JoBeth said. "We knew everything about Gracie that she wanted us to know. The loving friend with the biggest heart anyone could have was our Gracie. We knew the Gracie that could turn your bad day into a good one. We knew the Gracie that would listen to your problems and not be judgmental. We knew that Gracie, and that is all we needed to know about her."

Mr. Parker walked toward them and said, "Are there any more questions you have that I might be able to help you with?"

Sadie looked at the others and then said, "There will probably be many in the next few days, but right now, our heads are spinning. We will get back to you as soon as we have had time to take this all in."

They each shook Mr. Parker's hand, and swiftly out the door they went.

Cooper saw them and immediately walked in their direction. "Ladies, what might your next destination be?"

Sadie gave them each a glance and said, "It is so easy to read your minds."

She gave a quick giggle and said, "Cooper, we have a very special restaurant that we have been going to for years. It was a favorite of Gracie's. So that is where we would like to go. The address is...."

"I don't mean to interrupt, but I know where that special place is. I not only drive this limousine, but I did Miss Gracie's footwork for her. So I know a little bit about each of you, your likes, dislikes, and your dreams. Miss Gracie would talk to me as if I was a member of her family that she never had."

Tilly questioned, "Cooper, what do you mean that you did her footwork for her?"

"I ran errands, but Miss Gracie told me that I was helping her, and it was not like I was an errand boy. I am the one that had the pictures developed that she took at the beach. I am the one that went to the specialty shop and got the picture frames for her to give to each of you. I helped her do the things she was unable to do when she started getting sick. She kept me on the payroll when she didn't need my services, but she had a tender heart and wanted to help me. She was a very special lady."

"Yes, we knew that, but it seems we are just now finding out just how special she was," Sadie said.

"How long have you worked for Gracie?" Stella asked.

"It has been almost a year now. I was taking her back and forth to her doctor and then to the lawyer's office. She never talked about her illness. She never complained of being sick."

He paused as if he wanted to say something else.

He finally spoke, "I knew her for only a short time, but she always seemed so sad. She would smile, but her eyes didn't reflect the smile. The only way I can explain it was that she had sad eyes. Then when she came back from her weekend with all of you, she seemed so happy. Her eyes weren't sad anymore. I remember telling her that the trip seemed to be good for her. She smiled and told me that sometimes when you find out the truth about something, your heart fills with happiness. I didn't question what she meant."

Sadie knew exactly how Cooper felt. Gracie had believed all those years that she had killed her baby. Sadness had overtaken her, and she couldn't shed the guilt of what she thought she had done. When she had finally confessed her secret, Sadie was able to convince her Lindsey Grace had died on her own. Gracie's conscience was clear after all those years. Now, her mind, body, and soul were free from the guilt she had carried within herself.

"Now, if you ladies are ready to go, it would be a pleasure for me to drive you to your destination. You will be the last passengers I have."

Tilly quickly asked, "Why do you say that, Cooper?"

"I will be standing in the unemployment line starting tomorrow. There is not a lot of people in this world that need a limousine driver or someone to do special errands for them as Miss Gracie did."

The girls looked at one another and smiled. Once again, they were reading one another's minds.

Stella touched Cooper gently on the shoulder and said, "Would you consider being an advisor, errand person, driver, or whatever you want to call yourself for us? Gracie had confidence in you. That is all the reference we need."

"Ladies, you have made my day. It would give me great pleasure to extend my services to friends of Miss Gracie. In other words, you have made me a very happy man."

He opened the limousine door, bowed, and motioned for them to get in.

They sat down, and then suddenly, the talk with the lawyer finally started to sink in.

"What are we going to do with all this money?" Tilly confessed, "I can't even run a checkbook down the correct way."

JoBeth opened her envelope and gasped, "Do you realize that each of us is worth over five million dollars, and the money is still growing? Growing, that isn't even the correct word to use in this case. We have got to have help with this."

Sadie reassured them, "Mr. Parker can be trusted."

JoBeth looked puzzled and asked, "This might be a silly question, but I have got to ask you. Sadie, why did Mr. Parker call you Sadie Sue? You didn't even seem surprised or shocked, nor did you question him about it. Please fill us in on this little thing being called Sadie Sue."

Sadie sat back in the leather seat and looked out the window. She gathered enough strength not to cry and then said, "Gracie would call me Sadie Sue only when she wanted to talk to me about something serious or something important. I questioned her one time why she did, and she told me to get my full attention. Well, when Mr. Parker called me Sadie Sue, I knew that Gracie had discussed this name-calling with him. I knew right then that he could be trusted, and he would work for us as he did Gracie. We don't need to worry about him cheating us. No, we don't have the slightest clue on how to handle all this money, but with his help, we sure can learn."

"It is sort of like Gracie has put her trust in us to do what is right. Is that correct, Sadie Sue?" Tilly asked, slightly smiling.

"That's right, Tilly."

Suddenly, Cooper's voice came over the speaker, "Ladies, we have reached your destination."

Tilly reached toward the intercom, pushed the button, and said, "Thank you, Cooper. You are an excellent driver and a friend." Then she leaned back, crossed her arms against her chest, and smiled a conquering smile.

He stopped the limousine and, within seconds, was ready to open their door.

"What in the world does that big smile mean, Tilly?" Hannah asked.

"It means we got us, one great-looking driver." Tilly clarified while giggling.

"Hush, he will hear you," JoBeth snapped.

Her smile became bigger as she said in a flirting manner, "Who cares?"

They quickly got out and then gathered around one another. It seemed as if they didn't know exactly what to do.

"Well, at first, I thought this was a good idea. Now, I'm not so sure." Sadie admitted, with a worried look on her face.

"Well, I, for one, think we are doing the right thing. It is like we are paying the last respect to Gracie by going into the place we first met her and where we have shared so many good times," Stella pointed out proudly.

"We sure are going to get a lot of stares by walking in during the afternoon dinner meal, all dressed in black with pillbox hats with black veils," Tilly said while adjusting her hat.

Cooper spoke very softly and stated, "If I can be so bold, ladies. It will appear to everyone that you have just come back from a funeral. No one will think anything different."

He paused and then said in a powerful voice, "If anyone says anything out of the way, come out and get me!"

Tilly batted her big blue eyes at him and flirted, "You also make a very nice bodyguard."

Hannah grabbed Tilly's hand, pulled her toward the restaurant, and said, "My goodness, Tilly, quit your flirting. I have never seen you like this before."

She shook her head and continued, "Follow me. We are going inside and drink a cup of coffee in memory of Gracie."

This time the others did as Hannah said.

As they walked inside, Sadie couldn't help to paint a mental picture of them all sitting at their favorite table, laughing with Gracie. She tried to shake the emotion she was having, but as she looked at the others, she knew they were thinking the same thing.

"We can get through this, and the next time won't be quite as difficult," Stella said as she placed her hands gently on Sadie's back and gave her a slight push toward their favorite table.

They sat down in their usual chairs and looked directly at the empty chair. All eyes once again looked at Sadie for support.

"Well, ladies, I make a suggestion we take off our hats and place them in Gracie's chair."

"Good idea, Sadie. Then I think some of these people might quit their staring," Tilly bellowed, letting her voice get louder as she finished her sentence.

Tilly moved her leg from under the table just in case Sadie decided to give her a little warning for being so rude and loud. Instead, Sadie laughed as she watched Tilly shift in her chair.

"No warning kicks today, Tilly," Sadie assured her.

They each removed their pillbox hat and placed them in the chair.

"No tears, girls, please. We can cry it out behind closed doors and then no more tears. That is what Gracie requested, remember?" Hannah insisted.

Suddenly, Ida appeared with her pad and pencil.

She moved as close to each of them as she could and whispered, "You all look so nice. I know that you have been to Gracie's funeral. I wanted to go so badly when I read about it in the early morning paper. I pleaded with my money-hungry boss, but he wouldn't give in for me to go. I had thoughts about going anyway, but I knew he would fire me. I can't afford to lose this job. There would be no one that would hire an old woman like me. I'm sorry, I don't mean to be airing my dirty laundry on a sad day for all of you."

She paused, took a deep breath, and tried to continue, "I will be right back with the coffee." She turned quickly and walked away as if she was embarrassed.

"She looks as sad as we do about losing Gracie," Stella pointed out.

Sadie nodded, "Well, look at it like this. She has known Gracie for about as many years as we have, and she has been a part of us coming in here every week. Of course, she is going to miss her."

Ida returned with coffee cups and a large pot of coffee.

"Do you need menus this afternoon?" Ida asked as if she was trying to fight back the tears.

"Not today, Ida. We just want coffee. It is sort of our way of saying goodbye to Gracie," JoBeth said.

Ida started softly crying. She reached into her pocket, pulled out a handkerchief, and dabbed her eyes.

She apologized, "I am so sorry. I have tried very hard not to do that all day, but I just can't hold it back."

Sadie stood up, pulled another chair close to her, and said, "Ida, honey, sit with us, please."

Ida looked toward the front of the restaurant and whispered, "Only for a second, if my boss would happen to see me, I don't know what he would do. I will be taking early retirement in a few weeks due to my health, and he has been treating me like dirt. It is as if he is trying to find some reason to get rid of me. I am trying to hang on until I can start drawing my social security check. Then, I am going to tell him exactly how I feel about him."

A stern masculine voice rang out from the front of the restaurant, "Ida, your pick up is ready. Table two wants service now!"

Ida immediately jumped up from the chair with a concerned look on her face, "I am so sorry. I hope he didn't upset you."

Tilly stated sharply, "I hope he didn't upset you by screaming out your name like that. Does he realize he is making a fool out of himself by screaming across the restaurant?"

Ida quickly said, "The coffee is on me today. That way, I can also be doing it in memory of Gracie."

Then she raced toward the front of the restaurant as if she was a scared little rabbit running from the big bad hunter.

Stella blurted, "Poor Ida, she takes a lot off that male chauvinist pig,"

Suddenly, the group became silent.

Tilly was the first to speak. "I guess I am becoming soft in my old age, but I have an idea."

They all looked at one another and joined hands around the table. They each knew what the other was thinking.

"Who is going to be the one to ask Ida if she wants to join our group?" Hannah questioned.

"And who is going to be the one to tell her she doesn't have to worry about ever coming back in here to wait on other people or put up with that so-called boss?" Stella beamed.

Sadie said with tears running down her cheeks, "I just bet our Gracie is looking down from Heaven saying you go, girls. You picked the right one."

Tilly became very solemn and asked, "Do you think that Gracie knew what we...?"

"What are you trying to ask, Tilly? I don't know what you are talking about, and I really don't see why this subject needs to come up again," Sadie stated sternly.

"That's right, Tilly. This subject, whatever it was, does not need to be brought up again. No, not ever again as long as we all are on this earth!"

The others nodded in agreement. They became silent as if they were in their own little world thinking about what had just been decided.

Tilly finally leaned forward on her elbows, looked across the table, and said, "Well, who is going to be the one that tells Ida she is coming into a pile of money? Here she comes, and she looks like she needs some good news in her life."

Stella pointed to Sadie and said, "I vote Sadie tell her."

Sadie looked at the others. They smiled and nodded.

She immediately stood up, walked toward Ida, and guided her toward the bathroom.

"Oh, I hope Ida doesn't faint when Sadie tells her she is rich. She said she has been in poor health," Hannah stated, with a worried look on her face.

Tilly laughed, "It seems like I remember an old song that says something like, take this job and shove it. I hope she tells that boss of hers just that."

Suddenly, a scream came from the bathroom. The entire restaurant became stone-cold silent. Ida came running from the bathroom with Sadie right behind her. She ran straight toward their table.

"Well, I take it Sadie told you everything, Ida," Tilly said excitedly.

Sadie stood behind Ida, placed her arm on her shoulder, and sat her down in a chair. All eyes in the restaurant darted directly to them.

"Take a deep breath, Ida. We know it is a lot to try to take in. We are still not over the shock of it ourselves," JoBeth said.

"I can't believe this. I don't know what to do. I..." Ida tried to finish her sentence but was unable to speak.

A loud voice from the front of the restaurant yelled, "Ida, pick up for table three, now!"

Ida started to jump from the chair. Tilly pushed her gently back down.

Again, the same voice, "Ida, I said there is a pick up for table three. Come and get it now!"

Ida looked at the others as if she didn't know what to do.

Sadie said slowly, "Ida, you never have to carry another tray of food for anyone else unless you so desire. This job is history, and so is that man that has ordered you around like you were a dog for years. We would like you to come with us right now. We have a lot of talking to do. All this is new to us as well. But, we, as a group, can do this together."

"We are stronger together than we are as one," Tilly said, proudly repeating their motto.

Sadie smiled as she remembered the times they had said this very thing to Gracie.

JoBeth looked at Ida and said, "Well, girlfriend, what is it going to be?"

Ida smiled bigger than they had ever seen her smile. She jumped from the chair and said, "Take me out of here."

Stella got on the right side of Ida, and Hannah got on the left. They held tightly to her arms. The others followed behind. They walked right up to Ida's boss.

Ida removed her apron and threw it right in his face.

He grabbed for the apron, threw it on the floor, and said, "Ida, you are fired. Don't you ever walk back in my restaurant again."

They continued to walk toward the door. Ida was shaking from head to toe.

"I don't know what came over me," Ida sobbed in a shaky voice.

"You girls walk on out. I will be right there. I have a little something that I need to take care of," Tilly announced as she walked toward the counter.

As they were going out the door, Sadie turned and smiled at Tilly. She didn't know what she was going to tell the man, but she knew it was going to be a true Tilly statement.

She walked right up to Ida's boss. He had turned blood red in the face. It was apparent he was mad.

"I don't know what your little group of women has done to my waitress to make her walk out the way she did. Now, I am one waitress short with all these customers waiting on their food," he yelled in an outraged tone.

Tilly smiled and calmly pointed out, "Then maybe you need fewer customers."

She took several steps until she was almost in the center of the restaurant.

Tilly cleared her throat and loudly announced, "Excuse me, but I felt you might want to know that I just found a great big roach in my coffee."

She paused and then pretended to start crying, "It was floating belly up. I am so depressed over this that I am never going to step foot in this grade B restaurant again."

Quickly turning, she walked back to Ida's boss and calmly stated, "There you go. I hope that helped with your waitress situation."

Tilly watched as several of the customers looked into their coffee cups.

Ida's boss stood motionless. Tilly gave him a thumb's up, and out the door, she went. She walked directly to her friends, who were waiting with Cooper at the limousine.

Sadie looked at Tilly and said, "Something tells me we are going to have to find another restaurant to hold our weekly coffee club meetings."

Tilly grinned devilishly and agreed, "Yes, I think so, too."

Cooper held the door open while each one got in.

He slowly asked, "Ladies, where may I have the privilege of taking you now?"

"We need to go to Sadie's house. We have a lot of talking to do, and I am sure she is going to make a pot of coffee for everyone," Tilly said.

She paused for a minute and then politely asked, "Would you like to join us for coffee, Cooper?"

He nodded, smiled directly at Tilly, and carefully closed the door.

Ida sank into the luxurious comfort of the leather seat and questioned, "I can't believe it. What in the world have I done to deserve all this?"

Stella grabbed for Ida's hand, placed it in hers, and explained, "You were kind to an exceptional lady. A lady that didn't see dollar marks on anybody or anything. A lady that wasn't afraid to show she cared. A lady that carried hurt and pain on her shoulders and never complained. You, just like us, were fortunate enough to know a wonderful woman named Gracie."

As Cooper drove from the parking lot, Sadie looked back at the old building. It held many memories of the past for this group. This was the place the six women of the Southern Belle Breakfast Club had sat for hours at a time, dreaming their dreams, crying over past failures, and rejoicing over ordinary day accomplishments. But, more than anything, this group of women had shared a bond of friendship that could never be taken away from one another, even by death.

Sadie glanced at the others, drew a sharp breath, slowly closed her eyes, and wondered what other adventures were yet to unfold in their lives.

*Life can be an amazing journey,
especially with good
friends to journey with.*

~Phyllis f. McManus~